The Teething Intern

The Teething Intern

WASEEM HASSAN

authorHOUSE®

AuthorHouse™ LLC
1663 Liberty Drive
Bloomington, IN 47403
www.authorhouse.com
Phone: 1-800-839-8640

Published by AuthorHouse   12/02/2013

ISBN: 978-1-4918-2018-6 (sc)
ISBN: 978-1-4918-2019-3 (hc)
ISBN: 978-1-4918-2020-9 (e)

Library of Congress Control Number: 2013917413

1

It is 03:30 on a Saturday morning. I stand in casualty with three cases pending results, and three cases pending admission. Suddenly the doors of the hospital crash open; it's a three month old baby, completely flat. No pulse, dry as a bone. My head is spinning; I am still going on two cups of coffee, my supper.

My first instinct is to run for the door before it closes. My second is to grab the valium heading towards that fitting patient and just inject it in my arm. I choose the third which is trying to put a drip in this child that is already at heavens door.

Over the next half hour the baby has a drip up, fluid running into her bone marrow, we get a pulse, she is stable, she goes down to the ward. The fitting patient is now in lala land, where I would like to be. My three cases pending admission are all admitted now, finally. My three cases pending results are all normal and they are discharged with tto's.

It's a good call; no it's a great call. No one died, yet. I got to eat, well drink something and a baby is alive because of me. My MO or medical officer, Dr Okuvango aka dodge man is nowhere to be found, casualty is quiet. I look at my watch, its 5:40. I can still get some sleep before preparing for rounds if I am lucky.

Not to be, I put my head down 1 missisispi 2 missisipi 3 missisipi, phone rings, Sister in paeds ward. The baby I resused has crashed. I run down, to the wards. The baby is cold, pupils dilated, no pulse again, I look at my line. It is out. I try to put up a line while the nurse bags. I call dodge man. He says look at the clock and call it. The mother has tears sliding down her cheeks. She is not crying, she is not weeping. Her complexion is apoplectic. She looks me in the eye. Another one I will not forget.

Ward rounds are a nightmare. Half of my bloods have clotted. This means they all have to be repeated. Two more patients are waiting to be transferred to the no go zone, palliative HIV care and all I know is I need to find a bed. I look at my watch, it reads 09:55. The last few hours of that call as always are a blur. I look at my watch, its 12h55, Jenny; another intern on day shift saves my ass again and tells me to head off. She will take care of my shit, and boy is there a lot of shit, I am grateful though. I could not, would not have lasted much longer although I have had to before and will have to again. All in all I was on call for 30 hours, and then some, scary I know, but that's the norm here in South Africa.

I am a year and six months into my two year internship. At this point in my life, I can proudly say I am safe. Well, relatively safe. As a doctor that is.

I did not even introduce myself. Hi, I am Ali Sha. This is the story of my intern life thus far. I started writing this when I knew I had to find an outlet to survive the devastation of my everyday existence. Where to begin? It all started with a mad rush of matric final exams, everyone asking what you doing next year? This is truly the worst time of anybodies life. Anyone who has been through the matric experience or that final grad year can attest to this. You are tentative. You are afraid. Some afraid of failing. Some afraid of not accumulating enough points to begin lifes dreams. Me, I was just afraid I would/or would not get into medical school. Sometimes lifes journeys are decided with simple tests. I know what you are thinking. What a loser? But hey we all have problems. Some not as big as others, but they are important to that particular person. This I have learnt is called empathy. Walking in another mans shoes, and boy does it pain. You will know when you have done it too.

Since most of my family was either Doctors or Accountants, I did not have an easy way out of becoming the first actor in my family. You see, as an Indian and even more so as a Muslim we are taught to look at the practicalities of life. As I grew older I have learned that this is true for all races and creed. We are thought to dream small, live life small. Most of us programmed to get a good job, study hard, work your way up the ladder. The safe route. After reading the book rich dad poor dad, I realized that it was those who dreamt big and believed in themselves and their dreams; these were the people who lived their true success stories. And only some of them were seen on TV, not all. I guess there is still hope for this pessimist. Now many people have laughed at me for that. I did believe back then that I could have been the first breakthrough in history. The first Indian Muslim South African in Hollywood (back when I as 10 maybe). How drastically my outlook on life has changed since then. Anyway to become an actor in South Africa you would either have to have contacts, or be stunningly gorgeous (which are traits required in any profession as I later found out). But seriously can you imagine me telling my parents and my brother, that I am going to be an actor. The thought of it alone makes me piss in my pants. I have always had a problem fitting in with everyone which I have become accustomed to now. The less I say the less trouble I get into, same goes for the less I do. The only problem with this was I loved saying and doing things all the time. I was not a true extrovert but I had my opinions. They changed from time to time but the fundamentals were as solid as the earth which I was made from. I dreamed of being on television. A dark brown thin frail frame, times two pimples one on each cheek, tall (5 foot 8 inches if that counts), long straight hair, dark brown eyes. I mean, come on people blue and green eyes have been killed, its time for the dark brown to rise. It is time for normal to be cool. Here, here.

Then it happened, the call that changes ones destiny. It was a medical school, a prestigious one at that. I was in. Now I would not say I was intelligent. But what I gained in the field of intellect I lacked in just about every other field. Socially inept, maybe. Spiritually controlled, yes. Financially, dependent. A quick way of taking stock for me is to look at these fields. Social, financial, spiritual, intellectual and physical. I mean basically if you have these bases covered, you are doing alright. At that time I was not, and as time went on things did not get much better.

So here I am this normal cool guy. This normal cool guy, who started of with a 100% of his soul, when he left school. This normal cool guy, who on leaving medical school was full of soul. Now almost two years in as a practicing doctor in South Africa I have lost a bit of that soul. I think . . .

You know when times are tough in life and you become all nostalgic. You reminisce of the good old days. Everyone has a good old day. I cannot remember my last good old day. I do remember my last leave though. Ahh leave . . . vacation leave that is, I will come to that later.

I do remember my buddies from medical school. We had a dictum or questions, that I use everyday and will use everyday till I die. Who am I? What am I doing here? And did I have a nice day? I won't say I have found any answers yet but I am working on it. And I am slowly finding my way, my canvas is taking shape slowly but surely.

Now back to my friends. There was Surety man aka Jameel. He was always there when you needed a friend. He was the kind of guy everyone hated. First class A student, always with a beautiful girl on his arm, he wishes. He was a great conversationalist and good listener too, Ok pushing it there. If he had one pitfall, his kryptonite was woman. Don't get me wrong, he loved woman. He just sucked at social interactions with woman. None of us ever had the heart to tell him. He had the athletic frame six foot tall fair and handsome. He just had no idea what to do with it. I do believe through his varsity years this became more and more apparent. No matter how hard he tried he just could not get that balance. Still he was awesome guy and I miss having him around now at work. I think it would have been unfair for God to bless a man with so many things. Everyone and I mean everyone has a shortfall in some category. That I have learnt. Usually it is those you are most jealous of, that surprise you. Jameel qualified with me.

Then there was Kubin. Kubin was like your girlfriends or sisters food when she was learning how to cook. You had to take it in short spells. But as time wore on you got used to it and eventually you not only ate it, you liked it. He was loud, narcissistic and overly self confident. He was thoroughly entertaining to be around and that's why whenever I needed a pick me up, Kubin was my man and still is. He and I met on day three at medical school. He was hitting on some hot chick at the stairs of the great hall of Wits main campus. The conversation was that of a typical jock. Don't I know you from somewhere? The girl's reply, Yes you probably were at my recent engagement. I was nearby laughing. He asked me if I had a problem, I said no and walked away. An hour later we were put in the same tut group for chem 101 and we became sort of friends. He told me of his crazy expeditions of girls, drugs, and hours of a misspent youth. I would listen and laugh, knowing that possibly 90% of it was untrue. But all the same he was funny and he became a loyal friend.

And a most recent addition Stevie, a tall lanky white dude. He was a fairly new addition to my social circle. Nevertheless he was an invaluable one.

So, here I am post call on my way home. This is as we refer to it, the golden time. It is a time when a sense of relief sets in. You realize not only have you survived another call but you get to go home and do the four sacred rituals that is every human beings god given right. You get to shower, you get to shit, you get to eat, and you get to sleep. In that order. Post call, you smell. You look like road kill. A normal person should be able to spot the post call doctor 10 meters away. He is the guy with one lazy eye. He has drool over his scrubs. Oh yeah, I forgot he has scrubs on in the morning that look like they need a thorough hand wash. He keeps on asking the same dumb question. What time is it? He most probably is the man who will be performing your proposed surgery today. Just kidding, then again maybe?. He is usually the guy who will be taking your blood and doing your routine work up. And I am not kidding about that. He is me today. He was me.

Right about now I reach home. Home sweet home. As Gerald Durrel put it, a place of my family and other animals.

Home is quiet now. It is peaceful, except for the maid. In South Africa having a maid or domestic worker is fairly common, and we had Clementine, a lifesaver on most days and family now too. Clementine and I are like the pommies and the French. We had our hundred year war, but although we suffered massive casualties (my Levis jeans, my puma t-shirt, my prized possession, a chain from a former fling). We have penned our Geneva Convention. We are in a state of civil peace, well most of the time. You see Clementine had a couple of inconvenient habits. No. 1—You know that part of the morning when you are just floating in hyperspace, which is when she comes in to my room to get the dirty clothes and vacuum. No matter how I have attempted to sabotage her mission, she always finds a way in. I locked the door. She banged on it, till I was awake. I left the dirty clothes out on the floor outside my room. Mum seethed when visitors came over and saw this. Now I except she will come in, but as quietly as possible. And, no vacuuming till after ten. We also have a strange greeting in the morning. I look her in the eyes as she does me. We nod, we grunt, we move on. If I said I was I not a morning person that would be an under statement. I believe all work should start after nine. Come on who is with me. The hospital kick of is generally around 7h30 which to me translates to a 7h23 wake up call. Brush, wash, pee and go. Sometimes if I am lucky I can grab a muffin on the way out.

But then there is ever steady Dad, Abdul Sha. My father is a mans man. We have had our ups and downs. He has always been there for me solid as a rock. One thing is a dead certainty everyday, sure as the sun that rises; I will have my Dad making sure I read my prayers. My saving grace through the rough days. My dad was the type of man who was self made in every way. He knew what his strengths were and he stuck with that. And his strengths were my mum, amongst other things. Now many of you may find this amusing but I do believe modern man and that is man in the last fifty years or so has become a bit of a sell out. It's the female of the species who seem to be excelling now more than ever. And big ups to them. We have become mummies boys (including myself) and the macho self reliant, self aware alpha male has fallen a bit to the way side. My dad is up everyday at 5h00 does his daily morning prayer, sorts out the lunch and is of to work. He built up a business from scratch, made it and keeps running it like a 25 year old, except that my dad is well into his fifties. He is the sort of guy who quietly gets the job done. He is a constant gardener. The thing about my father, though is he probably has the right approach to life. He knows his responsibilities. He cares for his family and he lives in the moment, everyday is just another day to be grateful for. I do believe I envy him for this. It is difficult for me to understand his constant demeanor. But your feelings towards your parents are steady yet malleable. And so too people change, and my dad due to circumstance has changed over the years but I remember him the way he was when I was growing up.

It is just gone 2pm when the final step of my ritual kicks in. I lay down close my eyes and am instantly in rem sleep.

I awaken. It is getting dark outside. A little shiver slithers slowly down my back. It is chilly. Winter is on the way. I had that dream again, always the same dream. I am called to a resus, it's a person I know. I never see the face as it is turned away. I stand there not knowing what to do. I see the monitors bleeping, I hear the sisters screaming Doctor what do you want? I know I should act but I can't. I don't know whether it is I cant or I don't want to. The person dies, they cover the face and I wake up, shivering and cold.

It is supper time. Everyone is home now. There is the usual hustle and bustle of the kitchen. I can hear the pots clickety clanking and I am waiting for it. That moment before your name is going to be called; Ali come and eat.

This is a good time of the day. I sit down and I tell everyone about my day, they tell me of theirs. No one is allowed to do anything but eat, talk and listen. I have come to be filled by this gathering. It was not filling just from the food but for the soul. It was a routine but one of the happy ones. It is time to relax, be laughed at, have fights, make up, express opinions, everyday you never knew what you were going to get.

Some scientists say the way we are is pre-determined, genetically speaking. Some believe we are product of our environment. Most believe it is a mixture of the two. Now I have a third possibility, what if God enforces destiny upon us to mold us and change us as time goes by. I do believe this is what happened to my mother, Fathima Sha. My mother was a special woman. She was a very outgoing woman in her younger days. She had an old bunch of records that we used to dance to as kids. She used to take us to the movies with our friends. We had parties on our birthdays. I mean small immediate family parties. She was someone we could always talk to. However over the last couple years she has become enriched with a spiritual vitality. It has rubbed on from my dad. He was the first to bite the religious apple. You could say as most things occur, you wonder if there is a reason for them and I have the answer, time. Why did this happen? Why did this person change? They grew into it. In this case as in most, there were a number of causes. Experiences mold us into who we are. It was not an overnight phenomenon. First it began with my mother reading her morning prayers everyday on time. She would then soon read all her five daily prayers everyday on time. She would always be caught with an Islamic book in hand. She then started fasting every Monday and then every Thursday. I cannot say I did not notice it. It never bothered me or interfered with my life. My mother was always a devout Muslim. More than most I suppose. As a child, even as a young adult one never really contemplates ones death. It is not a thought that crosses your mind. It is like losing someone close to you. You don't realize that it will happen. It must happen. I believe you choose to suppress any notion that it will. When it does Kubler Ross's five stages kick in: Denial, one of the strongest human emotions. Anger often seen, rarely understood.

Bargaining, some thing kids and adults in corners do alike. Depression, one of the major problems of our society today and in the future. Acceptance, you want to, you will to, but for most of us it is more of autumn's leaves blowing by. I think many of us just keep on channeling through one of these five when tragedy strikes. We are in an elevator going up and down with these thoughts and emotions everyday. To let go, to hold on, is it not one and the same. And so it is the mystery that death shrouds us in, is as perplexing as what may follow it. Islamically we believe in life after death as do most of the major religions. Thus one is inclined to do good, be good, in this world, now, and reap the benefits later. I can't say I have done this to any great effect. Then again, I do fall into the category of youth wasted on the young. I just think of death as an event that will happen later. I am too young now. I have dreams to fulfill. I have places to be, people to meet. I have life to live. Most of us who have not been confronted with mortality feel this way. It is often too late when we do finally accept that death is not just a word. It is a finality that will come. It should not be carried like the shadow on ones back. It is not to be feared. It should be like a smile, something that you can control and can used to brighten the day. Death as a smile, most would say that is crazy. But, you can be prepared for this event. If you lived accordingly, death is but a smile. It is but a greeting to a new world, is it not?

The food for thought ends as does every supper, as does everyday. I stand up, walk over to the sink, and begin the wiping process as I usually do. Chores are here to make the time pass by. I do them as one does what one is accustomed to. I like to help clean up.

It is a wonderful experience to clean something that was once dirty. To make it new, almost. The soap and water runs through these dishes as a shower skims over your skin. I rub hard over the marks and most are removed. However some of these stains are permanent. No matter how hard I try I just cannot rid this plate of them. They are ingrained. They are apart of this plate now. They are a make-up, a dress me down. They are strength, a weakness. I know them well, struggle with them daily.

I vegetate the last few hours before bed. I believe 90% of man has become part vegetable. In front of the television I switch off, I disappear, and so does time. Rarely do I learn anything that will aid me in this life or the next. It is the cheap thrill of knowing what happened in this week's episode of the big bang theory. I sit there watching this show and sometimes I think of my patients. Mostly, I try to blot it out. The seductive bliss of a half hour without any contact is pivotal to my day. This is my time to unwind.

But, I see the faces; try to work out their problems.

Its bedtime, a time to rest before the craziness begins again. I go to my room. It is a peaceful place. It is warm, comfortable, and familiar. It smells of me although I don't know what I smell like; I know it smells of me. It was the room I grew in, it holds my past. I hate to say it but I have become attached to these bricks, paint and other objects. There is a soft glow, of a lampshade in the corner. On my bed stand is a picture of my buddies from med school. Next to that is a picture of my parents and brother. I don't really notice the spider in the corner of the ceiling. I just look forward to that moment when one jumps in to bed, when one is free from the day at last. The highlight of my day, ironically, sleep. Oh, how I take you for granted. My flower soft fluffy blanky pulled over me, in this dark quiet room. The feeling of floating on a cloud in utter silence. Time stands still here. I rest. I yearn for this rest. This is the forgiving rest. I close my eyes and sleep. A true joy to sleep easy.

2

I awaken two seconds before the alarm goes off on my phone. My body is programmed to wake up at this time. I wake up at this time on most days. The phone reads 06h57. I walk over to the bathroom look at myself in the mirror. There he is you handsome, sexy . . . what the hell is that? My right eyelid is swollen like Angelina Jolies lips. The white of my eyes is a crimson red. I spend five minutes with some ice over it. It improves by about a millimeter. I am a doctor and this was freaking me out. I call him, the Boss.

-Hello boss, I mean Professor Saloojee, It's me, Ali the intern covering casualty. I have a swollen right eye. It does not look too good. I was wondering . . .
-are your hands Ok?
-yes
-can you walk?
-yes
-can you see?
-yes
-so I guess I will see you at eight
-but Prof I just wanted to know . . . (The line was already dead) if I could come in a bit later, when my eye stops looking like a monkeys ass, the pink one.

I rock up to work, with my stethoscope, my bible (not what you think, it's my medical handbook), and my red eye. Oh man I forgot my white coat. I have two options here now. Face the grilling of a lifetime for being late while I go back home to get my lab coat or hope that there is one left in the change rooms at mains. Mains is short for the main theatre. The place horror stories are made of. This place smells of sweat of cyclists of the tour de France. It looks like prison except in prison you get food through your mouth and there are no tubes and bleeping machines around. Then of course there is the spacemen. I am one of them now. Every time a patient enters this freezer all I can think of is better you than me guy, better you than me. In our lovely third world meets the bush setting there is never a lab coat. There is a cream overall type jacket that once resembled a lab coat. It smells of old people for some reason (perhaps used by a previous generation) and it is also a true absorbent. I had one of these babies on last year and instead of acting as barrier it sucked up blood like toilet paper does you know what. I will go on about Mains another time. Right now I am late, and guess what no lab coat for me. I am done for. It has already begun the ward round. Prof G watches as I walk in with his heat seeker missile eyes, the clock reads 08h01.

-you are late Dr Sha.
-Yes Prof Saloojee
-Where is your lab coat
-Funny story that, I had a patient yesterday who . . . (white lie coming up)
-You don't give a damn about medicine, do you? (Getting a little loud here). You cowboys don't care about your families. You carry germs around like the mess that is your hair. What is that gel? You are a disgrace. How do they graduate you punks?

He goes on about what it was in his day. I will spare you the ten minute lecture. But I assure it was not pretty. I should have gone home and got my damn lab coat. Worse still as I was last and, I wasted ten minutes of our precious time with this lecture. I got the dreaded D ward. Themba turns to me:

-nice one Ali. Thanks for putting him in a good mood.

11

I have not known Themba too long. He has however managed to irritate and annoy me since we were partnered together. He is tall lanky black dude. He has a great array of one liners like the one he just gave me now. He at least does his work and disappears. I have had worse experiences. The rule we made on day one was whoever is last or messes up on ward rounds does D ward. It is the post intake ward. The way it works is that last night whoever was on call admitted a humongous number of patients to this ward the big D. Naturally that person on call did the bare minimum of investigations to look good and keep the patient alive till the morning, allowing a trigger happy MO who could have ordered every blood test known to man. The onus now falls on yours truly to pull bloods on derelict delirious and dying patients. It was going to be a long day.

You see what no one tells you in medical school, is that by the time you reach year five, you are at ground level of the medical towers. If you struggle through the next five years you will reach the next level. The level of the MO. The medical officer, he sits on level 1. whoop d doo! I know and boy do these guys on level 1 make you push tin. You sweat, you toil, you cry and that is on good days. We will come to the other levels another time.

Right now, I have work to do. You see most patients in D ward are not just sick. They are begging you to let them die, one mistake and they will die. I stare down at my list 10 bloods 1 LP(lumbar puncture) 2 pleural taps and 1 ascitic tap and a lot of paper work. I should be done in 3-4 hours or so then it's of to be mopped. Now, I don't mind taking blood from people. I walk up to my first victim like the vampire I am. He does not suspect it. He is too busy trying to breathe. This man is thin, wasted. He is breathing faster than the movement of the fan above him. He has sweat all over him as a car does the warm morning after a cold night. He looks at me. I avoid his eyes. I tell him:

-Tata igazi baba (I need blood), a little Zulu I do know.
-He just nods. At this point I don't think he cares.

Now, when you take blood, there are only two issues to consider. 1) A patient that moves 2) when there is no blood coming into that tube. When this happens you know you are in the pan, you will have to re-try and nobody likes that, especially the patient. The best patients to take

12

blood from are generally the sick patients as they don't fight you much. However on my last patient the dehydration is so bad, all her veins are flat. This means I will have to use an artery. Not fun. The problem is, I have had blood taken from me. I know it sucks. I know it is painful. Hell, I hate doing it. But someone has to and today that someone is me. I go arterial, poking away till I get enough blood to run the tests required. Oh ya, almost forgot most patients hate this one. Most tubes requires about 3-4 mls of blood and if a vein collapses or if you move, we might have to go back in, to get enough to run that test. I know, what you thinking. No we don't do that on purpose.

Bloods done, now it is time for the LP. Now I have had this procedure. So I know. This is up there as one of the most painful procedures. To have a needle pushed through to your spinal fluid is something out of a horror movie, except its real. Majority of the patients in the public sector in South Africa are black. Since the good old apartheid days (sarcasm), our burden of care has soared including the number of black patients. These patients are truly amazing. I take my hat of to them. They take each procedure like a man (including the women).

The deal with LP's is position, position, position. It is real estate man. You find your spot and as soon as the patient is relaxed enough, you go in.

A bit of timing is required. You don't want to go in when these powerful back muscles are tensing because you will not win. Generally these patients are clinically diagnosed as meningitis. They have monster head aches and the LP often brings some relief. However you ever try doing an LP on a well patient. It is a time consuming effort full procedure that can go wrong. This is one, not to be taken lightly. There was a patient once where an intern stressed and tired missed a couple of important steps on the exam. The LP done thereafter resulted in coning; the patient lost pressure in the skull area and later died. Suffice to say the family and the intern were never the same thereafter. But in the hospital that sees thousands of patients on a daily basis, these things do happen. First do no harm, right?

Ok, ward work done. Hey its only 12h55. Today I will have lunch. A quick lunch. The canteen is filled with familiar faces.

Bruce— hey Ali, heard the G-man nailed your ass this morning.

Me—   ya, forgot my lab coat and I did not know the side effects of Chloroquine.

Bruce— That oke is harsh man.

Me—   tell me about it.

Stevie— wat up? What happened to the eye?, did the G-man smack you one?

Me—   hey Stevie, how goes it, ya woke up on the wrong side of the bed. Is Mopped(medical out patients department) GCS 15 today? (GCS, medical term rated from 3-15 3=dead 15=good/normal)

Stevie— she is alive and kicking my friend. A firm 15.

We spend the next couple minutes discussing, patients and calls. Doctors have a bad habit. When around other doctors, all we do is talk shop. We can't help it; it is just all we know and a way to cope. We love asking questions, checking if we know things. We compare whose calls are worse. We talk about procedures, faster ways of doing things and diagnosing patients. We sometimes discuss funny incidents. But I think generally we all are just trying to cope. We make a lot of jokes. I mean let's face it we are dealing with a lot of stressful situations here. Humor and denial are all we have.

Mopd/ mopped/medical out patients department are all the same thing. This place is a war zone. Now let me explain to you Gomers are one thing from the house of god. I would give anything for that. Here we have an array of patients. We have first and foremost the druggies that are 50 plus. They must have every single drug amenable to them in the public sector. They will not leave till you give it to them. They know all the names. They know how they work and what they do. They probably don't need rub rub or diclofenac suppositories any more, but just writing up the prescription makes them feel better. These patients live for their medications. For them coming to the hospital is a monthly outing. They make a day of it. Packed sandwiches, newspaper, some knitting, and some backbiting about Aunty Julie's daughter. I will say that the queue is long and fair enough it can take a while. However the moment you tell them there is no need to come back or heaven forbid there is no need for this medication they will go ape on you. They will insist for a follow up and nag till every prescription is written. They are the easy customers though. The stretcher cases are the worst. There are those who are in bad shape and then there are the fakers. The fakers know that as triage dictates: a stretcher case gets seen first. They lie down and scream in agony. Initially these guys are hard to pick out in a crowd but soon you can see one a mile away. They are always entertaining to observe when they are not seen as urgently as possible. The real stretcher cases are the true emergencies. As interns for some reason unbeknown to me, we see these cases. Generally these patients require a full work up. They have multiple problems with no short term fix. The burden of infectious disease in sub Saharan Africa in a word or two is HIV and TB. The bane of a doctor's existence in the South African public medical service.

I hate these two diseases more than any thing in medicine. They mask so many other diseases and disease processes and they are always a differential in any case. Worst of all they are infectious meaning I can get them from patients too. Now I know this sounds bad but most stretcher patients that come in to the hospital are HIV positive. More than that most of these have either had TB, have TB, or are currently being treated for TB. It is sad. It is a melancholy that is felt deep within my heart that most of these patients will die from one these two. Our savior the ARV's(anti retrovirals) are being rolled out, but the damage is done and the repair of a nation is slow. I mean this is no small dent on the bumper. HIV is a head on collision. Close to half of the work force out there is afflicted in some way by this problem. And if you are not affected directly you know of someone who is. We are still not at the peak or pinnacle of the curve and the future looks very foggy.

While I was in pediatrics there was a child who was malnourished and HIV positive. Both her parents died of HIV related complications. She was seen to every day by her Gogo(grandma). She came to us as a baby and grew in the hospital. She was a hospital baby, born and bred here. This place was all she knew or had seen. As I worked in that ward and saw her every day I had a superficial attachment to this child. We were waiting to start her on ARV's. She died of a chest infection later that year. She never had a chance really. But it makes me wonder of all those children out there who do make it on to ARV's. What happens when Gogo dies? Who will take care of this child? Who will maintain this Childs daily medication routine? The thought scares me.

MOPD is reasonably quiet, as it is a Wednesday. The mid week is generally a quiet time in the hospital. The busy days are the Monday run and the Thursday/Friday rush. Monday is when hospitals in the periphery review their patients and realize, damn we have some problems here. Let's turf to a bigger center before this patient dies. The Thursday rush is when reasonably well geriatric patients are brought in with some dumb complaint. The relatives are intent on having them stay over at the hospital for the week end.

Today there are only five stretcher cases that are split between three interns. It should be a chilled afternoon. The one thing you never do in a hospital. Perhaps I can call it a golden rule. You should never expect a quiet period at any tine. You do this at you peril. This is why we as doctors are very cautious when using the Q word. The moment you use it, fate turns against you.

> Stevie— (walks in from lunch) Hey looks like things are pretty quiet here.
> Me— (for a moment, I wince, and then I notice the ambulance turn into the emergency ramp. In slow motion I look over to Stevie, (I am trying to stop swearing at him in my mind.) You know what you just did right, there goes the afternoon.
> Stevie— Oh shit, my bad.

It was not too bad, I guess. Your usual afternoon at mopped. A 17 year old matric student with boyfriend problems tells us she tries to "off herself", because life is too hard. Sister you have no idea what is in store for you. So on this day she decides to pop 30 panado's, (as it is the GP's choice). Now what many people might not know is that panado at a significant dose can really stuff your liver up. Yes, even good old panado can kill you. So we stabilize her, take the appropriate bloods, and get ready for the afternoon handover. Our esteemed colleagues or the MO's as we call them return after all the immediate action.

> Dodge man— Anything happen, Dr Sha.
> Me— Just a panado overdose, she is stable now. The plan is written up in he notes. There is just the usual back up of mopd.
> Dodge man— So, its OK then, I will se you guys tomorrow.
> Me— Ya, bye. (Thanks for the help).

Now you see the way the hospital works is that you (meaning me), the intern sees every thing that walks through the hospital door first. We triage the patients into categories. Generally speaking anything that requires admission must be seen by an MO. Ah, how I keep deluding myself. Most MO's are very difficult to locate (I generalize, maybe). Registrars on the other hand depending on their year of training can be very informative and a joy to work with. Don't get me wrong I have come across some amazing senior doctors. I have knowledge of majority of what I know from them practically and clinically speaking. However over the past few months I have noticed that the more confident and comfortable you are, the less you will see of them in a teacher-student role. I mean, is that not what internship is about anyway.

In O&G aka ogle and gyrate or Obstets and gynecology, I learnt how to do a Caesar or Caesarian section. I could do a Caesar in thirty minutes flat. I was taught how to do this from one man. The Peace man, his name is derived from the peace hand gestures which women know quite well in O&G. He was my registrar. He taught me, the essence of O&G. PV till your fore and middle fingers hurt. Always ask if you don't know and treat every woman like she was your mother or wife. Simple and easy to pick up, ya right. The truth be told I picked up on this mans passion for what he does. He loved his job. His work made him happy. It gave him peace. This is something that I am struggling to come to grips with but who can I talk to. Where do doctors go?

Peace man always had the right the answer. If he did not know the answer he did not bullshit. So often doctors bullshit. He would say to the patients, "I don't know." They respected his honesty. He treated every patient about the same. I know most of us as doctors don't treat patients equally. We are human and thus we are swayed by our own ingrained doctrines. We like to think we do but very rarely do, especially in public service.

What I liked about him most of all though, was the fact that he treated me like a doctor. I won't say an equal because I recognize this mans knowledge and experience far superseded my own Yet, he never spoke down to me or ordered me around (like interns often are by seniors). He wanted to teach me. I am glad he did. There was no task too big or too small. Often I have my seniors tell me on a procedure they have done a number of times before, "I think this is too difficult for an intern". He would run me through it. He would help me do it.

He would say," first just do it then master it." He did this with patience and with a smile. He knew I was afraid. I was a young naïve, fresh meat intern out of medical school. This opening batting session would make me or break me. I was the rookie without a clue. We have all been there, some time or another. I don't know what it is about us as people but we love hurting each other. We forget what it was like to be new. The dough, still soft in the oven. No heat or pressure over us. In the moments to come we will rise to the occasion. We all just want each other to flop. We want to be the only one. If we are the only ones, how does that benefit anyone? We have to pass knowledge on and stop being so competitive.

Many of us see our jobs as something we do but we don't realize our jobs often become who we are. Hell, we spend majority of our adult life doing it. I will say this, initially when I met peace man I hated him. He was firm, pushy, a know it all and he expected nothing less than what he gave. I was always too slow with my ward work. My drips used to be all blue jelcos (the smallest there is). My experience was poor and knowledge of O&G was like a distant load of feces, long since passed. It was learning how to walk/talk for the first time. I never got the chance to tell him, but I often think of him, Peace man. He gave me so much for so little.

He had a great philosophy though. It has stuck with me. He said, "For every one fact you have listened to, for every one skill you have learned, you have become safer. You will never reach 100%. In our profession, no one ever will. We should however be able to save those that can be, and do the best with all we possess hand, mind, and soul."

The peace man is gone now. His wife was killed in a hijacking episode while at a conference in Johannesburg. I heard the story through the grapevine some months after I had left O&G. I never spoke to him after I left O&G. I don't think he knows of the impact he had on me like so many good teachers, you only realize the truth in their words and actions after they are gone. He took his children and shipped of to Canada after becoming a consultant. I wish I could say it once though, "thank you, peace man. Thank you for being the doctor I wish I can aspire to be."

Then you have MO's like my mate here now in internal medicine, Dodge. He is not just a dodger but he is dodgy. He is from some other African country as are majority of the rural and even now urban doctors in South Africa. You see as resources flow from the poorer nations to the rich, from third world to first world, so too does this even rarer commodity the human resource. Most of the interns I am with now all have some sort of short or long term plan to move to greener pastures. The real reason is a mixture of crime, the exuberant amounts of money available overseas and better working environment. We all want to make a better life for our families and loved ones. It also is the lack of appreciation for the skill and effort we make here on a daily basis that plays a small part.

You see dodge man is a human resource that has moved from his country to the best of Africa, South Africa. Most of our MO's in the years to come will be foreigners. Some are good, some bad. My experience with dodge has not been a good one.

The first day when I basically ran casualty on my own was the wrong thing to do. Once your competency level is assessed you are given tasks that only supersede it. I have no idea how it works in the corporate world but here the levels of management are run like the mafia. A consultant is made man. He cannot be touched. He is above the law. You mess with a consultant at your peril. He has been there, done that, got the t shirts a couple of times. He runs things from above. Then the reg or registrar is the hit man. He is the last man on the ground, hard core, book wormed and skilled, usually. The buck stops at the reg on call. The MO is the knock around guy, generally has been there a long while and is well connected. He continuously does what he does and is used to it. The run around kids doing the donkey's job is where the intern is king. No job too big or stupid for us to do. The pay is done accordingly.

The provinces, hospitals, departments all have their specific niches. Thus once you are apart of them, you are one of them even if it is for a short period of time. When "shit" goes down, your department is who you stand with, come hell or high water. Even when you are just rotating as an intern. You better stand with your current department in an inter-departmental war which happens often. If you don't, it will not be forgotten.

Dodge man knew from day one I was OK to abuse. as you know the victim also lets the abuser get away with murder. He was very rarely around and if I did need him, I would call. When he answered he often deduced it was a situation I could not handle and he came in. These were few and far between. I don't think you learn too much like this. You do however become confident in your own abilities and one day it will just be you standing in a casualty alone (especially in Africa). I believe as an intern in any field the guidance and supervision is always needed and one should err on the side of more than less.

There was a man two weeks ago now, came in with history of a sudden fall. He was old 58 or so, he was Indian, and Mike assessed him. He was on call with Dodge. He was comatose and seemed to be stable. He was a GCS 10/15, Mike called dodge. He agreed with Mike's assessment. Mike labeled him as a stroke, as he had high blood pressure and was a type two diabetic. He was a smoker and had a previous mild stroke. All his signs pointed toward it too. The next day he seemed to be improving when I saw him in the ward. However, I missed something, Mike missed something, a twisted hip, that later was though to be a fractured hip. He had a clot that shot off to his brain and he died. The family was upset. They could not understand how their father, grandfather was getting better one day and was dead the next. Of course as in the public setting they accepted the outcome. I did wonder, though could I have done anything differently? Would I have changed this mans outcome? Dodge, did not even come out and see the patient. At the meeting he presented the case as ours. The blame cast onto us as a whole. I don't know if dodge would have picked up what we missed. I just feel we could have done more. I hate to admit it but watching the family cry was painful. I thought of my own father who is about that age. He would have been seen in a private hospital. He would have had better care. The racial discrimination was gone but now there was a new type of discrimination, the haves and have not's.

Dodge and I have had our encounters over the last few weeks. He knows I cover a lot of his load. You see most patients arrive at mopd in the morning. This is the time when everyone is light and fluffy. By the end of the day whoever does not have their ttto's is like a bull that has had his bottom spanked.

The tto or to take out is every out patients holy grail. Once they are armed with that prescription, they are half way there. The moment they leave the pharmacy they are all smiles. Now Stevie has this thing, he writes like a fart in the wind. Most of the time we cant read a word of his meds. Its there all right but no one can see it. Yet, pharmacy gets its right every time. The pharmacists can read any thing. They could decipher any doctors writing; probably take a course on it.

Now with that mopd patients take the cake. They are usually the sickest and dumbest patients of the lot. They come receive tto's and are satisfied.

And so the escalator of medicine continues. Patients initially go up. They then join the travolator where they swing in and out of hospital neither getting better nor do they get worse.

After a number of years depending on each individual patient's genetics and social habits, they then slowly go down the escalator till you don't see them anymore.

I guess that is modern medicine in a nut shell, well in third world countries, public service, anyway. They are the only place I have any experience in.

3

It was a warm winter's afternoon. Yes, you read correctly, you see in Kwa-Zulu Natal the winters close to the coast are like the summers of central Europe. I heard him come home the way he usually used to. He was a tall, graceful chap, my brother. If you did not know him too well you would think there was an air of conceitedness there. This was not so, far from it actually. He was the kind of guy who would help that old granny cross the road even if everyone laughed at him, (a long time ago now). He was a good man, in my eyes. He was wearing his guess jeans, the one I gave him for his birthday. He had his college sweater on. He punched me on the shoulder as he walked by, the way older brothers lovingly do, (I love you to man), as I kicked him back.

I was in grade 11 then. It was a trying time for me. I was disinterested in school, as most of us are at that age. I was working on my own personal image and I was trying to "be one of the boys". I was spending a lot of time sorting out my hair and collecting aftershaves. I wanted to be like him.

You see for my brother the world was his playground. He was a natural at most sport. I start with sports because it what defines a true man. Does it not? If we had some major melt down and we swiftly fell from grace into a time where we had to live as we did before telephones, television and Mcdonalds. I believe it would be those of us with the physical build and some mental stamina that will be able to survive.

Would we be able to catch our supper, cook it, and push through a catastrophic storm outside in the cold? Well I believe my brother would.

Now, I know what you are thinking. Everybody holds their family members up on a pedestal. We don't see any faults or imperfections.

My brother was my friend and close compatriot. He never left me out or put me down. He was unlike older brothers that my friends had, that seemed to tease, belittle, or pull rank on them. There was a three year difference between us. But it always felt a lot less to me.

There were summers spent playing cricket and soccer. Long hot days in the sun, where I perfected my forward defensive and fined tuned my dribbling skills. He taught me how to play. Movies and outings with his friends were however meetings that I missed. I had to, everyone needs their space and my parents forbid me as I was deemed too young to loaf around the mall. It is funny how, nowadays parents seem quite willing to sacrifice a child's free time by dropping them of at the mall with some money and friends. I know there is a lot of peer pressure from the child. But what happened to the days when we spent time together as families. They say looking at your child brings coolness to ones eyes, yet majority of the parents in the world today seem to be like guest appearances in the show of their children's lives. Time passes by and I do believe on some level the child resents this way of life. Then as the seasons change the child gets accustomed to this lifestyle and soon they are not children but young adults at age 10. It all starts at the mall.

So does this story. I don't know how or why it happened but it did. Now my brother as stated previously was a gentile handsome guy. He was confident and probably could have scored any chick he wanted, but why in the end he chose her, I will never understand.

The take away store was Wimpy, a place we frequented quite regularly with family and friend. She worked part time there as a waitress. Her father believed it would be a good learning experience of how to earn ones own money. Sorry, it was actually her stepfather. The guys used to go for ice creams and other deserts. They were all around the same age 17/18 pushing through the pain that was matric and focusing on what life after school would mean. Girls, getting rich, being famous, rainbow dreams, always fading with time.

I noted the smiles, the eye contact but thought nothing of it. Why would I suspect anything? She was good looking, well to me anyway. God has made someone for everybody. Well, that's what they say right.

I don't believe it. No, not because I am cynic but rather I believe I am a realist. I think we all just look around till we find some one who we like, maybe even fall in love. What we realize later, is that at this point in time that person is the right person for you and most of us, like that old t-shirt or black dress you can never gat rid of, hold to this ideal of love. The truth is we just find a partner, some one with whom we share space and time. This partner learns about us, through conversations, time and other people close to us. Soon they know most or all that is required. Initially there is the chemical romance but the passion must fade as every high has a low. Those that make it through the low have an interest, a clear goal that they want to achieve.

They want to be with you and if you are sharp enough you would know that this is rare thing. It's a big deal but then you have to ask your self, do you want to be with them? That's what I thought, OK give me a break. I am still in my early twenties.

So there she was, every visit to Wimpy was more food for thought then we knew. She was like 5 foot 6, soft light brown hair that ended just beyond her shoulder blades. Her eyes were a dark penetrating brown. She had very fine freckles on her face as someone who just shook one drop of pepper on their sunny side up. She was not quiet nor was she loud. She was a presence felt once arrived like a bus calling all passengers to get on board. She was friendly and talkative, very similar to my mum in some ways.

The first time I noticed that something was up when a lengthy conversation ensued between them over ordering a banana split.

Akbar—hi there.
She—   you again, you following me, or just staring.
Akbar—no, just getting some ice-cream, but it is a free country, I can look at whoever I want, right. I heard looking is free.
She—   well depends what you looking at?
Akbar—well, just the menu, for now anyway.
She—   I have seen you around, you a college boy, right.
Akbar—Yup, and you are part of the ice queens from the Girls high. (All my brothers friends gawking and giggling).
She—   who started this whole ice queen thing, hope it was not you guys.

Akbar— Nope not me, depends on who your sources are. I believe after this encounter things are warming up though, wouldn't you say.

She— Well that depends what you mean by warming up.

A few minutes later She arrived, and offloaded some ice and cream over my brothers pants. The reason I say ice and cream was first the ice fell upon his lap and then the cream part of his milk shake.

She—That's for calling me an ice queen and picking on my friends.

At first I think my bro was shocked. I was. But then he proceeded to take the ice cream and smear all over her face and clothes. It was hilarious. It was something out of a movie. And it set a gold standard for the tumultuous relationship that followed. And we could never go to Wimpy again, thanks bro.

A few things I would like to note from this encounter.

1) They had a genuine chemistry. (That kind of natural flirtation especially between teenagers never happens. This type of age group is well known for the most awkward and embarrassing interactions between a boy and a girl. I can testify to that.)

2) They were both alpha male and alpha female. Neither would back down.

3) They obviously had an attraction, but more than that a real liking for each other. That much was evident

4) When they were together nothing and no one else mattered. It was like the rest of us were invisible. They were in their own little bubble, a cocoon for two, no more no less.

5) There were only two problems that I could see and so could everyone else.

She was a non-muslim, and I guessed this because she was white.

4

It is a Thursday and I am on call. The psychology of an on call day always fascinates me. From the moment I open my eyes that morning I am depressed, mildly angry, and just a tad grouchy. Why did I choose this? The question I believe every doctor asks themselves at least once on every busy call day. You and only you alone are to blame. You chose to be a doctor. You chose to work 30 hour shifts. You chose to see sick people as a profession. You chose to be up at all hours of the night and morning. You chose to spend evenings hungry, thirsty, wearing ridiculous blue jail birds clothing. You chose all this, or did you?

I remember when I was young and I went to the doctor, my GP. I felt better just with Mummy saying, "Ali we are taking you to see the doctor." It was like I knew after I saw Dr Harry I would be on the path to recovery. The moment I stepped into that pristinely kept office, I was at peace. Despite my pounding headache, my rumbling tummy, my swollen glands, cuts, bruises or fractures I knew Dr Harry would know what to do. His words were gospel gold and I lapped it up like a cat does its milk every time. You get sick. You go to see this man with a white coat and funny walk man round his neck. He thumped you on the chest a couple a times maybe played with your tummy, or listened to the music of you breathing, and suddenly, Ah yes! He knew what was wrong. Of course sometimes you would have to undergo the dreaded injection but over the years I looked forward to it. Hell I even asked for it. In no time of an injection and some tablets you were as fit as fiddle.

This is what I believed doctors did. The pure naivety of it all. Now I realize what it takes to reach that position. Now I know what it is to deal with the real sick patients. Now I know why to be a doctor requires an oath and life long sacrifice that is definitely not every person's cup of tea.

You see the GP has been in the trenches. He has done his time in boot camp. He has seen about 70% of what is out there(common problems). He is adequately equipped to take care of the run of the mill general medical conditions. He has earned his status most of the time of a GP. But even for him the learning process has just begun. You see doctors unlike most professions are highly charged. You are dealing with the most dangerous entity on planet Earth, humans. It carries every burden possible. You need to keep up with the ever changing updates in management of conditions. There are always new better ways to do every aspect from diagnostics to therapeutics. Add to this the emotional burden of each patient. But most physicians agree the most difficult aspect is the loss of self in this sand and fog, and the loss of those closest to you in the process. This only happens to the good doctors. The rest of us learn to block it out. We learn not to care. It is not that we are bad people. It is not that we hate medicine. It is our defense mechanism. It is our way of functioning, staying alive, and surviving.

So there I was, hoping and praying like I do on every call day that at least the day work is light. A light day=more rest to push through a heavy night. Generally this never happens. I can honestly say that from my own experience for some reason, I cannot put my finger on it, but on call days are worse. I think your mind set is such you just see everything as being heavy and drawn out. Every one who is not on call conspires against you to leave more work behind to do when you are alone.

The round begins at 8am sharp. I am late again. My on call black strapped no name brand watch reads 08h11. I make up some excuse about traffic but dodge man expects nothing less from me and just gives me a disapproving nod. We move quite quickly through the round as we do when dodge does the round.

All in all, not too bad. I have 7 discharges. I have 10 bloods and 3 drips, one LP, some CT scans and Ultrasound to book, an echo and some follow up results. Oh ya, and one transfer back to a periphery hospital. An HIV positive renal or chronic kidney diseased patient that we cannot do any thing more for. Due to his HIV status and poor socioeconomic circumstances he will not get on to the program. This means he will not get dialysis; he will not get a transplant. He will die in a couple years, maybe months.

I push through the discharges quickly. The LP takes about 30 minutes to do.

The actual procedure takes me 10 minutes, but it takes the sisters about 10 minutes to find an LP needle and it takes them another 10 minutes to set up a trolley for me to work with.

I don't know how it works in first world countries or other third world countries for that matter, but in South Africa the logistics of practicing medicine is a nightmare. It is a never ending nightmare. It is very much real though. You don't suddenly wake up relieved that it was just a dream. You realize that you are already up and that is your life. It is my life. It is the life of many other doctors in South Africa and the world. It is especially so in poorer countries with no resources with no infrastructure. Places where the government has long forsaken its own people to line their own pockets. But what do I know?

You see simple paper work always takes forever. The reason being that most of the time there are no stocks. There are always shortages of stock. To take a simple blood can take 15 minutes. You have to wait for the right tube to be found or fetched. You have to physically write each form out and each blood test, Date, name, hospital number, time, oh the list is endless. But the cruncher there is no computer system in our province proudly South African, Kwazulu—Natal. I am praying, though.

They call chasing results when one does a test on patient and awaits the results of that test. We literally chase that result as one would chase the dragon. By the end of it, you have an adrenaline rush just from calling a lab technician and going through the rigmarole of getting each single result per patient, you realize how it is that so many MD's are drug abusers.

A typical conversation would be something like this:

Lab girl: hello, how are you?
Me: Hi there, its Dr Sha from ward M1, looking for Mr Khumalo's U&E result and Mr MKhizes FBC result.
Lab girl: uh, this is micro, you must phone chemistry and hematology.
         I will put you through to chemistry, hold on.
Me: listening to jingle bells in august while I await the transfer. The phone line suddenly goes dead

This means I have to start again. Let the re-dialing extravaganza begin.

Me: hello it's me, Dr Sha again. How are you?
Lab guy: heeelllooo, wat up.
Me: I need a chemistry result
Lab guy: hold on, it's coming up.
Me: jingle bells this hospital smells, wish the lab found my results today oh what fun it is to see Dr Sha win the day, hey!
Lab girl: helooo, howzit?
Me: hi, its Dr Sha, I am looking for a Mr Khumalo's U&E result.
Lab girl: OK, when was it taken?

Oh you are not gonna get me today, I am armed woman, got the patients file with me, and I got all the lab numbers and dates.

Me: it was taken two days ago, in the morning.
Lab girl: patient's hospital number . . .
Me: 550121
Lab girl: OK specimen was received and sent out.
Me: I checked the lab box and the patients file and the ward results box, there is no result there.
Lab girl: OK we keep a copy at reception. I will put you through to them.
Me: OK but, (line is already dead).

Another lab girl: how can I help you doctor?

Me: (sounds ominous). Hi there its Dr Sha, I am looking for a U&E result. The patients name is Mr N. Khumalo; it was taking two days ago, 550121. (Patience is wearing thin now.)
Other lab girl: Ok, hold on . . . it was sent out yesterday.
Me: yes I know but I can't seem to find the result.
Other lab girl: Ok, I will locate the copy.
                       A couple minutes later . . . I have it here.

A successful result chase ends in my favor. I get the other result, it takes twice as long. You see this paper system, requires dates. time, patients name and number and so on and so on. Oh how I wish the government would invest in this new technology called a computer system that could be used anywhere in the hospital anytime, province wide, awesome idea. Except it's already occurring in first world medicine.

What would life be like if you could see every patients result from their first admission? A history already on computer screen, wouldn't that be awesome. Ah but this KZN, South Africa, baby, and one can only hope. But I do hope, I do dream and that's what counts.

I push through the rest of my ward work and head of to have lunch before running of to casualty. There I meet dodge man, surprise, surprise.

> Dodge man: hey Dr Sha, you completed the ward work. Did you get all the blood results? How is Mr Khumalo's U&E's looking.

I resented this cat and mouse game. He knows I have the results and that his renal failure is worsening. He knows he should be discussed with a tertiary center for dialysis. This should be done by a senior Dr but the duty more than likely will fall to me. It really does astonish me how once you pass something everything thereafter seems beneath you. I guess I should not complain as I will probably do the same. Its human nature, in fact its genetic, you work to a position of seniority then you forget. You forget the sweat tears and strife it took to get you there. You then delegate and move on. I am generalizing though; you get a few people that really work from grass roots up. They are known through honor, and honored out of respect.

Nelson Mandela was such a man. I can't say I knew him much. At the time he came into power I was just entering my pubertal years, suffice to say I had other things on my mind. Now after reading a long walk to freedom, I realize as an adult the true greatness and selflessness of the man. A true public servant, a man of the people from the people but most importantly he was always for the people. Perhaps he is someone I should emulate or try to.

However you cannot ever compare yourself to the prophets of the past. You can only try and follow their examples. I hope the politicians of today honor him by trying . . . to follow that example.

Me: yup, I got the U&E, urea is up and the creatinine is above 600. I called our tertiary referral center spoke to the nephrologist there. He says we can refer the patient there.

Dodge: (he smiles at me). Ok, I will see you later, I swapped my call with Dr VW. It is you and me again tonight.

Me: (jingle bells, Jingle bells I am on call today, oh what fun it is to hear dodge man is here to stay) I hate having this tune in my head.

I meet up with Steveo at lunch. His spirits are high since his girlfriend is coming down for the week end. He has been telling me this every day since last week. I daydream of having a girlfriend of having something to look forward to.

Steveo: so you on call tonight bro?

Me: yup.

Steveo: hope its quiet for you.

The same old ritual that must be played out every time you tell someone you are on call. Whenever anyone is on call this is what is said, it is just like wishing strangers happy birthday when they tell you it's their birthday.

Steveo: so as I said my chick is comin down from Josies this weekend.

Me: uh huh. (While I gobble some big korn bites).

Steveo: I am thinking of going away to the coast man.

Me: oh ya. (As I gurgle some coke down my throat, very healthy lunch.)

Steveo: you know this area, what would you suggest?

Me: Umhlanga is a nice area. It's beautiful, close to the malls but pretty expensive, hotel wise.

Steveo: ya, I need to keep an eye on the budget.

Me: then there is Ballito, a lot more quiet and personal with some great town houses. Of course, you can always head to central Durbs. There is a lot to see and do there.

Steveo: so what would you suggest?

Me: it depends on what you want man

Steveo: ya, but what would you suggest?

Me: personally, I would head out north. I would go on drives throughout the midlands meander. There are a whole lot of these small agricultural farms that produce fresh veggies and fruit to taste and they show you how the entire process works for each farm. There is a beautiful strawberry farm. You can have some breakfast of strawberry waffles and fresh milk tea. There is this secluded little cheese farm where you can have some fresh feta goat cheese and wine, (Grape juice in my case) while you chill out on a hill top. Oh the scenery is mesmerizing. There are stretches of trees as many as the hair on your hand. The soft summer breeze will refresh you and slip straight through your outer clothes. You will feel truly relaxed and uplifted.

Steveo: Ok, I think I am sold.

Me: well, even if you still wanna take a drive to Durbs to the coast you can, it's only 45 minutes from the meander.

Steveo: ya, I guess so. I gotta run man, check whats happening in Casualty.

Me: ya, guess I better head of to MOPD.

Steveo: See you later man.

Me: See you.

The current arrangement of the group is that it is a bit heavy for someone to be on call and start of early in casualty. So when you are on call as I am on today you go to MOPD, till four then you head of to casualty. MOPD is its usual Dementor draining self. In Harry potter there are those dementors that drain all the happiness out of an individual, that is MOPD. After my afternoon of seeing hypertensive patients on chronic medications that include cough mixtures and asthma pumps (as they sometimes get breathless), a diabetic whose monthly sugar reading at the hospital is 24. The diabetic patient goes on to explain to me that he is feeling fine, what's the big fuss about. Last but not least there is an epileptic patient that is having seizures again.

You really cannot blame anyone for these common problems. If these patients had been counseled properly perhaps they would be patients. Perhaps they would take these diseases seriously. Perhaps, perhaps, perhaps.

I begin the grueling process of proper education and thus I only see 4 patients in two hours. According to our Mopd stats that is really slow going. This mopd sees an average of 300 patients a day. This number is split between 6-7 doctors. Today is a 6 day as there are two doctors off. One is post call and the other is sick. Yes, doctors get sick and funnily enough they get sick quite often in this place. I attribute it to burn out. In fact I can feel a bit of the flu coming on now. Reminder to self, need to take of 2 days of next month. Gotta stay healthy.

By the way I am just kidding, I don't do that if anyone asks. Any way, we as interns have 20 odd days annual leave a year and a couple sick days leave available over three years. Thus use wisely and cautiously, you never know when you might really need them.

Now, I have not seen my quota and this clinic is a ghost town at 16h45. What happens then, is all the patients that are left trudge like the seven dwarves over to casualty. There is sneezy, dopy, grumpy, grumpy, grumpy, big ears and grumpy. Oh ya, I forgot one grumpy. If I had to wait the whole day in one queue then as the sun disappears I was shafted to another queue, I would not be grumpy, I would be CRAZY, with anger that is. The best part is, guess who will be seeing these guys in casualty later? Yours truly.

I spend 20 minutes explaining to Mr Peters the difference between type 1 diabetes and type 2 diabetes and the fact that he might eventually require daily insulin injections to control his diabetes. He meets this startling revelation with resistance and denial. It's a normal human response.

Mr Ndabele is even more difficult, as someone explained to him that his thickened gums have been caused by the chronic medication he was on for his epilepsy. His idea of treating this problem was stopping the medication altogether. The result is seven stitches over his left cheek and countless attacks over the last couple months. I place him on some new meds and hope it also doesn't exhibit any major side effects. Deep down however I know this man will be back in casualty some day with seizures. The cheap medication and terrible side effects of many of the drugs often result in decreased compliance by the patients.

The worst patient however is Mrs Singh. She is your signature MOPD patient. I take one look at her 2000 page file and know I am in for it. Her repeat meds alone are over a page long. She starts of with the usual patient banter:

Mrs Singh: Hallo doctor, so young you are doctor.

Me: yes Hello Mrs Singh, I am Dr Sha I will be seeing you today.

Mrs Singh: You remind me of my nephew Sachin. He is just like you. You know he is studying to be an accountant.

Me: that's nice.

Mrs Singh: So tell me where are you from Dr?

Me: Oh from around here.

Mrs Singh: oh ya, where?

Me: just around . . .

Mrs Singh: who your father and mother?

Me: I don't think you will know them.

Mrs Singh: I know lots of people from around here. You know I was around when Indians had their own hospital. Those were better days.

Me: OK, Mrs Singh, are you well today? (Sure as hell looks like it)

Mrs Singh: funny you should ask, I got these pains over my body.

Me: where?

Mrs Singh: oh all over.

Me: where exactly?

Mrs Singh: In the front. In the back. I feel very weak doctor, can I have some vitamin tablets.

Me: ok, I think I will repeat you medications for your asthma, diabetes, hypertension and ischemic heart disease.

Mrs Singh: Dr, you know my husband died two years ago.

Me: I am sorry to hear that.

Mrs Singh: my daughter is moving to Jo'Burg next week end.

Me: Mrs Singh, any other medical complaints?

Mrs Singh: she got a nice job there.

Me: (I look at my watch, it reads 16h31)

Mrs Singh: She says I might have to stay with Aunty Anjeli, the neighbour soon. I can't live on my own. I am very sickly doctor. You know.

Mrs Singh continued to talk for the next ten minutes. I did not say anything. I did not listen either. All I did was what every doctor previously did, which was refill all her medications. Wait, I did add her vitamin tablets to the list, some rub rub for her "aching bones" and I told her to come back in 6 months. Funnily enough she thanked me and left. She was the only patient that thanked me that day. I know I did not deserve it. I felt like I let her down. Yet I know in truth it is the system that has her let her down. There is no psychologist on hand except once a week. I have tried to book a patient once before, it took the best part of 15 minutes. I did not have the time to help her the way she needed to be helped. I was already thinking of my call and all the patients left over while I was busy listening to this old ladies sad social problems.

I shrug it off and start heading towards casualty. I did my best, right.

Casualty is buzzing, it's already gone five o clock and the after hours drive is on like a scone.

MOPD has left me with 23 left over patients. Thanks Mrs Singh, ok I take that back. Patients always seem sicker at night. They look at you and they seem tearful, almost begging you to admit them. But don't fall prey to this eloquent and very successful plan learnt by every after hours patient.

You see the problem is beds and space. There are never enough beds. Thank God too, other wise we would continue admitting.

In my first year of internship, I used to sit in POPD(Pediatrics out patient dept or Popped= how you feel when you leave). My first couple calls I would see a child crying in pain with a snotty nose and a mother with those puppy dog eyes and I used to admit. Dr Nkosi taught me the difference between admitting out of pity and admitting those who need in patient care.

On one night I admitted till all beds were full. Then a baby came in with a severe pneumonia. He seemed a lot worse then a couple of the other admission I already sent up to the wards. Half hour later a 7 year old girl came in status asthmaticus (terrible asthma attack). The problem was we only had one oxygen canister in POPD. Dr Nkosi came down and we did our best, alternating the nebulizations and Oxygen. He was often called to high care but came down to monitor their progress. We did all we could. We gave the fluids antibiotics etc. We even decided to go up and see if there was any way we could pull a bed from somewhere. Nothing.

These children had nowhere else to go. The ambulance would take hours to come. Time they did not have. The baby with pneumonia did not make it the next day in POPD. Most of my admissions were discharged not long after. Maybe if he got one of those beds . . .

I guess we do our best and we learn as we go along. What else can one do?

So even though all these patients will inevitably want to be admitted as they have come from over 100km away and there is no way they can back home. I cannot admit anyone that is not close to death and then too, I have to make an informed decision.

For example, the 7th patient I see is Miss Madlala, she looks like Whoopi Goldbergs skeleton. I know this syndrome, I see it everyday. I read through her out patient's card. She has defaulted on her ARV's. She has a CD4 count of 7. She is as dry as the Sahara desert. I write her up for some IV fluids. I take some blood for FBC, U&E for what its worth. I know she cannot be admitted. I studied the ethics manual. I remember something about the greater good, vaguely. If admitted Mrs Madlala will take up a bed. She will take up this hospital bed for a long tine, with no positive outcome likely.

I carry on seeing to the rest of the left over MOPD patients. It takes from five to ten o'clock. I get through them without any major problems. I decide once I have seen them all, that it is time for some supper. A nice cold coke and a microwave warmed burger. The cold coke hits me like a 6 foot heavy weight boxer. I left it in the freezer. It gives me a slight buzz. Coke should be classified as schedule 4 drug. The warm burger hits the spot. For some reason when on call, you just become grateful for so many little things.

You are first and foremost grateful for your health. You see all these sick sick people. You realize how precious your health is. You promise to live a good life. You promise to eat, drink, say and do the right things starting tomorrow or the next day.

You think about all that free time you waste. You sit at home watching TV. You walk around doing nothing in a mall. You spend a lot of time thinking about doing things and going places but you never do. You spend a great deal of time sleeping and complaining.

You realize the importance of sustenance. You drink the water from your tap without really appreciating the miracle that this is. Every evening you have a warm freshly cooked meal, (Well just about every evening). You are so well off. You can choose where you want to eat. You complain about the price of things going up but you can still afford it, and you do spoil yourself often.

You go to bed in a house, a home. You have a nice warm bed. You wake up to a hot shower in the morning. You get too see your family daily (well I do). And spend time with friends who really know and care about you.

Do we really consciously absorb and understand these blessings?

Or do we just take them for granted?

There is however the human condition. We all are never satisfied. We can't be. We want more, need more, we have to be more. We are always trying to better ourselves or competing with others in some way.

As in my case the only thing missing was that special someone. The last kiss goodnight, early kiss good morning. I better start working quickly too. If mum has her way I will be marrying Aunty Sara's daughter next year.

As I was chomping on my chow, I look up and see, the man, Mbanjwa. Mbanjwa is an intern I have heard about. Well i lie i know him a bit. He is currently doing his surgery rotation. Supposedly if there was a prize for the intern of the year there would be no competition, he would win. He was a tall strapping Zulu man. He was sleek and muscular, an air of confidence. But he had the voice of a 6 year old girl, which was hilarious. He was also a kiss ass. He sucked to every senior and thus earned his recognition of being the best. As sucking up is something I could never do. There is this thick smooth chocolate milkshake "peoples" drink. It is called SuperM. It is sold at all the cafes. Mbanjwa was nicknamed SuperM in our intern circles as he was the "man" and for other reasons too.

Mbanjwa: hey Ali, how are you? (He knows my name, how does he know my name?)
Me: hey there Super . . ., Hey there Mbanjwa?
Mbanjwa: So how is your call going?

Me:	oh, not too bad. As you can, see just busy having a bite now.
Mbanjwa:	Ya, I just finished up with a resus in A1 now, we managed to bring the dude back.
Me;	(back from the dead, I say old chap, jolly well done). Oh ya, what happened man?
Mbanjwa:	well, I was doing my round and I saw this guy out of the corner of my eye. He was slipping into a coma. I had this sixth sense feel that doctors get, you know it right.
Me:	(oh ya, I get that feel all the time, usually I scratch it).
Mbanjwa:	Anyway I tell the sister to bring the resus trolley and BLEEP BLEEP
Me:	(saved by the pager), gotta go man will take you up on this thrilling story later man.

I walk towards casualty wondering which was worse, Mbanjwa's story or what waited me in casualty.

The answer was straight for ward the moment I saw my patient.

There she was as thin as a stick and as fragile as a twig. Her body habitus would make you guess she was in her early teens. Alas she was 28. She was HIV positive and she was breathing like someone who just won the comrades marathon. I didn't even have to examine her to guess that she had pneumonia. The chest X-ray would reveal she had TB before, maybe reactivated or reinfected with it now. And just to add insult to injury she probably had PCP, a common infection when your CD4 is sitting at <200. This was bad but the problems just began there. Her outpatient card was a mess.

From what I could gather it was a case of hospital hopping. A common past time for patients not happy with their diagnosis. The problem was that her follow up was shabby to put it mildly. Supposedly she was being treated for TB but she had no green card.

The green card, (invented by some genius in the health department) works like this. A patient with TB is diagnosed and treatment is started, they get a friend or family member to watch them take a pill everyday for 6 months(ya right) and this person ticks it off on a green card with months, days of the year, patients name etc. this is done till the treatment is complete. This DOTS or directly observed treatment or as I like to call it, with my patient serving as an example tonight Done my

Own Thing you Stupid is extremely effective in eradicating TB from the subcontinent. No wonder we have the highest rates of multi-drug resistant and extremely drug resistant TB in the world. As dots goes patient should have their treatment directly observed which "sometimes" does not happen. Well I really can not blame DOTS, patients have to take responsibility too but do they?

Now my patient will have to cough up sputum that will be sent to a lab, which will take a couple weeks to come back, with a culture result for TB and sensitivity of drugs that can kill TB. In the mean time my patient will be at home ticking or not ticking of her green card spreading TB amongst her fellow community members. Hell, it might even be you and me, well not likely if you have a good immunity.

So the process begins from scratch. After about half hour of sorting through this out patient card and using a nurse as an interpreter I gather the following information:

Name:	Happy (ironic name) Ndlovu
Main complaint:	cough which she has all the time, shortness of breath, a recent problem and probably the reason she cam to hospital today, "feeling sick all the time" and she needs a grant.
Past medical history:	diagnosed with HIV in 2005 at a clinic as she was getting sick often. A Cd4 was done only in 2006 when she was diagnosed with TB for the first time. Her cd4 then was 300 she thinks. She completed 6 months of treatment then. She was diagnosed with TB 3 months ago but her TB tablets were not working like before. She was still coughing and feeling sick.
Allergies:	none known
Social history:	she has 2 children; one is 4 the other 7. Both according to her are HIV negative. Father, fathers, or husband unknown. She lives over 150 km away from this hospital which she borrowed money from a friend to get to. She used to work as a maid but is too sick to do so now. She cries a bit as her she tells us her sister

died from aids and she does not know who will look after her children if she dies.

It is on this note that I make as detailed notes of this problem case as I can. I admit her to the wards with some of my best work in a long while.

I don't know why but from hundreds of patients that I have seen with similar problems, I just felt something for Happy. I had to make sure that this time things were done with some order and purpose.

The hours pass by; I get called in for the acute asthmatic, the drunken stuporous alcoholic 3am walk in and yet another parasuicide attempt. It is a quiet evening really and I am grateful. I don't call dodge man once. Hope you had a good night sleep dodge, once again.

As a senior, he goes off to sleep when things settle down, in his case 00h00.

My break will be when he comes back around 05h00, giving me 2-3 hours sleep.

5

My brother and Christine had an on and off relationship as most teenage love stories do. The surprising thing about theirs was that neither family ever found out. They were "seeing" each other for years before anyone realized it.

Christine was a real beautiful girl. She was blessed with timeless features. High cheek bones and soft curves. A medium upper body build. Strong muscular calves that allowed her to stretch her lanky legs. Flawless smile. God sent, not dentist made. I know what you thinking, I am not a perv, just very good at observations.

She was the epitome of all that my brother loathed. Opposites attract. The DIY female, the go-getter. A very driven and athletic bombshell. She did everything at pace and she was often way ahead of the pack. She was a spawn of the woman's liberation movement, yet still down to earth. She had some Afrikaner background from her mums side. Family was pretty important in her life too as a consequence. She wanted to be a success no matter what.

As I slept in the same room as my brother, those early years I was kept in the loop purely due to proximity. The late night phone calls, where some nights they laughed, some they fought, some she cried. The perfume scented letters that he kept in a hidden place which of course I knew and invaded.

Initially they were just kids having fun I suppose. The incidents that occurred with time however showed that their early infatuations had been replaced with some thing deeper and more meaningful.

I remember one afternoon at a school rugby match where my brother was ridiculed and called racist names. He had hate speech thrown at him in school many a time, we all do, but he never reacted. Yet on this occasion the moment Tim Joubert stooped so low as to mock his girlfriend. My brother saw red. He was not the fighting type. Although he was out numbered, even though I pitched in with a punch or two, we caught a bit of a hiding. All for Christine's pride.

He was angry and hurt by words. It was not something I had not seen in my brother ever before. It frightened me. Luckily the fight was short lived. Some drunken parents pulled us apart and we lived to fight another day.

I don't know why but he seemed to be more and more engrossed in her.

She was like a novel that just got better and better the more you read. Soon he was watching pansy movies, going to plays. He would even go and watch her play hockey. He lost some friends and his group became smaller and smaller till one day it just included one, her.

The truth is though that most couples do tend to spend more and more time alone as time goes on. I would say it is true of all higher order species but especially notable in humans. Most animals have their packs, herds, family as do we. It is what defines us. Our group of few nourishes us when we are young, strengthens us as we grow strong, and cherishes us as we grow old.

It was around my brother's final schooling year that it finally came round to my parents that my brother was with one "gornie". It was the end of an era. The post mortem of ones schooling life comes down to your matric results and your matric ball.

Of course these events are taboo and Islamically completely forbidden. Yet some how my brother as he always did made a plan and snuck out. He had his partner in crime but on that particular night he was not only seen by God but by Uncle Asmal too. My fathers friend, a man of great stature in the local community. He owned a bakery and in the early hours of that Saturday morning, my brother was busted, big time.

My father came in with the disrespect of ones family and religion speech. My mother spent some time sobbing then the anger took over. My brother at the age of 18 was not too old for a fully loaded open hand five finger times two if you please. The first talking to always lasts a long time. Every child knows that moment a parent finds out information for which they disapprove. That first session is the worst. You do what my brother did expertly every time. You remain silent; you listen, and well at least try to be above the alarm bells running in that space between your ears. You answer direct questions as simply and as forthright as possible.

Dad: so, where were you last night my boy? (At this point his tone is still controlled, and his voice is not yet strained).

Bro: I went out to the ball.

Dad: Did I not distinctly tell you that you cannot go?

Bro: yes, you did.

Mum: (Sniffing in the background).

Dad: so why did you disobey me boy?

Bro: I had to. I promised my friends.

Dad: so your friends are more important than your family now, right I see.

Mum: Why beta (son)? Why?

Bro: I am sorry Ma.

Mum: You have disgraced your family and our name. The entire community will know about your philandering. You lucky it was only Uncle Asmal that saw you and not Aunty Jameela as well. You were running around like a mad thing after midnight with one gorni as well. Have you no shame? Do you not care of the consequences? You only think of yourself, and your own selfish pleasures.

Dad: what is your relationship with this girl?

Bro: her name is.

Dad: I did not ask what her name is.

Bro: we are just close friends papa. Just close friends.

Mum: what did you do at this ball? Did you drink beer, were you smoking, doing drugs? Huh, huh . . .

Bro: no, it was just a farewell party to all those leaving school.

Dad: we may be old but we are not stupid. We know what happens. Where was the after party? Why didn't you come home straight after the ball?

Bro: I was coerced into going but I wanted to anyway. I did not drink beer or smoke or do drugs there.

Dad: why do you disappoint us? Why did you disobey us?

Bro: I have always done what you have asked of me. I just had this one thing I had to do, this last goodbye, can you not understand that.

Dad: No I cannot, I will speak to you again later. You have hurt your mother and me very deeply.

What occurred there after was quite more "than a talk to later". The story goes as I found out some time later on, that my brother's indiscretion became known to the entire community. As is the case in closely knit communities if someone farts everyone smells it. I guess these things do happen. Children and teenagers will do wrong every now and then. But the question is: what is an acceptable flaw to one person, to one group, to one nation is never the same. My father was a stern man. He was a deeply religious man too. Our family pride was irrecoverably injured.

Akbar was deemed unfit to go off to medical school in Johannesburg as was planned. He was as my father put it "too weak willed for his own good". Akbar made a promise to Christine that he would be there and that due to the circumstances, that night, would be their last night together. The circumstances were numerous. She was not an Indian, she was not Muslim, and she was a couple months older than my brother. Her family was also just as set in their ways as ours. They were catholic and of English descent. It was a tragedy, waiting to happen. As is usually the case the last meeting is the one that is the fire starter.

The last night where they were to say goodbye resulted in destined changes to all our lives. My father of course became a lot stricter and so too my brother and myself to a certain extent rebelled more and more.

It is as proven, if you place an animal in a large holding, he will placidly move around finding comfort in his space and freedom. However you place that same animal in a corner, he will fight till he dies to breathe, to find that inch of space again, and he will bide his time till he does.

6

It was the weekend baby. My first weekend off this month. I do believe that I have wasted so many free moments in my youth that when the time does present itself now in my working years I have to make the most of it.

Stage one—the first part is the planning. This started earlier in the month. I know what you are thinking, what a bunch of nerds. The problem is as most adults find out unless you don't work or you are your own boss, it is very difficult to organize a meeting with all your buddies. So, I got calls from the boys on availability. This was our week end.

Stage 2— the etiquette-It would start of with an early morning big boy breakfast at the wimpy in Durbs. This is a breakfast fit for kings. You have your strong cup of coffee that wakes you up for the rest of the day. You have mother natures best, thick beefy Borewors, oily fatty patti and your eggs, fried onions, fresh tomatoes and French fries. The healthier side is a glass of coke, a compliment to any meal.

I forget the best part, the company.

On this particular week end there were five of us. It was the usual suspects: Kubin, Jameel, Steveo and I. The addition this week end was Samed or Sam who wanted to have a (politically correct) Durban experience. Whatever that meant?

The day started of with an early morning drive with Steveo and I leaving Maritzburg at about 7am. It takes about an hour to get from Maritzburg to Durbs. Jameels flight was landing at about 7h40, so I was about ten minutes early. Don't get me wrong I obey the rules of the road, especially when there are cops and cameras around. Everyone has their vices and even doctors are not perfect. So there we were, Steveo smoking away like a chimney and me speeding on the high way. My Toyota Tazz crying in fifth gear at 160km/hr, and Steveo telling me about how he psyched himself out of proposing to his girlfriend. This had happened a couple a weeks ago.

Steveo— So there we were, the sun was setting, and it was a beautiful day on the north coast. The weekend had been perfect, not a single fight all weekend. We had great food, I saw some action and we woke up naked in each others arm. I start telling her about how I am getting older and at 28 a man needs to start taking life seriously.

Me: (I forget Steveo is three years older than me as he did three years Bcom before swapping over to medicine. He could not see himself as an accountant for the rest of his life.)

Steveo— she looks deep into my eyes and she tells me she loves me.

Me— (he stops talking) so, what did you say?

Steveo— I froze man. I don't know why but I just did not know what to do. I felt like running away. I was wishing that the whole thing was just a dream.

Me— (now I don't know why it is but everyone makes a big deal of this "I Love You". You either love someone or you don't and if you do you tell them and if you don't you don't tell them. I think it's just a way of lying to ones self that all of a sudden they are pure and everything is real. I have never had sex with a woman But I tell you this if you can swap fluids with someone, sleep with them alone and you are afraid of saying three words to that person, you are only lying to yourself.)

Steveo— the silence became awkward and I got up and walked away. The drive home she acted like nothing happened but things just have not been the same since. I mean we went out but she does not look at me or kiss me like she used to.

Me— so, do you love her?

Steveo— I don't know, I am just so confused man.

Me— what are you confused about?

Steveo— I mean is that it. Is this the last girl I will ever be with? What do I do once she says yes! I do, I will be trapped with her forever man.

Me— so you don't love her then?

Steveo— no, I do but I just don't know if I am ready for that next thing anymore.

Me: and what would that next thing be, Steveo?

Steveo— you know marriage and kids and settling down.

Me— well I have a couple questions for you, don't answer me, answer these questions in your own mind. How would you feel if you let Sheila go and somebody else married her? How would you feel if you saw her a couple years down the line, will you regret letting her go? Does this woman make you happy? Are you able to be yourself around her? Will you miss her after you move on? I mean these are the questions you have to ask yourself, man. These are the questions.

Steveo— Yoh bro that is deep shit right there man. This is way too deep a conversation for a Saturday morning. But thanks for the input boet. So, whose gonna win today the blue bulls or the sharks.

Me— well that is a no brainer man, Sharks forever man.

We scooter on down to the airport. The Durban airport was crazy busy. It was month end, so it was choc-a-block. Its funny how here, at the sliding door, people come in and go out. Ce la vie. We live only to move forward and when we move forward we can't help but always look back.

There is the usual family of 30 dropping of one Indian Aunty for her trip back up to Johannesburg. The businessman, that comes home for the weekend. He runs into the arms of his wife, and grabs his kids and kisses them. An old couple, visiting their son or daughter. They walk slowly toward each other and embrace. They start the carrying and offloading of baggage physical and metaphysical. An out of towner looking for a taxi, or maybe a board with his name on it. Two lovers sprint toward each other. With a rose in hand, a passionate glance, strong deep smooching follows.

We make our way towards the domestic arrivals. Suddenly I hear someone scream my name. I turn around to see a familiar face. It is my mothers close friends daughter, a 45th cutting family connection. We went to primary school together. We were good friends back then. But as we moved on to high school, we saw each other less and less. Our circle of friends changed and we basically lost contact. We became the hi and bye type of friend. The type you unexpectedly meet in a public place. You say a few words, relate to the person you are really with at the time, how you know this other person. Then you ask where we going for lunch? And you move on.

Her— Asalaamu alaykum(slmz), so Ali long time no see, how you keeping?

Me— Wa alaykummus sallam (Wslmz) Im Ok. You know carrying on.

Her— mum was telling me just the other day how proud everyone is of you. I hear you doing your internship at home. It must be really nice to be back huh.

Me— Ya, its Ok. So what you up to?

Her— well, I have finished my Bcom and honors. I was working up in Josies for a while but mummy wants me back home. I am actually down this weekend to sort out a job here. I guess in our case all roads lead to home huh.

Me— (While I nod in agreement with a goofy look on my face. I see out of the corner of my eye, Steveo walking up toward me. His swagger and childish thumbs up behind her worries me. I need to break this conversation of before he gets here. He has the uncanny ability of making situations awkward.)
Anyway I best be gettin on my bicycle.

Steveo— hi there Ali and who is this foxy lady?

Her— Hi my name is Khatija. I am a distant cousin, well friend of Ali's.

Stevo— Hi I am Stephen. I am a new friend of Ali's.

48

Me—   (oh shit, too late.) So ya nice catching up . . . (It was a waste of time; my voice was now a mere whisper. It had begun the usual talk around you and about you, even though you right there. They had covered upbringing and place of birth when I luckily looked at my watch and found a way out.)

Me—   so we better get going, picking up a friend from the arrivals area.

Steveo— Ali this is the arrivals area.

Me—   (nice one, Ali)

Khatija— well my brother is on his way to fetch me. I guess I better be off. Nice meeting you Stephen.

Stephen—my friends call me Steveo, and that is what you are now.

Khatija— ok, and hope to hear from you Ali.

Me—   ya, sure thing alright then, Slmz

Khayija— Wslmz.

As she walks away, her dark black hair gets caught in a breeze. She turns and waves. Her dark brown eyes are very soft and sincere. Flawless face and open mouth smile makes me realize it was bad I never got in touch in Joburg. You see she tried to contact a bunch of times in Josies, for meetings with other friends and family from back home. I don't know why but I was always busy with something, exams, assignments etc. Perhaps I really just wanted to keep to myself. I did not want to be that guy from home anymore. I was my alter ego. I was someone new and fresh in Josies. No one knew me. I did not know anyone. Thus I re-invented myself. I could be anyone. I could be me or a better version of me. So i thought.

Steveo— she is nice man and she is hot too. You indian guys have it so good man.

Me—   ya ya, shut up, lets go find Jameel.

He was easy to spot. The only person wearing shorts and a sleeveless top. You see Josies and a Durban winter are completely different experiences. I found this out the hard way my first year in Josies. I remember thinking what the hell am I doing here that first year? I gave up all the comforts of home. Good food, washing and ironing done for you. Great weather, and of course the beach. It was a sacrifice made for a dream and I soon got used to it. However the cold winters were something you never really become accustomed with. Those mornings, the moment you throw of that blanket you feel the cold bite at your bones. You walk in slow motion toward the bathroom. The moment your bum hits that pan, you know this is it, its real I am in hell and it has frozen over. The first year of Josies was like a winter for me but it would not stay that way.

Jameel— what up boys?

Steveo— Howzit ma main man?

Me— Slmz how you keeping man? Put some clothes on damn it, this is not summer, you know. Have some respect.

Jameel— So how are we gonna paint the town red this weekend.

Steveo— where are you from the 60s, no one says that anymore.

Jameel: well I am bringing old sayings back

Steveo— ok then, we have plans, my friend, very good plans that will be revealed in good time.

Jameel— Ok, sounds good. I love this side of the world man. The sun is out. Its 22 degrees and they call this winter. Gotta love this place. "I love this place." screaming out to the world.

Me— (As Jameel continues telling every person we pass how he loves this place, I start thinking about our plans for the day.)

Steveo— So china, where you wanna go for breakfast.

Jameel— do we even have to ask that question?

Steveo— Let me just call the other guys. Let them know we have the package and that we will meet them at the rendezvous point.

Me— So in other words we picked up Jameel and we will meet them for breakfast at Wimpy in town.

Steveo— why you gotta kill my vibe man?

And so the day begins.

7

The post breakfast synopsis was five guys that were happy. Bellies full, minds empty we decided to take a walk along the coast before the highlight of the day.

The beach had its time for walking and this was not it. A typical Indian experience though, except for Jameel who was from Johannesburg, the rest of us were wearing jeans with tekkies and t-shirts. The sun was beating down. It felt like a hot summer's day. Yet it was the middle of winter.

There were beautiful babes chillin out in their bikinis. There was an old man begging for some change with a cigarette in hand. The jesters trying to entertain, with different tricks, and asking for donations. The beautiful sand art along the walk way was always interesting. The local structures and logos of Durban and South Africa. Usually showing off the big five, a serenade of political figures and, of course some satire of international film stars. There was one of J.Lo's huge ass as she sun bathes. There was a clever one with Thabo Mbeki and Jacob Zuma. The two of them shaking hands with "arms deal" written on their arms.

We had our Dinky donuts. The sticky hot chocolate and caramel over flowing on this little bun, like a volcano erupting the moment you bite into it, your body just relishes the High carb sugar rush. We bought two trays which worked out to about 2-3 donuts per person but in actual fact I only had one. I turned to watch this guy on a skateboard and when I turned back they were all gone. What can I say? That's boys for you. So I bought another tray, I put one in my mouth and once again I look up to see a surfer ride a wave, and lo and behold when I turn back it's all gone.

Me—   Kubin, you hog.

Kubin—   you gotta take care of your donuts man.

Sam—   please don't tell me this is all you do.

Me—   no, no no, this is just the beginning my friend. We still have some put-put to play and some bowling and then.

Sam—   what am I hanging around with a bunch of gays . . .

Steveo—   uncool man, what if I was gay.

Sam—   I am not sitting near the white dude from now on.

Jameel—   Ok boys out with it, I know you guys have some hideous plan for my birthday so just do what you guys gotta do now and lets get it over with.

Me—   oh shit, you mean it's your birthday. I totally forgot mate (in my bad Australian accent). And the truth was I did forget.

Sam—   looks at Jameel and says oh ya we have something planned something you boys are never gonna forget, don't think we forgot your birthday was a couple weeks ago, Ali.

Me—   (I look at him and wonder what on earth is this guy going on about.)

Sam—   (smiles and winks at me) Ali I think you are also gonna be celebrating your birthday tonight, my boy.

Kubin—   we have a little something special planned for you guys. Just one piece of advice, please just go with the flow and don't be a bunch of wussy's, right.

Me—   Steveo you know anything about this . . .

Steveo—   I know a little bit about a little bit, but unfortunately I am on call tomorrow, so I will be heading of with some other mates after the game, but you guys enjoy.

Jameel and I just looked at each and laughed. It was a nervous laugh. The kind of laugh that occurs as a kid and you are all in on a joke till someone pulls your pants down and you realize the joke is on you.

On that mysterious note we headed of towards Kings Park for the highlight of the day. The big game, Bulls vs Sharks. We came down every now and then to Durbs and usually we watched what ever sport was on at the time. Yet I have to admit the atmosphere of a Sharks game at Kings Park is something else. For the fans it is a religious experience.

We got there about two hours before kick off and still there was no parking. Driving around looking for parking must be one of the most frustrating things in the world. Car guards looked ominous every where we went, sweating and thirsty we stopped to buy a cold drink from one of the vendors. As is always the case, he asked us if we were looking for parking. We said, yes. He said for fifty bucks he will make a plan. We split the costs. And he did. He showed us to this little private parking area, something for VIP's I suppose and we were set. We still had a half hour before game time. That is the funny thing about Durban and with Indians in general. Everyone assumes that we are corrupt and that we make plans. We plot and scheme. And although we do, a lot of the time things just happen. Sometimes these great opportunities just present themselves and no one is going to say No to them.

We walk into the stadium. We are met by this blasting crazy, booming atmosphere. Over fifty thousand people in one venue, feels like it today anyway. There are kids running around with banners. There are adults well on their way to being drunk at three in the afternoon. The music is blaring; the cheerleaders are dazzling and dancing. It is an event, a spectacle that has become all types of sport. Live entertainment for the masses, and boy do we soak it up.

We move to our seats and begin behaving like animals in a zoo. Shouting and screaming Sharks forever, Sharks forever. I don't know but the Sharks are apart of my life for that moment in time, all any one cares about is the sharks winning.

There are so many more important things in life. The players of the Sharks don't know me. Hell, they probably don't even care about me and my puny existence. But somehow I feel an energy and release at this ground that I want to make the dreary and desperate Hospitals and its patients disappear.

The game kicks of to a roar of the crowd. Every one is merry and singing. It is a given that most of the fans are here week in week out. I watch a lot of sports on television. Being here live, is something else.

Kubin and Steveo are on their way to a higher state, and Sam was smoking something that did not smell of cigarettes. They were all in an extra jovial and happy mood into the first half. The Sharks need to win this match to stay in the hunt for a semi-final position. Apart from a few real sober supporters biting their nails with the sharks down 17 points to three with less than five minutes left in the first half, the rest of the crowd is in seventh heaven and nothing is going to bring them down.

I wonder about the way we all spend our working week waiting for the week end to come to a Sharks game and unwind. We just cannot wait to sit with a boerewors roll, an ice cold can and nothing but a spectacle. Is this all we live for? Is this what we work towards?

The game reaches a climax in the second half with some inspirational play by Scrum half Ruan Pienaar and Fly half Fransie Steyn. With Seven minutes to go the scores are level at 27 each. I don't know what it is about believing in someone, some thing so much that you know they will come through for you. I guess as a fan, you feel apart of something bigger than yourself. You are affiliated to this team even if it is pure geographical coincidence or patriotism. These players in some way were apart of us. They were us and we were them. They gave us hope of what we could be and we gave them the courage to give off better. It was an enormous symbiotic relationship that will only grow with investment, both in time and with exorbitant amounts of money.

This particular game was an absolute cruncher. Probably the best of the season, I just could not believe that I was actually here for this one, at the Shark tank. It was thrilling and it was strangely euphoric. The adrenaline of the spectators and the players reached fever pitch in the last three minutes of the game.

Then it happened, you would not believe me if I tell you that time stood still as Fransie Steyn picked up a penalty, had a look up, and as the sun shone down on him, he smacked it through the posts from his own half to win the game for the sharks. It secured us a semi-final birth. To say the stadium went berserk is an understatement of note.

What a game? What a moment? What entertainment?

The referee blew the final whistle and just like that it was all over, but the laughter and merriment lingered. I am sure it will for most well into the night and late into Sunday afternoon.

As we filed out of the stadium like ants that had savored their nourishment and now scurried away, I realized something very important. I was addicted, and I would be back for more. Who knows I might even be here when the sharks finally win the currie cup again?

The boys however other then Jameel and I were in a state. Steveo who at half time was already caught on the big screen biting a fellow supporter's upper buttock, was busy sucking his thumb. Don't ask me why? Kubin, probably the man who consumed the most alcohol was ironically still looking 50/50. He actually seemed Ok. I guess as they say his body was accustomed to this, "his body could handle it". Sam seemed to be in a world of his own. He continued to answer questions in monosyllables. It was unlike him, since he was usually quite a loud and proud guy.

I was not at all concerned about the current state of my buddies. Through my varsity years and many more of being the designated driver I had seen it all before. I did however for good measure just check in with everyone. A simple hey guys who is up for some Spur steak. In guy talk this translated to: are you Ok enough to eat yet? Everybody answered in the affirmative, except for Sam who pulled me aside. Sam turned to me slowly and said in a soft barely audible tone, "tonight my friend I pay you back in kind, it will be a night you will never forget."

Steveo was just about ready to depart with some other guys. He was on call tomorrow so he only drank half of what he usually does. He was somewhat reluctant and dare I say it, sad to leave us.

Steveo— It is swak that I won't be around for tonight's fun. Ali and Jameel, hope you guys enjoy. I had my say in the venue and I trust you will have a good time.

Kubin— shut up man. You are going to give it away. I will call you later. Now piss of back home and call us when you reach dumb ass.

Steveo— Just wish I could have been there but not meant to be. Got stuff I gotta do. Cheers rascals.

Me— see you on Monday man, take it easy.

Sam— don worry, we will make sure that it happens dude, as planned.

Jameel—see you Steveo, till next time mate.

I watched as Steveo walked away with some of his other mates. I was just hoping that it was not the guy with the panty on his head that was driving. Steveo waved in the distance and now we were down to four.

It was of to the steak house for some prime cut medium rare decadent steak. When you are a student you are always trying to save a buck here and there. You might even be doing these menial jobs of waitressing and handing out flyers. You do these things to pay of loans, to make ends meet. You do them because you have to, and you eat crap, dress as best you can and you really never splash out.

After my first pay cheque I realized one thing. With no responsibilities or real commitments I was really going to enjoy these years of making some money on myself. I would buy myself the clothes I always wanted to wear and eat good food. And I would treat those who had always been there for me.

So when we sat down at Spur and I said to the guys, "order what you want Jameel it's on me." Everybody looked up and laughed.

Jameel—you know I earn the same amount as you.
Me—   that's why next time it's my birthday its on you.
Jameel—thanks man.
Kubin—Now boys do we have something planned for you. As you all know its Jameels birthday today. Happy Birthday again mate. And of course we did not do the ritual of play a ridiculous prank on him as we usually do.
Sam—   the reason being.
Kubin—well the reason being is that we are growing up now and its time for big boy stuff.
Me—   ok now you guys are scaring me.
Kubin—Lest I forget we missed your birthday in January this year as well.
Sam—   so tonight is an ode to the two virgins in our inner circle.
Me—   Ok I told you guys, I am never going to do anything illegal.
Jameel—Ya, me too.
Sam—   Don't worry you wussies its legal and it will be a night you will never forget. That I promise you
Kubin—its all been set so just enjoy.

Then Kubin and Sam looked at each other and unison shouted out

"Tonight we go titty ballin."

At this point Sam and Kubin are inconsolable with laughter. Beneath the two cackling Hyenas Jameel and I look at each other. Jameel smiles and says are you guys messing with us or what? I wonder to myself what the hell is titty ballin?

An hour later there we are, outside this seedy neon lit joint. This particular place has a club and a strip joint in one. According to Kubin it was heaven on earth. It was going to be a first for me.

The word apprehensive just did not fully cover the shivering and shaking of my nervous body and system. The reason was quite simple. I knew this was wrong. I knew I should not be here. Apart of me was inquisitive and curious like the teenage boy watching a sex scene on TV only to be walked in by one of his parents. You know it was dangerous, you know you might get caught but you do it anyway. You do it because you just have to see. You have to experience this for yourself. I also could not let the guys down. Yet I found myself, as we walked toward the entrance drifting to an alarming thought.

What would my parents think if they found out?

From being a first hand witness of what transpired with my brother. I gathered the consequences were life altering. I coaxed myself into believing that I deserved this. Hell I was a doctor now. I was older. I had lived and studied in Jo'burg. I had never done any major wrong in that time. Well just about. I deserved this one night, right. It was probably shaytaan in my head slowly pushing, urging me on. As we reached the till after waiting about ten minutes in a queue of middle aged guys and a couple of girls: I saw Jameel out of the corner of my eye looking curiously at me.

Jameel—Ali, just relax and enjoy. It's a once off thing. Calm down and don't be so uptight. Go with the flow and have fun, tonight is our night.

I gazed at the sky and asked God to forgive me. On auto pilot I paid the R100 entrance fee to this Obese Gawky twenty something white female. She looked at me and said, "First time huh". I smiled and said "yes."

She told me that the rules were simple. I was not allowed to touch unless I paid or was told to. I had to pay at least one girl for a dance and since it was a "birthday treat" I would get one free personal dance, which was already paid for. And I was told to please control myself and not "piss my pants". Kubin yelled out, "cant promise anything there."

The club itself on entrance was exactly what I expected and worse. There where groups of people and more groups of people. Some dancing, some at a bar chatting, some in dim lit corners. Even in the club I noted people divided along racial lines. Blacks with blacks, whites with whites, Indians well you know.

I don't know how people communicate in a club as I could barely hear myself think.

It was all Doof Doof Doof. Sam asked me something and I just nodded. He disappeared thereafter. Everyone seemed to be in some sort of trance. They seemed without expression; it was as if they were there, but not really there. Now outside it was cold, but in here it was humid and boiling hot. A group of girls in front of us seemed to be dancing in their under wear. I noted that just about every pair of male eyes were on them as they swayed to these psychedelic pulsating thumps.

I had to admit it was quite a sensory explosion. My sympathetic nervous system was in overdrive. Kubin was already on the floor shaking his head and making convulsive movements with his body. He seemed to be in his element. He was like an animal released into its natural environment. The bright translucent lights that switched on and off seemed to excite people. The colored smoke acted like a huge filter cigarette inhaled and exhaled by every one. The DJ was like a judge above everyone passing down laws that people celebrated with hands that shot up in the air that waved around without a care. Everyone seemed calm and easy even though the noise and lights made it seem like it was the end of the world. This disaster area was chaos and this crowd was happy to be in the middle of it.

In our student years some of the guys used to go clubbing on some weekends. I never went. In fact they never asked me. Tonight since I was the designated driver and they were supposedly treating me for my birthday I had to come, or did I? Had I been a victim of peer pressure, and were my friends still my friends if our ideals were different?

I looked at my watch and half hour had already passed. It was already just passed midnight. I had not seen Sam in a while and when he returned there were three things I noted. One he had a girl on his arm that was a white teenager definitely not more than 16. Two he handed me a drink and he handed one to Jameel that smelt of alcohol. Three, his zip was undone.

He introduced her as Nancy and said she was his girlfriend for the night. Whatever that meant, I do not know. Jameel started drinking but I held back for some reason. Kubin actively maneuvered of the dance floor and shouted something in Sam's ear. Sam in turn shouted I assume the same message into Jameels ear. Jameel said to me "we movin on, follow Kuben".

We walked to the far corner of the dance floor where a sign in bright neon pink read, the "Karma Sutra". Enough said.

We walked up a faded pink carpeted staircase through some beads into a smaller room. We were searched again by this black body builder. My four limbs together matched the size of his one bicep. He just tapped me over the legs, the abdomen than under arms and nodded toward the door.

We entered this huge hall. There were about twenty round tables facing a stage with a pole in the middle of it. Every thing here was garish and although it was a lot more quiet and subtle. I felt more uneasy here then I did in the club. We walked toward a centrally situated table. I still had not sipped my drink. The rest of the guys were on their second including Jameel.

A butch female that would pass for a male except for the two bulges on her chest asks me if I want anything to drink or smoke. I just nodded my head horizontally.

A song comes on which I remember from a previous year "don't ya wish your girlfriend was hot like me." Whilst everyone is singing along about 15 scantily dressed, make up covered, fully loaded bosom wizened ladies stroll onto the center stage. They dance seductively and point at random men in the crowd as his buddies cheer him on and he stands and dances with them. Kubin is picked out from our table but both he and Sam go up. Sam with his girlfriend in arm, Kubin with a powder blue dressed (well, underwear) colored female doing what appeared to be some form of rave dance to this really slow song. I resigned myself to the fact that these boys were as high as the kites we played with as kids. And what was I doing here?

After about ten minutes of watching a guy from each group being picked up by one of these showgirls I was sweating in anticipation of the inevitable. Sam said that they had already organized everything.

They walked toward us. Jameel and I looked at each other, Jameel with a grin from ear to ear. I can only imagine that I looked like Joey from Friends with a dumb grin on my face. Now it goes without saying that up close these were attractive woman. A young white female not more than 30 with blonde hair and black streaks took Jameel by the hand. They disappeared into the VIP area. A tall slender white female slides in next to me. She has long dark black hair and a minimal amount of make up. I don't like a lot of make up but for the rest of her she was not really my cup of tea. She looks liked she was probably in her late thirties. Her features are definitely not South African. There is a thick scent of cheap perfume that drapes her as close as the black camisole she is wearing. She smiles a warm wide smile that reveals a perfect set of white pearly teeth. She moves closer to me and whispers in my ear "hello".

> Her— My name is Ivana and you are? (In a thick Russian accent, I assume it's Russian).
>
> Me— hi there, I am . . . I am Steve. (I don't know why I lied but I just did not want to give my real name.)
>
> Ivana— your friend tell you Ali, and it your birthday. Why you lie to me? Huh pumpkin.
>
> Me— (note to self, never lie, not ever, even to a stripper, as you will always get caught. I look over to Sam and Kubin. They are watching me with chimpanzee like features and intent; I just wish I could slap them now. (I decide to go with the truth from now on.) I am scared. I am nervous. I have never done anything like this before. And my friends brought me here under protest. That's the truth.
>
> Ivana— doesn't worry love Ivana will take care of you. I will calm you down then I will spice you up.
>
> Me— I smile. It's a fake smile. It's a smile when you know you should smile and you do, on cue. So what do we do now?
>
> Ivana— Now I take you for dance.

She grabs my hand and leads to the VIP area. My buddies behind me all whistling and screaming. "Go Ali, It's your birthday, Go Ali, It's your birthday." We walk into a small room as big as a toilet cubicle she delicately places me on a chair in the middle. Mirrors are all around me, and I try to set my hair right.

> Ivana— How old you are Ali?

Me—   I am 25 and you?

Ivana— how old you think I am.

Me: (oh shit, don't lie), 35.

Ivana— yes, lets go with this. Now just relax and keep your eyes on me and let me entertain you.

At that point I could not help thinking that this woman is a stripper. I am in a strip club. How crazy is that?

I also realize that from the entrance and fees that were posted up, this private dance cost my buddies a minimum of R350. Actually depending on what she was going to do, it could still go up.

She takes a blind fold and covers my eyes. Then the music begins. Funnily enough it is a Sade song—Smooth operator, how apt?

I feel her warm hands unbutton my shirt. My first instinct is to grab her hands and tell her stop. But then I say what the f.? And go with the flow.

She only unbuttons the top few buttons of my shirt and delicately touches me all over my chest. Her finger nails are long and for some reason I began thinking of doing medical exams on patients. I was thinking at that moment, this is probably what it feels like when I tell my patients to let me examine them. Well I obviously don't touch them like this but they still must feel a bit vulnerable and naked. Its funny how clothing is that last barrier and how we take it for granted nowadays. She takes of the blind fold. She exhales a warm breath close to my face. It is a kind of cherry flavored aroma to it.

I open my eyes to see that she has changed and is wearing a gown beneath which is a black lace bikini=like set. It is sexy and I am mildly turned on. She removes each piece of clothing with ease and expertise. It is an art and I am her audience. And I am in awe. She has a beautiful figure and I should know. I see naked woman all the time but never like this. Once she is only wearing a panty and bra. She sits on my lap. She is lighter than a feather. She removes the bra and takes my hands. She places it firmly on both her breasts and nods approvingly. Due to my inexperience I grope a bit, deep and hard at first, she pulls back. I wait for the slap that is to come. Yet it does not. Instead she takes my hand and just about teaches me this art of fondling and caressing. However the doctor in me has picked up something. From my grope and revisiting that initial area just behind her left nipple, I feel a lump. It is a definite lump. It is firm and tethered to the deep underlying tissue. I have felt this before and though I might be wrong and hopefully I am, but this could be something.

The rest of the show continues without my mind continually drifting to one question. Should I tell her? I believe Ivana picks up on this vibe and after dancing around and on me a couple times she stops.

Ivana—do you not like my dance?

Me— No, no Ivana it was great, brilliant, I really enjoyed it. But the thing is, I am a Doctor and I would like to ask you something.

Ivana—What is it?

Me— I felt a lump in your breast and I suggest you see a doctor to have it checked out as soon as possible.

Ivana—oh, Ok, where?

Me— here it is here.

I spend the next couple minutes asking her a couple more questions and furthering my examination until our consult is rudely interrupted. The body guard pushes through the curtain at the moment I have my hand in her axilla. He grabs me and picks me up in one swift movement. I swear a little bit of urine had stained my underwear at that point. Luckily Ivana screamed that it is Ok and came to my rescue. I gave my showgirl some advice and said a referral to a surgeon would be a good idea. I knew one in Durban, and gave her my number just in case she has a problem. At the end of it she looked at me strangely.

Ivana—you know I was not going to come to work tonight. But Boss calls me and says he is short tonight and he need me. The girl who was to dance for you, the girl Kubin want was off sick. So I stood in but I say thank you comrade for all your help.

Me— well God has a reason for everything, hey. I also nearly did not make tonight. But I am glad I did come. Good luck and take care.

I walked out with Ivana. The rest of the guys seemed a lot more intoxicated then when I went I in. I looked at my watch and it read

03h13. It was time to head back home. Sam's girlfriend had moved on to a huge black guy at the bar. Sam was on the dance floor. He was shaking his hands up and down and bobbing his head back and forth. Jameel was lying face down at the table with some form of liquid dripping from his mouth. Kubin was the only one that was still able to talk in a sane manner.

Kubin— So you have fun, Bro.

Me— Ya I guess you could say that. I just can't escape my work,

Kubin— what the hell are you talking about?

Me— nothing, so can we go now.

Kubin— Ali you are one crazy bloke. You know you were in there for over 20 minutes.

Me— Ya I know, but nothing really happened.

Kubin— you don't have to kiss and tell to me.

Me— Thanks man, but I know that.

Kubin— no, no, no you will have to kiss and tell to all of us once we are all sober.

Me— whatever, now let's bounce. I will say two things though.

1-This is a first and last for me.

2-Allah please forgive me, but as they say you work in mysterious ways.

8

You know the feeling. We all have it. Some of us more often than others, everyone including Bill gates has had it. Yes, I am talking about that dreaded Monday morning return to work. It makes the week end seem like a blur. It is almost like whatever happened on the weekend was just a fantasy, a daydream.

During my rotation of Obstetrics and Gynecology O and G or ogle and grope, the weekends at work made it seem like you were in perpetual cycle of unaltered monotony. Every woman you saw was in labor. You did Per Vaginal exam (PV) after PV and Caesar after Caesar, trust me PVs are no fun, and the worst of it was that Monday morning after working just about the entire week end you had to present the cases that came in and how you managed every one of them. For good measure the consultants (Dr Garvey, you ass wipe) will ask you questions on any given topic and make snide remarks at whatever you answer. Then after the meeting if you are stationed in labor ward you head straight back to PV's and Caesars.

Those weekends were also like a dream, well a nightmare. You are your work and your work is you and it becomes you. It follows you everywhere. And that is how medicine is. Other jobs have work and a life outside work. Medicines work is life. And trust me that concept takes a bit of getting used to and most never get it.

But I was picking it up slowly as I had learned this weekend. No matter where you go or what you are doing for some reason it follows you. Funnily enough the more you try to avoid it, the more it is in your face. Every family function there is an Uncle or Aunt with a problem and a pain, some are a pain in the neck, others I feel sorry for. And it always ends up the same way.

Me—	I think you should have that checked out by your doctor, Aunty Fowzie.
Aunty Fowzie—	But aren't you a doctor, can't you write a small script for me.
Me—	No I am still an intern, I am not allowed to write scripts outside the hospital yet.
Aunty Fowzie—	Oh Ok then, I will have to come to the hospital, you can organize for me there. Uncle Essop also having problem with his eyes.
Me—	(oh ya, well take him to an optometrist then) Oh ya, you can always come by the hospital but I cannot promise anything, OK.
Aunty Fowzie—	No problem Betaa, we will see you at the hospital then, maybe we will come Monday, I just have to convince Uncle Essop.

At this point I know it is a lost cause, so I smile and I know they will come and I know I will find a way to help them. I will do this not just because they are my family, but because they are in need and I have some knowledge. I have a responsibility to use this knowledge and do the right thing for all my patients and anyone I can help. It is not the choice of being good that is difficult. It is continuously doing good over an extended period of time that becomes tedious.

I reach the hospital two minutes late and head up to the first floor lecture theatre. I have actually done quiet well today, almost here on time. The meeting has just started and we review the problem cases admitted over the weekend. Those that were on call get grilled over their management and things they missed or should have done. My mind is still cast back to a very weird and wacky weekend experience. My phone buzzes, everyone in the room looks toward me (damn, forgot to switch it to silent). It's a message from Kubin. It's quite amazing how your close friends and family always seem to be thinking of you the moment you thinking of them. The message reads:

Watzup Niggs? (On account of my darker skin, I take no offense.) I know you busy thinking of those Boobies over the weekend, you sick bastard. I was too. Hope to see you again soon man. The weekend was of the hook. It was a blast. Take it easy at work today and if you get it easy, take it twice.

I am grateful to have crazy friends like Kubin. He serves as a gauge as to how normal my life really is, every time I meet up with him, I just feel grateful. However I cannot deny whatever we do together is always entertaining.

I know the Monday drill though. Once the meeting is over, it's of to the ward, to do the round. Monday rounds are usually a killer as there are a whole lot of new admissions from the weekend. The worst part is sometimes because the weekend is run with less staff: the patients can take a turn for the worse. It is a terrible feeling walking in to a ward on Monday, when you left a patient that was getting better on Friday to find that on Monday they are not there any more. I don't know why but the patients and everyone just seem sicker on Monday.

The meeting is over within 30 minutes. I was completely zoned out through most of it. Russian strippers, diagnosing breast cancer (maybe), awesome rugby, good food and great friends. A far cry from where I am right now, but that is life, got to take the highs with the lows. Oh shit, Stacy comes up to me; this means only one thing she wants to swap calls again. I swear a fort night does not go by without Stacy wanting to swap calls.

Stacy— Ali I see here you are on call tomorrow. Would you mind swapping with me for Wednesday? My boyfriend's sister is going to be down from the UK.

Me— I will look at it and let you know by the end of today Stacy.

Stacy— OK cool, thanks Ali.
Then it's the german, another consultant. Let the sparring begin.

German—So I see you were late again, (just loud enough for every one to hear.)

Me— Ya, I was two minutes late.

German—Liar, you were four minutes late. (Voice rising)

Me—   (OK, stay cool. He is having one of those days. Do not
           get dirty.) My watch said 08h02 but you may be right. I
           apologize for my tardiness.
           (The saying goes pigs like fighting and if you get in a
           fight with a pig, both of you will get dirty, and the pig
           will like it.)
German—I am going to be watching you Dr Sha. (As the entire
           department looks on).

As much as dodge man is never to be found, the german is always on
my ass. We call him the German aka Dr Heiter as he always wants things
done to perfection. He is cold and callous to colleagues and patients
alike. He is a surgeon. So he is goal orientated.

He has taken a particular liking to me. I have no idea why but some
people just want everything and everyone to be perfect. I wish I could
just tell him off some day. I know exactly what I would say but I guess I
just don't have the marbles for it. He is always picking on me. Everyone
has someone who gives them beans at work. All I know is I have a couple
months to go.

I look at the roster, great it's another morning with the old man. Let
the questioning begin. I start my trek toward the medical wards. The old
man is already waiting with his white coat. The tragedy of today is that I
see Super M there with him. I scratch my head and wonder what the hell
is Mbanjwa doing here? He is supposed to be doing his Surgery rotation.

Super M—   hi Ali. How are you doing?
Me—   I am OK. So what you doing here, I thought you were
            doing surgery.
Super M—   well funny you should ask but I actually am on leave
            today. Since my bus back home only leaves tonight,
            I thought I would come learn some true pearls here
            from Dr Naidoo. I really love medicine, don't you, it is
            just so vast.
Me—   For a second, I wanted to burst out laughing. Then I
            thought I would tell this guy he can stop sucking up
            because a) his lips are swelling, b) he is making the rest
            of us look like ass c) it is a known fact that he is the
            best and most dedicated intern around. I keep it all

inside, smile and tell him that medicine is not one of my favorites.

Dr Naidoo— I tell you Dr Mbanjwa you remind me a lot of myself as young doctor. Don't lose that desire and drive my boy. You should watch this chap Dr Sha he is headed for great things.

Me— (Dr Naidoo thereafter launched into yet another soliloquy of what medicine has become and how it used to be in his hey day. I switch of after a minute, start thinking about whether it is a good idea to swap that call with Stacy. It goes quiet and I see both Dr Naidoo and Super M staring at me.

What to do? Did he just ask me a question? The probability is very high. Just agree it usually works.)

I can't agree with you more Dr Naidoo.

Dr Naidoo— Agree about what, I asked you where the ward list of patients, and new admissions.

Me— Oh ya, OK I will just get that.

I scurry off like a busy little bee and know that I come of looking like an idiot but I guess it's a Monday, just keep on rollin with the punches.

The ward round goes as expected, moves through at a snails pace. It is the usual suspects on a weekend internal medicine admission. Every patient that was admitted is wasted, really sick and probably ready to slam dunk that bucket.

Of the 21 admissions to our ward 14 are HIV positive and 7 are on ARV's. It is the usual HIV suspects, a host of pneumonias caused by PCP, TB, and some viral, I am sure. Then there is one each of Cryptococcal meningitis and TB meningitis. There is also one patient with gastroenteritis that was too dehydrated to send home, also by the looks of his bloods in acute renal failure.

Of the non HIV patients we also have the usual suspects. We have an eighty year old who suffered a stroke. We have three patients with diabetes who thought they would just let their blood sugar levels slide for the weekend. Then of course there were two non ST elevated MI's or heart attack victims.

And there was one other patient a white male in a public hospital, I cannot say I saw this too often but at the same time this was becoming more and more common.

As medical aids become more and more expensive, patients are turning to the over burdened, ever ready public sector.

You see the way it works on South Africa and many countries around the world is you pay a private medical aid company that gives you cover. This cover is dependent on the amount of money you put in and on your choice of cover.

For example, you may choose only hospital care. This would mean that for seeing a doctor, a specialist, a dentist or getting medication from a pharmacist you would have to pay out of your own pocket. In fact anything not requiring admission for a serious problem in a private hospital, you will have to sort out yourself.

The other end of the spectrum is complete cover and this covers everything to a certain point. That point is when in a certain time period you have maxed out that medical aid. Trust me, they may not tell you but you can and may max out your medical aid.

In between the above two there are a whole variety of other options to choose from, but the bottom line is they will fall between full cover and just hospital emergency cover.

The reality is that with the rising medical prices and the everyday use of medical aid, most patients either cannot afford medical aid or use it till they don't have anything left. Suddenly the medical private sector is unaffordable or unavailable, and guess where everyone ends up.

This is the case with Mr Edwards. He used to be able to afford those crazy private sector prices, but he can't anymore. So here he was, and as far as I was concerned he was the only interesting patient here today. He had what looked on chest XRay to be an interstitial lung disease. Due to his age we did some blood culture and sputum cultures and we covered him with antibiotics too. He would need to see a Pulmonologist.

For some reason Mr Edwards and I seemed to hit off. He also had a dry sense of humor and a love for the lowest form of wit, sarcasm.

He called Dr Naidoo, a patch Adams wanna be (my sentiment exactly) and could not believe that Super M would give up vacation time to continue working. He also said that I was too young to be working in a hospital and that I should go back to school or partying.

All things considered it was an average morning. Of the many questions asked we nailed Dr Naidoo today. I would say Super M answered about 90% but my 10 % was still awesome.

Over the weekend we lost only 4 patients from our ward.

By lost, I mean they died. Just clearing things up.

Normally we lose about 1-2 patients a week end.

That is actual lost, we admit them and they disappear, no really, they probably get up and go home, or someone kidnaps them and harvests their organs, just kidding, I think.

It's sad. It's a reality. Even sadder is that you get used to it, it becomes a norm and slowly the wall is up. As you can see other then Mr Edwards who really stood out, I don't remember the patients names, I just remember conditions and how to cure or help the patient in some way. It's that wall I tell you, it keeps us going, though. And that in the end is what everyone needs.

The rest of the day just kind of dissipates as it usually does on a Monday. True to his word Super M stays the whole day, even helps out in casualty. Despite being a goody two shoes I was glad he did as it was a busy day and he basically halved my workload. I thanked him at day end and "bought him" a Bar One for the trip home. I decided that since I was doing nothing on Wednesday anyway that I would swap calls with Stacy. Of course I let it play out a while, well till I saw her at lunch and then I said yes I would swap. She bought me a chocolate too, a Bar One. I don't particularly like Bar Ones so you know what I did with it.

9

My brother's first year at varsity was when his love blossomed. It was not something that happened overnight. It was rather like the degree he was doing. It took a lot of work time and understanding. He was at first overwhelmed with his emotions, but like his work once he became accustomed to it he began to thrive.

I had an idea things were on the up very early on. Hey I may have been in grade 10 at the time, but I could notice the subtle changes that were occurring. Well to be honest we shared a room and my brother could not hide much from me. My parents were oblivious. I believe my mother had an idea early on but she was in complete denial. Most parents are like that when they hold their kids up on a pedestal and suddenly they are brought back down to earth. "My child taking drugs, never, you must be mistaken".

I really do not know the details just the snippets of what I heard and the small instances when I saw them together. I know this much is true, it was the best of times and yet, it was worst of times for big brother.

As is the case in most relationships as I have found out in my experience. On a daily basis it changes and molds itself into what you and your partner make it. Initially my brother's grounding was a tragedy. I don't know why he wanted to do medicine but after that night when fate intervened, he never spoke of it again. Thinking back now, I know he would have been a better doctor than me. He was a kind caring individual that was both mentally and physically strong. He was deemed, as my parents put it, not able to handle the responsibilities that came with freedom.

His years as a Bcom student served as a catalyst for him to spend a lot of time with Christine. The irony was that by keeping him close and allowing him to study in our small town, he saw her everyday. She studied through the university too, a business admin course.

They obviously became a lot more secretive and although it was known to their close friends and probably quiet a few others, it never really broke out. I found out when I was browsing through my brother's cell phone, I could always break his security passwords. There were these long SMS cellphone conversations, places they would meet, the usual missing you, missing you too.

It is hard to say when someone falls in love. I guess you really cannot choose the whys and hows of it but you can control it. As is the case with anything that is right and wrong.

I never thought he disobeyed my parents on purpose. I don't think he knew how far or deep he was till it was too late. You promise people things and if you are brought up right like my brother was, you can not go back on your word.

Later on, he would tell me of how they would spend afternoons just talking and laughing. They were off the same generation. They grew up in the same time frame, in this small city. Apartheid was over and it was not just curiosity. There was a genuine liking for each other initially that grew like a warren buffet investment into something huge. They would obviously always be in a place with very few people but he promised me that their relationship was never physical in those early years. I believed him. He was my brother.

He was always at the top his class. He studied hard. He read his prayers daily. He listened to my parents and rarely outright disobeyed them. He was a good son. He went out with his friends often and my parents always allowed it. He was always going out to play sport, watch a movie, going out to watch soccer with the guys. So, my father thought it was all done and dusted. Far from it.

Christine who I met every now and then always treated me like a lost puppy. She would talk to me in this playful baby voice, ruffle my hair. It was our thing. At first she annoyed me but the more I got to know her, the more I really liked her. I could see what my brother saw in her. In a weird way she reminded me of mum. I told him that once and he booted me, so I never said it again. But she was just like mum.

She was studying and doing well in her degree too. She was strong willed yet at the same time had this great sense of empathy and humanity.

Her friends on the other hand and a lot of the whites on campus were shocked. Even though it was over, there it will always be. White is right, the top, the best. Whatever they do is the gold standard. It was a mentality that was hard to break after years of environmental programming. As an Indian we were always in the middle. Perhaps that is where we will always be psychologically, anyway.

We don't say too much. We don't like confrontation. This is evident by Gandhi's Satyagraha strategy. We are passive by nature. But mistake this passiveness for weakness at your peril. We are as resolute as they come.

In South Africa though, we will always be in the middle. Pre and post apartheid, it is a predicament we have accepted. In the past it was outright white rule. Now it is just about outright black. I say just about, because we are classified as black. However in the line up of affirmative action, we are still neither at the front nor the back. We still keep on thriving. We still hold our trinity of God, family and financial security as major priorities.

Although apartheid was over, the repercussions still linger and will for a long while. Deep wounds and scars always remain.

Her friends very rarely spoke to my brother or any of us. She also was in the process of keeping this relationship on the low down. Her parents knew nothing of my brother. She never told them anything and I guess she had her reasons. Her mother was of Afrikaner descent. The woman takes care of the man and is family orientated. The wife is always keen to please and support. This was Christine's mum Marie. Marie was a housewife mostly.

Her step dad on the other hand was an Englishmen. He was full of history and debonair style. (Stereotyping a bit much.) He was a teacher. First at a private school and then he became a public school deputy headmaster.

He had worked there for many years.

She had a sister who died young from a leukemia. Her only brother had moved to London that year she started varsity. She had a small amount of family in town. He was moving to study, work and travel in Europe. He was also going to visit family there. Of all her family, Christine was closest to her brother. They grew up together under the stern watch of their father and the loving kindness of their mum. They shared their secrets and dreams as brothers and sisters do. Her father died of a heart attack and her mother remarried years later.

However as her brother left early that year, Christine did not tell him too much about Akbar.

It was not a big deal yet, but as time went on the relationship matured into something they never expected or perhaps something they did all along.

My brother did not speak too much of her at home for obvious reasons but soon the age old Indian question would be raised.

After that first year at varsity, it started to creep in.

The first occasion was at Eid. Eid is that time of the year when Muslim families get together and everyone is happy and it is a joyous occasion. It marks the end of the fasting month of Ramadaan.

We fast during the month of Ramadaan from sunrise to sunset. Then at night we perform extra prayers after breaking our fast. I know the reasons behind it and I understand them and accept them. But the truth is when I think about my religion Islam, the logic and sense of it all is what truly comforts me.

Fasting humbles me. It makes me realize the importance of being grateful and not taking a minute for granted. The day without food and drink makes you think about the small things. Not only those less fortunate than you, but about all the people who have less than you.

You place problems in order of priority and it is only then you see the gravity of your life's "major problems". You take all these minor hassles and blow them out of proportion and wonder what life must be like, thinking when or where your next meal will come from.

During that month you become totally immersed in your duties and all the trivialities of daily life fade away. You know that time is precious and so too every action, thus you have to make every second of it count, for good.

And at the end of it, is Eid. A celebration for the sacrifices made during that month. You get to meet your family and friends. You celebrate together and exchange gifts.

It was at this time in my brothers second year at varsity, that they asked him when he was going to get married.

You see once the Aunties get you, you are cornered like a bug about to get squashed.

Aunty Sara:	Fathima how old is Akbar now?
Akbar:	I am 21, Aunty Sara.
Aunty Nasreen:	So anyone special in your life Akbar.
Akbar:	No, not yet.
Aunty Sara:	I know a very nice girl, Aunty Fathima. She is a nice homely girl. She is just finishing school, comes from a good family, wealthy family. They will definitely agree to the match, should I organize a meet?
Akbar:	No, definitely not. I am not ready for that.
Mum:	he is still young.
Aunty Nasreen:	Ya leave him be, he is still only 21.
Mum:	I think he will tell us when he is ready.
Akbar:	Just speak of me as if I am a ghost in the room.
Aunty Nasreen:	You remember Mohseen, he is getting married, he is only 22 as well. He is marrying Aunty Sumaya's daughter, they make a very good match. She is starting her teaching career at that primary school near the park. He has just got a job at that accounting firm down town.
Akbar:	I guess that was right for him. It might be right for many other guys but it is just not right for me.
Mum:	you know how these kids are these days.

My brother left the room, and it fell silent.

Everyone knew of the episode that took place at the end of matric. It was a small town and news travels. Everyone knew and wondered at that gathering, what it all meant. The outburst did not help either.

These were my Aunties and although meddling and curious, they wanted what they thought would be best for my brother.

At that point although he was still young, everyone including my Mum began to wonder. Of course I knew the truth. I did not have to wonder, I became apprehensive.

What was going to happen?
This was no fairy tale, this was real life.
I knew as well as my brother it was an impossible situation.
It was an impossible love, which would only end in sadness.
But as they say love is blind?
To those involved anyway.
And love hurts.
To those innocent bystanders caught in cupid's crossfire.

10

Old man Botha was a hoot. He really was a laugh a minute, down to earth, stubborn and crazy old coot.

He had the same type of humor as me. As dry as the Sahara and always flowing like the Victoria Falls.

The first day we met I liked him. He was a likable man. He was in his sixties. He had a worn face of a man that spent a lot of time in the sun, and clear pale blue eyes. He had lived through so many tragedies that he had given up waiting for the good. He lost his wife in tragic circumstances. Their only child, Susan died from a rare bone cancer, another statistic. He worked in Jo'burg for many years but after his wife's death he moved back to his first love, the midlands. He grew up here and missed its warmer climate and freshness.

He was always making fun of everyone especially me. He spoke fluent Zulu (something I wish I could do). Thus he always had a crowd of fellow patients to share his jokes with.

Typical ones included, "are you trying to make potholes in my hand or are you gonna find a vein?"(IV Line)

- what time is the nurse gonna play and hide and seek with my ass again (suppository)
- Is it time for boiled, butchered and banal? (breakfast, lunch, supper)
- I love this bed; it keeps me up all night, so I can look sicker in the morning.

- If only the sisters could realize this is not a market place but a hospital. (Sisters generally scream when they talk)
- So did the mod squad figure out what's wrong with me yet?(at our morning rounds)

But generally he was a quite a pleasant fellow.

Initially we thought he had a community acquired pneumonia but as that was not clearing up, the differentials became more ominous, as his renal function was not pretty either.

For some odd reason, I spent a lot time talking to Mr. Botha. Sometimes he asked interesting questions, other times he told me entertaining stories. Soon I realized he was a patient that I had truly bonded with, perhaps even over stepped the line a bit. We would discuss chess, a game he was exceptional at. I was a novice but was picking up fast. Just a couple moves a day, he was mentoring me in a way.

As I was allocated this ward duty for a month, I saw him every morning. It was different being around someone with impeccable insight. It was different being able to communicate open and freely with a patient.

I had dealt with non black patients before. I had dealt with smart patients before but this was a first for me. This was a man I spent my free time with.

He was opinionated. However he was not a racist, far from it. He was someone who had lost a child and a spouse. Both of them, in cruel circumstances. Yet he kept going. He was a far cry from the majority of patients I had seen and dealt with so far.

Unjani Baba?
Uhlalapi GoGo?
Hlugu la?
Vula?
Bega Phezulu?
Hlala phansi?
Hamba lo stombe

It was just catch phrases. Most of them words I had picked up along the way.

I used the brief histories with clinical exams and whatever body language and facial expressions I could notice to formulate diagnoses and managements.

Sometimes you get lucky and there is a nurse available.

I mean let's be reasonable, it's a country with more than 10 official languages.

I could not understand how people harm and kill each other for not being able to speak a language.

Ironically this strategy of minimal interaction and communication has worked well overall. World wide doctors are notorious for brief histories and poor listening skills. I was just another doctor to add to the list.

Mr Botha had a particular interest in religion and politics.

According to him:

South Africa could have been the best country to live in the world, till apartheid came and stuffed it up. It divided the very thing that made South Africa unique, unity in diversity, something we still strive for today, as evident by our national anthem.

However since 1994 we had made some huge steps forward but equally large steps back. We are still a young democracy and time is on our side. However that which we need most is what we lack year after year. Since Mr Mandela, we have no leadership, no inspiration.

Like all young democracies we were still caught in that age old twist of fate. We put into power the people who we think will do the best for all, but actually they are doing the best for themselves. The amount of corruption and crime in South Africa is sickening.

The scariest thing about the crime is the level of violence and the absolute power of the state that even though corruption is exposed daily, nothing can be done about it.

Thus standards have slowly dropped, in the most important avenues being education, health and safety and security. The pillars by which a countries care of its people are measured.

Justice is a joke; murderers and killers sometimes find life better in prison than out of it. The finances of country are critical and we have spent a huge amount on weapons to keep us safe from whom, and to attack what?

The engine of the country, human resources in the highest office have all looked to greener pastures.

But in the end let's face it, most of us are born South Africans, we are African. Our skin colors may be different, our tongues may speak different languages but we all love this land, this place, we call home and it will always be home and it will always call to us.

When Mr Botha spoke like that it stirred something inside of me. Even nurses and other doctors would engage in conversation and debate with him.

He had close relationships with black workers growing up and even as a farmer later on.

He knew more about the culture and way of life of my patient demographic than I did.

His father was a farmer too, a man good with his hands. He grew up in the Ou Kaap, and later moved to the Midlands in Kwazulu Natal.

His dad had a small estate and made wine for the local community. Apartheid was in full swing in those years, so maids and slave like labor was quite common. Ironically it was this close interaction, which forged close relationships between him and black people. As a child he did not see the gross inequities and I guess we did not either. Not until you are much older and still, even though you had these uneasy cold awkward minutes, you turned away blind and deaf with a sick taste in your mouth.

He told me of stories. Some the same, some different, like the one of a worker, that was hauled from the farm for being "part of the ANC". They, men in their uniforms came like predators searching for prey, hungry for blood. They came to the farm when the sun was at its zenith. They grabbed him in the fields, pushed him against the earth. They hit him with batons amid protest from his family and friends. They showed his dad papers and whispered in his ears. He looked on, not a word. He was now their prisoner and so it was. We are all prisoners of the state. Different in our level of imprisonment but prisoners nonetheless.

All you had to do was look at their eyes as they hauled this man like a sack of potatoes into the back of a Bakkie. The crowd stared with intense hatred, disdain and anger. But they did not do a thing, they would just bite their tongue, and bide their time.

It was not the first time it happened, nor the last. These were common occurrences; white people accepted them as being normal. The enemies had to be found and killed.

But as Mr Botha grew, he questioned the action, a lot. What if this man was just trying to make a living, get by? The workers live on the plantation; they live with you, grow with you, and effectively make you rich

Why would you want these people tortured and killed?

When they were in fact the very people that helped you live?

The relationship of power was a relative one then and now that the tide has turned to watch Mr Botha interact with the fellow patients made me smile.

It was a naughty smile. This white boere speaking Zulu and making fun of the current government, the previous government and the government yet to come. However it was this same government that was currently assisting him take care of his deterioration in health.

There was a fascination that I had with Mr Botha, inexplicable connection. The kind you watch unfold: as a child dropped of at kindergarten on day one makes friends. It is not as random as it seems how you are drawn to certain people. Why do we feel a certain empathy toward one person and not another. Most of the time psychologists link it to your childhood, but every so often like the bees that make honey it is a pure miracle.

Mr Botha's stay at the hospital was highlight for me. A little distraction to my daily routine.

11

It was crazy to think that although fundamentally the world had progressed, some things never change.

Some, well most people do a double take when a young white woman and black man hold hands and kiss each other.

The executive man sneers at the new female CEO of the company. Although well qualified and experienced she still has that little extra to prove and more to sacrifice.

What we do not understand we fear? What we cannot understand we label as wrong? What we do is right? Only our group is right! And it always will be.

And we teach children this too. The baton is passed on, and the circle keeps spinning.

The world has spun around for many years, yet it took just about 2000 years to abolish slavery, to see that all men are equal. Hell, globally that is still a problem and always will be.

My brother found this out the hard way.

It became an obvious fact that Akbar and Christine were now an item. Their close friends knew it. They knew that this kind of love was dangerous.

It is the kind that everyone knows is wrong and 99% would never get involved in it. The 1% that does, half way into the relationship call it quits.

But there are those special few that truly know that nothing will allow them to feel that pulse of life and breathe of air like this love. In our town the communities were small and they spoke like fire does with wood. At this time post apartheid the wounds were healing but the scars were still fresh and raw.

I was watching this tragedy unfold like a sad song that played in the background from a depressing scene in a movie.

It all started as it usually does with a strong sense of denial that is dissolved into shock.

Akbar and Christine tried to hide from themselves. They tried and tried but could not.

It is like a fat person who knows they are fat, but cannot help eating that cookie. A wife who is repetitively beaten by her husband but always goes back to him. A man in love, who will do anything for that woman. Anything.

Now in small towns it is impossible to get away with the cat and mouse game. Everyone knows everyone's business. They want to know it. The entertainment really lies in the community and its secrets and lies. The gossip is a seed that grows and sometimes like a vine just spreads and constricts.

As always it was a protagonist that sets the ball in motion.

My uncle, a very religious man came down from Ladysmith over the 10th of Muharram to spend time with the family. He came with his annual gifts and cheerful demeanor. Uncle Ahmed and Aunty Rabiya were always welcome guests. We had many good times at their farm in Ladysmith.

Akbar and my Uncle Ahmed were also quite close. They had a special kinship. Both were elder brothers and both were born on the 7 of May. They looked alike. Tall, just about 6ft, a tanned complexion with rich brown eyes and a perfect nose. My uncle with a thick bushy beard. Akbar with his goatie and light mustache. Thin curled lips and muscular physique.

It started through some harmless gossip. If there ever is such a thing. As per usual a lot of the families were around over the weekend. Akbar was notably absent studying again at the library . . .

Aunty Sara came in with her latest gossip story. One of our distant relatives in town, bored with nothing to do, I think.

Aunty Rabiya:	Salaams. How you been keeping Sara.
Aunty Sara:	oh very well and you Rabiya. I have not seen you in a long time.
Aunty Rabiya:	oh I am well.
Aunty Sara:	I see the kids and Ahmed are well. How are things in Ladysmith?

Twenty minutes of pleasantries and past times relived later . . .

Aunty Sara:	I would not have believed it if I did not see it with my own eyes, there they were holding hands, whispering sweet nothings in each others ears.
Aunty Rabiya:	Did you tell Aunty Fathima?
Aunty Sara:	No it's none of my business.
Aunty Rabiya:	So then why did your daughter go to the library to see if it was true?
Aunty Sara:	She had to see it for her self. You know Akbar. Or should I say do we really know Akbar at all . . .
Aunty Rabiya:	well I think we should tell Fathima. She has a right to know.
Aunty Sara:	I am not really close family. It would not be my place to say anything.

The mouse trap was really set by Aunty Sara that day as we later worked out. Aunty Rabiya did not say anything to Mum. However she did say something to Uncle Ahmed. He in turn said something to Dad.

Dad lost it, his pride was injured, he could not bear that Akbar had disobeyed him. Thus he denied it.

It was safe to say a small rift had developed between the close relationship my father had with his brother. The rest of their trip was tentative.

Of course as is custom my father never said anything to anyone about what occurred. He had to find out for himself. It is strange how we we take out our anger on the bearer of bad news, rather than look at the news objectively.

My father was so sure of himself that he went of to the library to see for himself.

A week later when Akbar said he was of to the library my father left to see if he was there and with whom.

It so happened that my father could not find Akbar there. He went to the University Commerce library. No sign of him. He asked around and found out that Akbar was at the Admin building. He went down the road to the building and there they were.

In his shock, he did nothing but just watched.

I can't say what it was exactly that made him snap.

The lies and loss of knowing his son. The hiding and the mistrust. The tale being told to him by his brother who lived well over 150km away. The loss of integrity, honesty in his eldest. His prized possession sitting at the table holding a white non Muslims girls hand. My Dads confidence in Akbar was broken.

It was just wrong on so many levels. He came home that evening and he was silent till supper.

Dad: so Akbar how is the studies going?

Akbar: that's a first Dad, you asking about my studies?

Dad: it is your final year, next year you begin working.

Akbar: yes, almost done.

Dad: how is the commerce library, you spend a lot of time there?
      (Akbar stops eating and looks up at my Father, stares at him. He knows. We all know.)

Akbar: Calmy, my brother replies, Yeah I do. I love the library.

Dad: don't get smart with me boy, you still live in my house. I saw you son, I saw you today and you broke my heart into a million little pieces. You have lied to me; you have destroyed the trust between us. (his voice getting ever louder and more powerful). I cannot even look at you.

Akbar: (head down. Tears welling up in his eyes.) Mum tell him. Is all he could whisper.

Dad: Mouth open, eyes wide, you knew about this Fathima.

Akbar; well at least I can speak to her. We all can

Mum: I found out one afternoon, when I saw them walking together. Bisley road was closed and I had to take Radison drive to pick up some groceries. I confronted him and he told me that he just needs time. But I did not know that he was this serious about her. I did not want to push him away. The last time we spoke to him like this you know what happened. I cannot see my child starve himself and be sick. So I listened to him and told him that he had to end it. I told him he had till he graduates.

Dad: well it's simple what must be done. You will break it of with her, graduate and work. And then you will marry someone more suited, someone in your taqdeer. In time you will heal and we will find you someone who is suitable to this family.

Akbar: He screams out, No I love her, always will. There is nothing you can do that will ever change that. This is my taqdeer. You cannot dictate my future.

Dad: I am sorry son, but do not test my patience on this issue. You have already irrevocably destroyed our families name and reputation. I cannot believe what you have done. I look at you and wonder how far from the tree you have fallen.

Akbar: what reputation dad. No one cares or really cares about us, except us. Why cant you just listen to me, hear me out. Why is your life so black and white?

Dad;   This is because there is no gray in the life of a muslim my son, you have learnt right from wrong and as your father while I am still alive I will guide you the best way I see fit. I am trying to protect you from yourself. I am trying to save you from a life of pain and sadness in this world and the next. Do you not understand that?

Akbar: No, I don't. I won't.

Dad: as I said do not test me son.

Akbar got up and left the table. The rest of us just looked on.

It was like two alpha male lions out in the jungle waiting to face off. Akbar was older now. He was a man. He was finishing up his studies but at the time to be honest I was still confused. I did not understand how he could go against my father's wishes like that.

Over the next couple days not much happened. My father assumed it was over. I did too,

Then it happened. We went to the mall to buy some ice creams. It was just dad, mum and I. My holiday was coming to an end. I was busy savoring my strawberry swirl when I saw him walking towards us. Hand in hand with her.

I mean libraries were one thing but this was public. This was crazy. It was loco, man.

It was an act of defiance. It was bold. It was brave yet ultimately it was sad. Ironically no one said anything. Akbar walked up to us like he was strolling in a park.

Akbar: slmz everyone this is my close friend Christine. I am sure you all know her.

Christine this is my father and mother, Ayub and Fathima. You know my brother. So where are you guys of to?

My father did not say a word. He looked past him like a fly on the wall.

All my mother said was, you have no shame, you have gone too far Akbar.

I was in shock. Christine just smiled but as we walked by, she looked worried.

I stayed, to talk to Akbar.

Me: hi Christine.
Christine: hi Ali.
Me: so tell me whose genius idea was this?
Christine: It was Akbars.
Akbar: I just cannot hide this anymore Ali. No one seems to want to give in.
Me: you know dad. He is not going to see things your way. I don't think he ever will.
Akbar: no I will make him.
Me: I dunno bro. he was not impressed. He has that glazed weary eye as well. Be prepared for the backlash.
Akbar: I am prepared for anything. We love each other. Why can't they see that?
Christine: I just don't know how to speak to your parents and mine for that matter.
Me: so what did your family have to say?
Christine; they know of Akbar . . . I guess I am still working on it.
Me: how long do you guys expect to work on it . . .
Akbar: the rest of our lives probably . . .

When they looked at each other. When they were lost like that in each others eyes, i felt so many different emotions for them. Fear. Shame. Sorrow. None of them were positive. Smiling and happy, they walked on. I was apprehensive. I was squeamish. I just don't think they were seeing things 20/20 at this point. They were in love and they were blind. I was not.

Me: you guys have to cool things down for a while. No one is going to understand or just let this slide. Trust me. Now is the time to lay low. Not to be bold. We live in a small community and consequences of actions here are far reaching.

Akbar: well we are willing to take that chance. We believe in each other, we trust each other. I know it is going to work out, it will be alright Christine.

Christine: ya, everyone will get over it eventually.

Their optimism was almost strong enough to believe in. It was like a strong coffee that was decaffeinated, it lacked the resonance of true conviction.

My parents reaction was however quite different. As it was with my family, the assault on my brother was carefully thought out and full proof.

I had my part to play, I was to ask my brother to let Christie go or else?

I would do this with a close family friend Molana Moosa.

We cornered him at home a couple days later after Jummah salaah. Friday is a special day for us. As the Christians have Sunday mass, Jewish faith Sabbath Saturday, Friday was Jummah Mubarak.

It was a day like everyday but more special in that we had our Khutbahs

(Lectures at mosque) on how to better ourselves and our lives. I know most people see religion as something you do but as Muslims it should be something you live and breathe in, everyday in and out. No exceptions.

Thus that Friday was deemed as a good point to start. To marry a non-muslim had its regulations. But a Muslim man could marry a woman of the book, although it did not happen often nowadays. My brother knew his religion well as most of us do, and he knew this.

So there we were on Friday afternoon, my brother and Molana Moosa, and I with three cups of hot Chai(tea).

We started talking about following the right path, suppressing ones Nafs(desires) doing what is right. To be honest though, I sat there feeling like a hypocrite.

I was no perfect Muslim, sure I read the Quraan, and read my Salaah, but I did wrong on a daily basis.

How could I expect my brother to be perfect?

We all had our shortcomings. I guess the truth is we are just afraid. We did not want my brother to go astray. We wanted him to remain one of us. We wanted similar not different. And we knew that in the long run this relationship would only bring him sadness, which would bring us sadness. Sure we could act and go along but would Christine ever be accepted, I don't know. What about their kids to come too?

But to him all this adversity and strife was worth it. For her, he would fight.

Molana Moosa:	So, Brother Akbar, your father was telling me you have this girl in your life.
Akbar:	Yes Molana Moosa, she is Christian and white. We intend on making Nikah.
Molana Moosa:	you know that the blessings of your parents are pivotal to having a happy life.
Akbar:	I know this. I have tried speaking to them and reasoning with them but they will not listen. All they want is for me to break it of.
Molana Moosa;	why won't you break it of?
Akbar:	Because I love her. I have a made promise and I will keep it.
Molana Moosa:	love is not everything in this world brother. You must remember you love for Allah first then your parents too. Your brothers love too (I nod accordingly). They know you best. They have raised you. They have taken care of you. They are your key to happiness in this life and the next.

Akbar:	I am not doing anything wrong. I can marry this woman and I believe we will be happy together. In time my parents will see the virtues and the reasons why I love this woman.
Molana Moosa:	Your parents have sent me to prevent this; they specifically sent me to talk you out of it, to talk some sense into you. There are many other paths for you to travel. You have a responsibility to do what is right as a Muslim.
Akbar: I know.	But I also know which path I have chosen. I will not be able to live with myself in any capacity. If I do not live MY! Life. My parents who love me will have to respect that. Thank you for coming Molana Moosa but I think that will be all.
Me:	Akbar, are you sure?
Akbar:	thanks for worrying about me so much Bro but I have made up my mind. I know I will always be a Muslim and if Allah wishes so will Christine. But I want to make it clear, I will not give up on her nor will I be told to, ever. Neither of us will be forced into submission.

I never thought that would happen at the time but it did. Akbar made his call.

My Father had other plans though.

He went to see Christine's father on the other side of town in the predominantly white area. It was sad what apartheid did to us. It stripped the very fiber of unity and solidarity. The areas where originally demarcated to keep us separate and that it has. Long after apartheid in majority of small town South Africa those demarcations remain like oil and water.

My Father spilt the beans on the relationship and on everything that was going on. He did not lie or paint a picture. What he said we will never know. Nonetheless when a stranger comes home it is one thing. However when it's an Indian man wearing a Juba (Islamic robe) and mosque hat with a long beard and strong scent of musk, it must be worrying. Worse still he tells you stories of his son and your daughter holding hands and walking around the town mall together: I know that would anger any father and injure his pride. The problem with it is, I know my father. He is a very intelligent man and he always has a plan.

As they say n' boere maak n' plan, and the addition to that maar n'charo het n' plan.

His plan was a number of serious conversations with Christine's dad John. After all the conversations with the Molana did not work. Talking and giving ultimatums did not either. It was clear only a congregation of the parents were required.

Parents can do crazy things for their children, sometimes in other peoples eyes it might not always seem like the best thing for them. But hey they are not your kids and we all have our own garden to tend too.

And the end result was the disappearance of Christine.

12

It is funny how stupid, simple things are taken for granted everyday. The simple air you breathe in and out. How often have you taken a breath and wondered about this miracle, or the fact that you can walk and see, amazing huh.

Well the reason I bring up this topic is not because I am trying to be all philosophical, or coercing you to thank whatever higher being you believe in but to remind you.

After last nights intake I have an awesome total of three patients as new admissions. Before I jumped for joy, I should have seen the state of these three patients. A 49 year old male with newly diagnosed thyroid issues likely in thyrotoxicosis. A 67 year old female with a deep venous thrombosis or DVT. Last but not least, a type 2 diabetic that had a septic foot and was going blind.

I have dealt with these kinds of patients before but since Mr Botha, for some odd reason every now and then I look at my patients in a different light.

Mr Botha and his unknown illness was becoming a good internal med case for me.

His kidney function was completely abnormal, then his glucose levels were through the roof. He was developing some leg swelling too. I was still waiting on lots of his results as most were sent out to a tertiary hospital.

Mr Botha: so Dr Sha, would you like some IV fluids today, I got some to spare.
Me: no thanks Mr Botha.
Mr Botha: why the long face today, I am the one who is dying here.
Me: Agh, just work and some family problems.
Mr Botha: ya, I heard about your friend. Sorry about that.
Me: what friend?
Mr Botha: Stevie.
Me: oh ya, shit forgot to speak to him.
Mr Botha: well you should.
Me: why what did he say?
Mr Botha: I think you should find out personally.
Me: well no good news Mr Botha.
Mr Botha: any bad news.
Me: no bad news either.
Mr Botha: well, that's a plus.
Me: I am afraid you gonna be here a bit longer. We need to do more tests.
Mr Botha: I am getting used to Mr Khumalo's snoring and the kitchens lovely rendition of chicken ala king.
Me: Mr Botha that's cabbage.
Mr Botha: exactly!
Me: guess I will speak to you later.
Mr Botha: don't worry about it. I will be right here.

I had forgotten all about Stevie boy. About a month ago Stevie boy was taking bloods at something like four in the morning on this wasted chronic gastro HIV positive bottom of the barrel patient. He got the bloods and after putting in the IV line, the patient pulled his hand, and the needle accidentally went directly into Stevies finger.

He had to take prophylaxis now.

The dreaded anti-retrovirals, the worst medications under the sun.

Not only do you have severe gastro and you are nauseous all the time but on top of having the flu, you are expected to come to work, do your calls and perform like nothing happened. That is what pisses me off.

These tablets are no fun. I tell you I have been on them and I don't wish them on my worst enemy.

Of course they (the experts, other doctors) tell you that it reduces your risk of contracting HIV by a couple percentage points.

It is a true test of physical and mental stamina. The worst part is the wait. You know the risk is extremely low, but it is human nature. You just can't stop thinking about the what ifs. That is when you realize how you take all the glorious blessings at your disposal for granted.

I remember my encounter. There I was doing a lumbar puncture. As the cubicles are so small and people are working on top of each other, it happened.

The sister bumps me from behind while my needle is still in place, and the CSF spits like a fire flame into my unprotected eye.

The thing about is we are all very careful, well most of us. I have seen super M that idiot be a hero and resus a patient without gloves.

The rest of us usually have our goggles on and gloves on and we are draped, looking like Martians. But the one time you forget to do something, good old Murphy has to act.

And so it was. First you have to check if the patient is HIV positive, in my case a no brainer. Second you check yourself, nerve racking if you know what you have done in your own private life. I was negative, and then you are on the ARV's awaiting re-tests over a year.

And that is just HIV; we don't even check hepatitis B, C which are even more common.

Then you have to wait for the patients Cd4 count plus minus viral load. It is a gauge as to how infective the patient was/is. My patient had a cd4 of 50 so I was all in, triple therapy. Stevies was less than 50, so he was all in too.

One month later after you have puked, and pissed out your backside. You sit in that chair.

Initially you don't think of it. Then you think about why you did not do this and that. I guess it is like any accident. You play it over and over in your mind. If only I was more cautious. If I did this or that. But once it's done, the toothpaste is out of the tube.

Then you get angry. I was angry at the government, for these messed up small cubicles, for not rolling out ARV's earlier, for making me work in these circumstances.

But as you sit in that chair, awaiting your result, there is feeling of apprehension. There you were, a doctor trying to help people. Now what if . . . the roles are reversed. I was just thinking it's a death sentence.

I was more nervous than my final exam. I was negative and still am, but what if . . . and really what can you do thereafter. What would you do?

So I went looking for Stevie, as that 6 week test was pretty important.

I could not find him anywhere.

It took me about a half hour and there he was sitting on the floor outside next to his car listening to his Ipod. I could hear the song, every bodies changing—keane.

Stevie: it was positive.
Me: what do you mean it was positive?
Stevie: I mean I am HIV positive man.
Me: what the hell? You are joking right?
Stevie: No I am dead serious.
Me: (mind the pun). So you tested and what happened?
Stveie: I am telling you man it was f . . . in positive!!!
Me: where at staff clinic. Please man, come on.
Stevie: well sister Bhengu was not in. The new sister said I was positive.
Me: (I was stumped. Speechless.) Then it hit me, maybe she is not reading it correctly. We went down to the clinic and sure enough she was not properly trained yet and had read Stevies result incorrectly and 3 other tests that morning. Luckily I showed her how to read the results, she was a new nurse, just graduated and since the clinic was short today, she was slotted in at the last minute and was reading a test she was not used to.

We retested him and he was negative but still skeptical.

We both sat there next to his car in silence for a while. We may as well have been in the middle of the Atlantic Ocean drowning.

Now I was a bit shocked myself. I have never thought of this scenario in my mind ever. I had seen people being counseled. Shit, I have counseled patients before but this was different. This was my friend. This was a doctor. I was a doctor. It could happen to me.

Me: what can I do?
Stevie: he just looked at me blankly?

95

Me: (now there are many ways to broach this kind of problem but as a doctor in my humble opinion. Positive reinforcement works best.)

Look, these tests here are reliable. But if you want to make sure, let's go to one of the private labs and sort this out once and for all.

Stevie: for the first time that day, there was an expression of purpose. He looked at me and his eyes said lets do it.

Me: come on man, let's go.

So off we went to the private labs there on the outskirts of the city central in our lunch time. Well a bit of extended lunch, the other interns would cover us, they knew how serious this was. It was quiet, air conditioned and sobering. The only thought running through my mind was that this could have been me. It scared the shit out of me.

Stevie went and got the most up to date test available. He paid a nice sum for it as well. It would take some time to get the result. So we waited.

We sat in silence but we were at full volume.

Here we were literally taking a chance with our lives everyday. We did not think about it. We just did it. It was the same as fireman, running into the flames, it was daring, it was dangerous and somebody had to do it.

But if you asked that fireman's family if they would like him home for Christmas, you know what the answer would be.

We did these crazy things with the thought of an accident right at the back of the mind.

1 in a million, huh it will never happen to me, but there is always the one. And that one could very well be you.

Stevie: I spoke to my family and my girlfriend, about this scare
Me: oh yeah, what they say?
Stevie: well my mum just started crying.
Me: and . . .
Stevie: well my girlfriend she did not say anything. She just hung up.
Me: and then I said the worst thing possible . . .

Are you Ok?

Stevie: I am just a bit shaken. If this were positive I would not know what to do with myself man. I mean you have all these hopes and dreams. You just want to go back, but you can't. And the irony is by doing good, you get punished. I just don't think I will be able to handle it man.

We sit. We wait. We wait. And time crawls by like an ant making its way across your huge garden.

The sister walks in and says Dr Farel.

Stevie: yes mam
Sister: we have your results.

Would you mind stepping in here please, would you like your partner to come with?

We look at each other. We would laugh, in fact we should laugh. But all we manage is a secret smile. We don't say anything. We just walk in to the room, with sister.

The Sister turns to him and says a whole lot of words. I am just waiting for the important ones. I am sure Steve is too. I can't help it, but at this time, think of my patients and what they must go through. At least the sister spoke English. At least she had the courtesy to try and explain fully the repercussions of this result.

Sister: (she opens the paper)
Stevie and I wait with baited breathe.
Sister: it's negative. But we have done a p24 test which will take a couple a days. But this test is 99% sensitive.

We walk out. We don't say anything.

Stevie looks into the distance. He smiles but at the same time his eyes are a tad misty.

Stevie: thanks for coming man. I appreciate it. Check you tomorrow.
Me: sure thing, don't worry about it. See you tomorrow man

His p24 also came back negative, and we knew all was OK.

And that was that. As doctors we all hope that is that, but we all are exposed to viruses and bacteria everyday. We are in the frontline, and our poor families are probably exposed too. Goes with the job as they say, and you chose it, right?

Or did you, choose to work in disastrous conditions with no protective supplies. I don't know but I do it.

13

Mr Botha and Mr Khumalo were having their usual arguments on the pros and cons of democracy and the current state of South Africa. It was always entertaining and interesting to watch. Since they called each other B and K. I mean come on; it does not get any better than that.

Mr Botha: what is democracy K(Mr Khumalo) but a body overridden by the head. Sure, you have the hands that do all the dirty work-department of labor, your liver and kidneys-department of health, your heart-justice, your feet-transport, your eyes, ears and mouth—art and culture your bowels-finance,

Me: yip, what goes in must come out.

Mr Botha: But at the end of the day, it's the head or the brain that controls everything, right. Democracy originally was pure. Nowadays it's a bidding war, for those in power to remain in power and ensure power through whatever means possible, and by whatever deals possible.

Mr Khumalo: so you are saying it is a dictatorship masquerading as a democracy, B.

Mr Botha: exactly.

Mr Khumalo: well then how do you explain America electing a black president.

Mr Botha: well it is true. I have to admit that was due to a number of circumstances. The people of America wanted change and they voted for it.

Mr Khumalo: and that my friend is the power of democracy as we witnessed in our country, the power to change.

Mr Botha: but you have to admit the darker recesses of mans mind like a political body will always take hold.

Mr Khumalo: well that I cannot deny. Everyone craves power and hates to lose it. However there is no system that betters democracy.

Mr Botha: the Chinese will dispute that point. And the way the world is going they have a strong case.

Mr Khumalo: I do believe that also has a lot to do with the way their economies are run. There is a big difference. Time has shown that the capitalist market in the long term benefits very few.

Mr Botha: You are right there.

Me: ah, finally something the two of you agree on.

It was fascinating that these two highly intelligent individuals ended up here in ward 16 medical male. The stories were sad. Mr Botha's private medical aid exhausted on his daughters chronic Leukemia. He had no alternative. Mr Khumalo was here by default. He had medical aid but while changing to another private care aid he was found to have a pre existing condition and thus was ruled out. His chronic renal failure was now our responsibility and with his recurrent bladder infections, he was here quite often.

To be honest I think they had no better place to be.

It was the case for a vast majority of patients. I mean think about it. You had a warm bed (well reasonably), decent food (sometimes), and people to talk to and some one to check on you all the time.

Whats not to love?

This is how people become institutionalized.

Well there is that small insignificant problem of being poor and dying.

But other than that little hiccup it was awesome.

I was whizzing through my rounds now six weeks into medicine and I was settled. It takes about six weeks to get into a block.

Things were OK. I heard from my brother after a long time. He said he was doing well. He sounded sincere this time.

And there was the party. It was Johara's annual party. My cousin Jojo has been having a party every year for as long as I can remember.

Although it is something my parents don't really celebrate openly like everyone else. Since it was my aunts daughter (from my mothers side), I was always allowed to go.

It is quite funny how we overlook things for family in certain respects but not in others.

The reason I have grown to love this party is the chicks. My cousin always invites her friends. It is one of the only places I can speak to a girl without the gazing eyes of a grown up or the innuendo of something more serious.

This party was my one for the week. My one refers to the one thing I look forward to. Its that one thing you have. The one thing to look for ward to in the week. The highlight in the week. The one thing you need to get you through the week. The high of the week. Sometimes it might even be the highlight of a month, of a year.

You find these little things to get you through the week. The drab and dreary. The monotony of day to day being. You wake up. You get into your car. You sit in the traffic that just gets worse every year. You drop the kids of at school and then you are at that boring job. The job that gives you joy once a month, payday. You gossip with your co-workers, talk about the game last night. Suddenly the day is over. You go home complain about having the same meals every week. You switch on the television and fall asleep to wake up to the next day.

But I had this party. This week, this month, it was my one.

For some it's a holiday. For others it's that weekend away. For you it might even be a party, or even time with the family or special someone. It is that thing out of the ordinary that you hold onto like a drug because there is that natural high before and after.

Getting ready, the planning, what to wear? Who would be there? What you might do there? Sure you go, sure you forget and look forward to the next ONE, but you need it. You need it to push through.

At the same time that it was exciting, it was pure melancholy that mine was a party at family.

I could not make it last year as I was on call. Another event that was missed due to being on call. I remember it, because it was a weekend call and I could not get anyone to swap calls with.

Waking up on a Sunday to go to work at eight in the morning and if you are lucky, you may get to have some lunch, supper and three—four hours sleep. I mean hey, it is an important shift job, someone has to do it, and as my mother always tells me "you chose it", but it is never fun.

When you miss most of the public holidays, family functions and weddings. When everything you do, or want to attend requires planning and begging others to cover for you. I know most of the time it's a sacrifice for a couple of years but at the same time, it is a sacrifice.

I wish there was another way, but you realize when you on call very quickly, you are needed. One doctor short really might mean that some patients might not make it. I am not saying this out of a God complex, but trust me when I say, you take away the number of the work force, and people die. It hurts especially when its people that could be saved.

I mean most of the time on call, when I am there, I go through the motions, and I work. I feel fulfilled. It is OK. Every now and then there is a patient that stands out, that makes your day/night.

But recently the more patients I see, these chronic sick patients that are good people. They were probably once very productive people. But when I see them dying. I feel hopeless. I just don't the see the big difference i/ we are making. And then I am not OK again. But slowly I am coming to terms with it.

It is just no matter how hard I try, I can never separate the two. This work, this job, this life, this calling.

All I know is that I wake up each day and I go and do the best I can. That's about all I can say and do.

I remember when I was doing my pediatric block we had a ward for forgotten kids. There was a group of children between the ages of two weeks and ten years. They came into hospital most of them really unwell, with the usual host of social and economic factors.

The repertoire includes Mother or father dead or dying. Most of their parents are HIV positive CD4 counts (a measure of how severe the disease progression is, usually above 400 is good). These patients had CD4 counts of 1-50 and most of them had TB for a start and a host of other problems. They did not have food, they did not have money, they had no real support.

Now, I have parents and family, I have a full home cooked meal everyday. I have money to buy over the counter anti nausea meds etc. I have I have I have . . . but these people the patients of South Africa, Africa, poverty stricken of the world are have nots.

I don't think about it for too long though. I just feel more guilty, so I leave it like a black hole in the corner of my mind.

It just makes me sad.

So the gogos bring these kids in and we admit and once admitted its with us they stay. They are here for good, dropped of at hospital day care. There was this kid Jabu Mkhize admitted 12/02/04 I wrote notes on his file 12/10/04. His family was lost. The social workers cannot find homes for all these children.

Most of them are sick and some die, some live, some get a lot better, waiting for a place to call home.

This could be the explanation of the government's tardiness in the role out on ARV's. Thousands of orphans with no homes, no family, majority of them with no realistic future.

Jabu stayed till early 2005, he was then moved to one of these Child Homes. The truth is I am not sure, will there be a happy ending for him?

The reason I say that is when he left he was on an ARV regimen and was on his second month of TB treatment.

He was doing well in hospital, but once they leave, it seems its just a downhill slope.

I have seen it happen many times. A child is admitted or even a pensioner. You treat them. They leave the hospital in a fairly stable condition. Less than fortnight later, they come back worse than before.

The truth is sometimes we don't have enough beds. At the same time once a patient is admitted you can't ship them out till they are completely worked up and sorted out. Well you can but that's just not cricket mate.

So in fact we have a ward with about 7-10 social cases out 25 medical beds. All, waiting for a home. Some get lucky, their families remember them and they come take them home. Others are just left waiting for placement.

These people are taking up space for other sick patients. Sometimes it's a real tough call to make but what can you do?

As a doctor here, you are a social worker too, some days you are counselor, some days you have to play the nurse or dietitian too.

The problem is you were not really trained for all these other extraneous problems, so depending on your own personality ethics and morals, you do what you can.

I just can't help feeling that often it's just not enough, but hey that's the system and I am an ant in the middle of the Kalahari Desert.

But I am looking for other ants, to help save the world, yeah right!

14

It's a Saturday night party, but what to wear, what to wear.

It is an amazing fact that the human condition allows us to indulge in stupidity. For some of us it is every now and then, for others it is everyday.

I have a cupboard full of clothes, a lot of new stuff. I got a cool array of smart casual shirts and authentic Diesel jeans (which I paid a small fortune for), but alas as the time approaches I look at this awesome smorgasbord of fashion I have and think like a little girl I have nothing to wear.

I must boldly go where everyman now feminized completely goes. I must head to the malls, let the shopping extravaganza begin.

Now everyone has their own way of shopping. Mine is analytical, it relies on age old traditions, a polished sense of style, and of course the place with the biggest sale and cheapest shit. Hey I am a metro-sexual, don't hate the player . . .

I had a mission. From my very limited knowledge I noted that polar necks something I have worn in the past to be ridiculed for all eternity was definitely out. I also noted that leather was definitely out. It would be a cold day in hell before I wore anything leather.

For some crazy reason and correct me if I am wrong I wear things that are comfortable. Some things fair enough you won't wear on a Sunday afternoon. But the clothing I wear is not of the creed "I can't wait to take this off", and even though my heels pain so much I feel like crying, God Damn I look good.

Most of the ladies can take that pain. High heels, enough said.

I liked my dark blue jeans versatile and suave. I think a simple but elegant black shirt. Yes and a neat frat boy jersey with my Soviet glasses. It says hey I am a doctor, yet I am cool sophisticated young and available.

I am ready, but just as I make my move to leave the mall, I bump into her again, Khathija.

Khatija:	Slmz Ali, so nice to see you.
Me:	Wslmz hey there, howzit goin?
Khatija:	So, I am not the only one doing some last minute shopping for the party.
Me:	(how could I forget, Jojo and Khatija were second cousins. I guess since I have been out of the family loop for a while I had forgotten who would be there.)
	Ya, you know how it is busy at work, had to sneak away to get something for the party.
Khathija:	so what did you get?
Me:	well it's going to have to be a surprise.
Khathija:	ooh I like surprises.
Me:	the way she is smiling with a natural soft glow and holding that pose, eyes directly looking into mine and body moving forward, make me wonder . . . Are we flirting?

I mean I have flirted before and I will flirt again, well actually I am not sure what this is. I mean she is my second cousins cousin twice removed, so in a way we are family, kind of.

And then her mum comes into the picture, Aunty Sara.

Aunty Sara:	Slmz Ali so nice to see you. It is so difficult to find parking here. You know these malls just keep getting busier and busier. So how are mum and dad?
Me:	Wslmz, mum and dad are fine.
Aunty Sara:	you coming to the party tonight.

Me:	Yup, I will be there. It will be nice to see everyone. It has been a while.
Aunty Sara:	guess we will see you later dear, got some serious shopping to do.
Khathija:	Ya, I will see you later. She whispers just as her mother is out of hearing distance, cant wait to see that surprise.
Me:	I greet and walk on nonchalantly, I smile and think its on baby its on like Donkey Kong.

But Khathija although beautiful is just not my personality type. But girls into you are always a good thing, confidence booster.

The day has become one of those obsessive compulsive ones. You try to be perfect but you just can't.

You are trying to get the perfect hair style that accentuates your jaw line and manly features. You have combed your hair a dozen times and smelt all your perfumes a couple of times and chosen.

The hype is here as I said its infective, Saturday night fever. Its meat/ meet night. I am in heading into the butcher shop and I have to find the rarest and most exquisitely tender piece of juicy fillet steak. Jojo will have invited all her friends from varsity and it is the only place where one can mingle and chat to these chicks in peace.

There is always some innuendo and problem when this kind of scene takes place without parents and family nearby.

Truth be told, I am just a little lonely. I mean I have my friends and stuff, but they have their own lives too. And I speak to my parents and brother but I miss having that someone special in my life.

Me:	Mum I am ready to go, guess I will see you guys later.
Mum:	Ali come here.
Me:	What up mum?
Dad:	Come here son.
Me:	yes mum and dad (as I walk over to the lounge)
Dad:	remember now we let you go there because we know how you look forward to this, but be responsible and don't do anything stupid.
Me:	(I want to say dad, what do you think I am 12. I can take care of myself.) Instead I just nod and walk on.
Dad:	asalaamu alykum

Me: walaykum salaam.

I jump in my car push play on the radio—nothing like some Paul Oakenfold to get the pulse going and get ready mentally.

Be cool, act cool, you are cool.

I pull up to the house. It is situated on top of a hill with only a few houses around. It is a wealthy area. The lights are bright and I walk straight through as the gate is open. It is a cream and beige colored house that has a Tuscan theme to it. For some reason the surtee class are obsessed with the Italians.

Oh ya, I almost completely forgot. There are divisions here in South Africa, As time has gone on, it has gotten better. I only worked it out a couple of years ago. I was in class at university all self conscience and of course trying to act cool. I tried to strike up a confession with the most beautiful girl I had ever seen. I was never short of confidence but as I said I was always aware of myself. I always question myself but I am confident when it comes to relating and interacting with people. Her name was Shubnam. She was stunning. A true star.

Shubnam: (she sits down in the middle of the aisle)
Me: ˙I walk up and sit next to her and say Slmz I am Ali, she smiles politely gets up and walks to the next row and sits down.

I sit there wondering whether its just me.

Then this dude Aslam, (he is fair, a surtee, also rich, drives a Golf Gti). He does what looks like is the exact same thing I did and she does not get up. She does not move, they talk and talk, and two years later, they were married. It was an interesting experience to say the least. That was not the first or last time. There are levels of how fierce or weird people get based on color, creed and status.

You get some people that may greet. That is how far they go. Then you get some that greet and allow you talk to them, but that is as far as they go. If they catch you talking to their daughter they kill you. Sure I am being a bit extreme but it is still a loose caste system, and trust me its still in India and it still is embalmed in Indians worldwide, but its getting better I hope. I guess we will see.

I mean in the 21ˢᵗ century can we still continue basing social interactions on color and what your grandfathers father did. That is sad but true.

Somethings are hard to see passed and the caste system is one of them.

It was as always based on class and color. The richer and fairer you are the higher up you were. In a way it was really stupid and naïve. Its not inherent I don't think but learnt and passes down generation after generation. Yet again sometimes I wonder the need to be superior to someone else. It supersedes many other needs. It gives a false comfort of self. It took thousands of years to abolish slavery. It took a while longer to actually believe that all men are equal and that women have rights too.

Of course every religion knows about and teaches it including Islam, but do we ever practice what we preach? Do we ever follow what has been taught?

So back to the divisions. Yes, as was the custom in India. We continue to some degree to have a caste system, still there, like the scratch on a car that has aged with time.

There were the surtees, merman's, urdus, cocknies etc. all with their own languages and some customs but inevitably and some thing we have come to realize is that we were all Muslim. The divisions have been there since I was a kid but they have slowly improved with time. It begs the question of, if there was unity how much more could man have accomplished. We are all still trying to be number one though.

As stated each group has its niche, but I have noticed subtle differences. People nowadays realize that even though the man your white daughter is planning on marrying is black or white, if he is a good man who loves and cares for your daughter, what does it really matter? By people i mean less than 5% of us.

My dad was Urdu speaking and my mum was surtee, so there was a taboo already with our family background.

So too with the caste system which is slowly remolding itself from the black and white into a rainbow. I was happy to see my friend Aslam a surtee guy marry Mumtaz an Urdu speaking girl. He did it and although his parents were not over the moon about it, they accepted his choice. Now they are one big happy family, I think, one can never be sure as the pommies say, innit.

In the end I knew I would have to please my parents to some extent. Your parents blessing is an important part of the whole process. Trust me

I know. And somehow if you don't get it, there will always be something missing.

So Jojo was on the surtee side of the family, if lines need to be drawn.

The house was bustling like a bazaar; I could smell the meat on the braai stand.

Me: Slmz Aslam, howzit man?

Aslam: Ali, nice to see you bro.

Me: what you doing in maritzburg?

Aslam: well Mumtaz's brother and Johara are kind of courting each other.

Me: oh, ok.(means they are likely getting married soon).

Aslam: and you hows the doctors life treating you?

Before I could jump whole heartedly into that answer. I saw her.

She was wearing a blue Shalwaar kames. She had shoulder length dark brown hair and her smile was infectious. She looked out of the corner of her eye and then carried on talking to another girl. She was fresh, different, she was warm and her face was flushed with expression. I just had to talk her. I had this feeling many times before but for some reason I had this expectation that something was going to happen tonight. Now I knew what.

Me: ya nice catching up with you Aslam.

Aslam: I would be careful with that one if I were you.

Me: what do you mean, a lot of guys have been bitten by her while she is here.

Aslam: well I am not one for gossip, best you find out on your own. See you around Ali.

Me: ya sure thing.

Now you know how it is when someone warns you or gives you some good advice. But you are just in another place altogether at the time and you don't hear a word they say. All you hear or see is what you want to. You are blinded by your raging hormones, and your ego.

Since my cousin was with her right now I knew my chances of a solid introduction was on. I had to make my move now.

Me: Slmz Jojo. Happy birthday, I got you a little something something.

Jojo: Wslmz, so now that you are a doctor you forfeit your family huh.

       When was the last time you came over?

Me: I was looking at Jojo, talking to Jojo but the corner of my eyes could not be torn away from her like Julius Malema is drawn to corruption claims.

Of course Jojo was beautiful as ever. Contrary to what people think not all Muslims marry their cousins. And I would never see her as anything more than a cousin. I know the feeling is mutual. She was wearing a halter neck white top and skinny shiny Levi jeans.(the reason I knew it was Levis, as only a Levi sat that good), I know I am a bad boy, sometimes we all go a little crazy. I could not believe that her father would have allowed it.

She wearing some kajal and her hands were covered in mendhi or henna. She was small next to the lynx next to her but no less attractive but as stated she was my cousin.

Ah she looks over, time for the introduction.

Jojo: Anya, this is my cousin . . .

While I am busy processing this unusual name Anya, as that is exactly what I would like to do. Someone screams my name and comes through the crowd to meet me.

It is none other than . . .

Khathija: Ali what are you doing here?

Me: just as I reach my hand out to shake Anya's, she pulls away.

Khatija: Slmz I am Khatija.

Anya: Slmz I am Anya.

Me: before I could even get a word in there, these two were having their own conversation and it pissed me off.

Khatija: wow that is a rich American accent.

Anya: well it's actually Canadian. My dad is from there, but he is originally from India.

Khatija:	and your mum?
Anya:	well she is actually my South African connection.
Khatija:	so what are you doing In South Africa?
Anya:	well actually my dad is working here now on business for a bit, so I am just down studying at the University on an exchange basis finishing my thesis on cultural diversities of the world.
Jojo:	that's where she bumped into me and her crazy tour of KZN and South Africa began, we have been having girls nights ever since.
Me:	yeah I bet.

You know when you say something and straight away you regret it. Well that was one of those moments. The first thing I go and say is Yeah I bet, my chances statistically have dropped to below 10%, so much for first impressions.

Me:	need to redeem myself, time for some smooth operating.
Slmz:	I am Ali, Ali Sha, ala bond James bond.
Khatija:	well he is just Ali to those close to him
Me:	at this point I am like what the hell? Khatija just leave us alone and let me get my groove on, coz right now you are killing me.
Anya:	Ali, cool name?
Khathija:	it's a pretty common name here.
Me:	(I am in quick sand and Khatija is throwing in more water.)
Jojo:	yeah where did you get that name and surname act? You're not James Bond.
Me:	(and Jojo is throwing on the sand.)
Khatjia:	from his friends probably. All boys think they are James Bond.
Jojo:	wow Khatija heard you are a teacher at that primary school, how is it?

And just like that, they got into a conversation about education for 10 minutes with me just saying yeah, all the time.

Me: (what is this girls gone bad, were they trying to sabotage me?)

Me: well I am doctor. (Time to do some repairs)

Anya: oh yeah, you look pretty young.

Me: just doing my internship.

Anya: that must be something.

Me: (and the comeback is complete.) Ya it is quite difficult to take care of patients here in South Africa.

Anya: So anyway when is this party getting started?

Jojo: oh yes that reminds me of the cake. Anya, come with me. And just like that they were gone.
          I look around and it's just me and Khatija again.

Khatija: so you were saying its difficult being a doctor in South Africa.

Me: yeah, but my mind was already drifting. I got a whiff of her perfume as she walked away, one that I do know, one of my favorites, but a rare one.

Khatija: what is it with guys and foreign chicks? You know she is just soaking up everybodies attention.

Me: sounds like you are a bit jealous Khatija.

Khatija: No, not really.

Me: I decided to cut the chit chat and find some place to just be alone for a moment. Just going to bathroom I told her, but I did not, I went out and sat in my car. Should I stay or should I go?

I thought about it for a few minutes. I guess I should just have fun and enjoy the evening. I decided to reduce the volume of time I spent with the ladies especially her, thus reducing the pressure of the evening.

I took a slow labored walk back inside. The party had continued on. They had brought out the cake. There was the usual sing—a-long happy birthday song. Then Jojos mum said how proud she was of her. Her daughter would soon be a chartered accountant. It was then that I realized how old we all were. If Jojo was now 26, my 26th was on the way.

I grabbed a can of Coke and headed outside in search of some testosterone. I missed my boys on nights like this, I am sure we as a group would find this whole experience very amusing.

Most of the faces outside I knew but they were strangely different. Uncle Ayub was at the braai stand. He looked older, and he spoke a lot about how bad things were. I knew I was the same. Hell as Indians in general we were all the same. We just complained and condemned but at the heart of it like all South Africans we were just concerned.

Uncle Ayub: what is this country becoming if you can't go to the beach on a Sunday afternoon with your family? You heard Juns was mugged there on Durban beach front. They took everything.

Uncle Qayum: ya, I heard about it, can't say I was not surprised, though.

A couple of weeks ago Fathima Bibi and I were walking to the Wimpy in Queen Street. There was this one suspicious looking character that came, he eyed us walk into the shop from our car. As we walked out I saw the same guy again loitering around our car. Then just as we neared our car, he ran and grabbed Fathi's bag. He disappeared into the bazaar, gone. Luckily she left her phone at home and she did not have much cash on her. The scary thing is, we jumped in the car all despondent and miserable and no one around even batted an eye lash. I swear everyone just accepts this as the norm now.

Listening to the conversation made me angry and sad at the same time and for different reasons. Angry because of the conversation and the fact that this was all I ever heard and read about in the news from people on the radio. It was everywhere. It made me sad as there was just no change.

Nothing was changing or maybe it was just getting worse. The scary part for me was, what am I or anyone of us here doing about it? The same as everyone else, nothing, just complaining.

But I was not going to tell them my sad stories about the hospital or wallow in the petty crime and mellow dramatic happenings of the sports world. Although on any other occasion I would.

No sir, I was on a recognizance mission here. I had to gather information before my next meet with the fiery beauty.

Me: slmz Uncle Ayub
Uncle Ayub: Ali, how is my young Dr Sha doing?

Me:	Alhamdulillah.
Me:	so how thongs at are work, I mean things at work. (My mind was somewhere else)
Uncle Ayub:	looks at me quizzically, it's OK. So how is the state of our public hospitals? Rabia and I had a boy that was sick at work. We took him to Ebersdale, it was shocking. Ali I would not go to that hospital if I was breathing my last breath and I had a knife sticking out of my chest and the worst asthmatic ever, I would never set foot in that hospital.
Me:	(a—uncle Ayub you should be dead if you have all that shit happening to you and b—its safe to say I wont be seeing you around any public hospital anytime soon)
Uncle Ayub;	I just make shukr everyday that we can afford private medical care.

It took another twenty minutes of mundane topics that included as always a free consultation around a toe nail infection and something about a grey hair patch. I finally had to go in to the house to avoid any further torture.

Just before leaving though I got my Intel.

Me:	so uncle Ayub, who is that girl Anya?
Uncle Ayub:	oh so you met Anya, she is from Canada; her father took in a transfer to work with some diplomatic aid. He does some political work, I think.
Me:	so will she i mean they be going back soon?
Uncle Ayub:	well you never know with these politicians. She has really taken to Johara, stays overnight here quite a bit.
Me:	But someone said she was here studying.
Uncle Ayub:	oh ya, she is doing some social sciences course, but I don't think she knows that all the good money is in accounting or engineering or medicine. Don't you agree, Ali?
Me:	Yeah yeah, I was distracted.

I could hear some feet shuffling and I saw Aunty Rabi carrying out the presents so I hurried to the main tent. I had bought her a guess bag from Manchester road, it was a fake but it was as real as it got and I doubt anyone would spot the difference. I know I'm a cheap skate. I could not afford 100% genuine guess wear for second cousins yet.

Jojo was opening her presents and I could not help but notice Taahir, Jojo's cousin from the other side of the family chatting up Anya. I had to make my move, fast so I walked over to join in the festivities. This concealed menacing bad doctor act was backfiring and my recog mission had revealed nothing much.

Anya: Taahir, When did you get back?
Taahir: well I came in last Tuesday. It was amazing. It was first trip
         to Europe. It was an unforgettable experience. I mean I only
         got to see Paris and London but it is most definitely the best
         trip I have ever had.

Taahir was a tall lanky Fair skinned, polar bear. Well he was big and clever like a monkey. He was an act sci man. From what I remember. I was just angry that my chances were all but gone now.

He was more in her class. They were too similar. Two angels talking under the effervescent light of the fluorescent tubes in this gaudy white tent.

The whole scene made me sick.

And here is the present from Ali.

Me: dope too late to run, all eyes on me now.
Jojo: she opens cautiously and seems pleased, wow, its really cool.
Me: ah she did not notice.
Jojo: you doctors must be earning well to but this expansive stuff.
Me;   I just smiled and waved, smile and wave.
Anya: Ali that is a really cool gift, how thoughtful.
Ali: well I saw it and just thought, this is Jojo.
Anya: ah that is really sweet.
Ali: back in the game.
Anya: so what you going to be up to on Saturday. We were
         thinking of going for a movie. If that is ok with you, Taahir.
Taahir: oh yeah sure, the more the merrier.

Me: slmz Taahir.(snigger)
Taahir: wslmz.(snigger too).

He and I both knew what this was now. It was a show down. She was looking for the alpha male and that was . . .

Khathija: so I heard you guys going for a movie on Saturday, what time?

I could not believe this. She was back.

Anya: Ya you should come too Khatija. It will be nice to go out again.
Khatija: I was just joking. I don't think my dad will allow me to come.
Me: Shoo, close one.

Jojo had finished her present proceedings and had come to join the four of us. Looking around the room I could see the piercing eyes of everyone on our little group. It made me uneasy. It was to be expected. Boys and girls of a similar age talking in a group, could only mean one thing right? Wrong! Well, Right! It was crazy but some things don't change. Boys will be boys and girls will be girls and the aunties and uncles . . .

As the night wore on we spoke a lot. We had a lot in common, the five of us, and we kept the conversations going. It was Khatija who provided the comic relief, unknowingly to her. It was Anya that provided the beauty and grace. Taahir was not bad either, I accepted his intellectual wit and it grew on me. Friends and family came by and left wishing Jojo.

Taahir was the first to leave. He had to catch up on some sleep. It was already past midnight. Then it was Khatija and her family. She was going to find out if her father would let her come with us to the movies.

Soon it was just the three of us. I stayed to help with the cleaning and packing of trestles and other menial work of course. Out of the goodness of my heart, yeah right.

As soon as Jojo left I went into the zone.

Me: so Anya, any boyfriends back in Canada.

Anya: no, never had a boyfriend. (She blushed, I think)

Me: so how long do you think you will be here?

Anya: well not too long I hope.

Me: do you like it that much?

Anya: I just hate the crime and the poverty and the hopelessness.

Me: ya, you should come to the hospital, now there is all three in one.

Anya: what do you mean?

Me: well the crime is that all these impoverished people have a hopeless healthcare system.

Anya: she giggled.

Me: I could not believe she liked my weird sense of humor. I hope you had nice time tonight.

Anya: well between you and Taahir I was thoroughly entertained.

Me: (well there it was. Honors even I guess.)

Everything was packed. I thanked Uncle Ayub and Aunty Rabia for inviting me. They thanked me for staying and helping out. It was past one now.

Jojo walked me out. Anya was already gone up. She was staying over but was too tired.

Jojo: thanks for the bag Ali.

Me: no problem.

Jojo and I had always been close but it had been a while. Should I or shouldnt I? Oh what the hell?

Me: Jojo, I want to ask you something.

Jojo: don't even start.

Me: what?

Jojo: every guy that sees her wants to be with her.

Me: how did you know?

Jojo: it's obvious. Taahir already asked me too and a couple guys at varsity.

Me: oh Ok.

I resigned myself to the fact that it was a lost cause. I felt hopeless. Again.

I jumped in my car and thought about the evening on my way home. It was fun and I had a nice time. It was a good evening and that is what I took away.

15

It was hard to say why an old black man that was a firm ANC member got on so well with an old white boere. But Mr Botha and Mr Khumalo were like salt and pepper. They played chess and talked politics. They played minor pranks on the sisters; it was unlike any ward or work I had been accustomed to.

Initially I was unhappy, with my assignment to male ward, but now I was really enjoying it. I was enjoying work. It was the first time in two years. I was looking forward to my ward rounds. I had most of patients under control and I was answering most of the questions on ward rounds.

Things were looking up. As always we were brought down to earth. Our results for Mr Botha had come back. He had Systemic lupus erythmetosis. It was a late diagnosis. And I knew a lot of organ damage had already been done.

Mr Khumalo on the other hand had developed some abnormal liver tests. We were awaiting his booking for a ct scan of his abdomen. He would have to be transferred to a tertiary institute for this to occur. So he would be waiting for a while.

Every time I had been given ward duty so far, it was just a whole lot of numbers, death certificates and AIDS, AIDS, and more AIDS.

Most of the patients I could not understand or did not have the time to understand.

Now I had two patients that kept me going even when things were down. And they were interesting cases, not just HIV/AIDS. I was enjoying the ward as we had cover from a few foreign students. They were placed in OPD, so I just had my ward to look after, which was awesome.

The foreign students were a real blessing, they added a lot to the team. They helped with calls and day work. I knew they were reveling in the clinical experience. They were fresh and had not been at all tainted yet.

They were a couple from Germany, Kurt and Karen.

It was almost lunch time, so I was of to the canteen.

Can you believe it; I was actually taking lunch regularly half hour at a time now?

Stevie: howzit my boy?

Me: it has been a while since I had seen Stevie and boy did he look like shit.

After the HIV scare, he had been sick for a couple days.

Me: I am OK, man. So what is up or down? You don't look so hot man.

Stevie: I tell you man, you have a knack of picking up on people's vibes. It would be nice to talk to you some time. But I see Mother Theresa and Florence Nightingale heading our way.

Me: aren't those the two new foreign students?

Stevie: ya, they are hell bent on saving the world. It makes me sick.

Me: ya I can see that.

Stevie. No really man, they are always trying to do things by the book and going the extra mile for every patient. They are like us when we first started medicine.

Me: oh yeah I remember that, full of hope and dreams of changing the world.

Kurt: hi my name is Kurt and this is Karen, we are the foreign students working in OPD.

Me: Hi there. (Kurt and Karen obviously were german. Even before he spoke, I don't see too many ash blonde male and females with sparkling blue eyes in our setting.)

So how are you guys finding South Africa and our humble MOPD.

Kurt: It is brilliant. We learn so much in short time here.
Karen: only problem is the Zulu?
Me: well that's a problem for me too.
Stevie: gotta go, my lunch time is over, speak to you tonight, maybe at seven or so, over at Frankies.
Me: sure thing man, catch you later.
Kurt: we have been having good a time here.
Karen: everyone is helpful and friendly.
Me: so is it like anything you expected?
Karen: yes and no.
Kurt: there is so much of HIV and TB.
Karen: and there are always so many patients.
Kurt: but the hospital has most of the basic investigations.
Karen: and the lab and sisters work quite well for a third world setting.
Me: so where about from Germany are you?
Kurt: we are from Bonn, originally, but we have moved around a lot.
Karen: we have worked only in Germany but have enjoyed our experience here so far.
Me: so how long do you guys intend on staying?
Karen: well we should be here for three months.
Me: well I would like to say welcome and thanks, I really appreciate all your help. You have saved me from OPD.
Karen: we love OPD
Me: well I have to admit, that is probably the first and last time I will hear that.
       So how have the other interns in OPD been?

(They look at each other and remain quite.)

Me: well don't look too much into our behaviour. It's just been a tough two years. I will see you guys around. I am running male medical ward D, so I am pretty sure I will be seeing a lot of your admissions.
       How long have you guys been here anyway?

Kurt: oh it's just our first week, but today is our second day in OPD.

Karen: nice meeting you.

I make my way to do an afternoon look at blood results and changes in patient's conditions, and of course morning admissions.

Sister Khuzwayo who runs the ward with me is waiting as I enter. She does not look happy. Sister Khuzwayo only approaches when there are real problems, so this must be serious.

Me: Sawubona sister, what is the problem?

Sr K: We had 7 free beds, now we have none.

Me: what 7 admission since my round and lunch. That is crazy.

Sr K: most of them are social cases. You have to look and decide.

I am handed 7 files. I walk over to the patients beds and begin a busy afternoon.

An hour and a half later, I find one of these patients was a genuine admission. There are 3 gastroenteritic patients, which we usually rehydrate in OPD, and then send home. The problem is we need bed for patients we can help save. I know it sounds sick to turn people away but that is exactly what we do.

It is like ICU, where you only have a finite number of beds and patients are chosen on the belief that you admit and treat those with the greatest probability of survival.

The only difference is that we have to hold this principle for the entire hospital, or a lot of people that could live to see the sun tomorrow, don't.

Generally it takes some time to learn how to screen patients in this way, who might die anyway despite admission, who can be worked up and if they will survive the time of work up to diagnosis to treatment.

It is something you just learn with time.

The one true admission was query meningitis that on the CSF results showed a bacterial meningitis, so this patient should be an in patent.

The three other patients one a stroke, that seems to have had a stroke according to the history for more than a week. The two others are defaulters on PTB treatment.

I discuss the admission with Dr R(the rag man) and he agrees with me. Only the one requires admission.

The others are transferred out. The two defaulters are referred to their closest local TB hospital clinics for daily streptomycin injections and work up of any resistance.

The three gastro patients had AIDS with CD4 of less than 50, they were stage fours and all had not yet stared ARV's. The out look was bleak. They received their rehydration and were discharged, still awaiting to get on to ARV's.

The stroke patient had an elective CT scan booked and was discharged.

I spoke to Sr Khuzwayo. She seemed pleased.

The problem was we both knew going into an afternoon intake with no beds was a nightmare that neither of us needed.

The last thing I did was check the list of who these patients were admitted by, and why they were not screened.

They were all admitted by Kurt and Karen.

I would have to speak to them, now I knew what Stevie was talking about.

I could not go through this rigmarole everyday.

I look at my watch, it says 16h05. The day is officially over but as usual I still have a bit to do.

I have to break the news to Mr Botha, now that we have a diagnosis.

Me: Hi there Mr B, I have some good news and some bad news. What do you want first?

Mr B: I think I will take the bad news first.

Me: well it's a two in one, really. I have a diagnosis finally and I am afraid it's SLE, systemic lupus erythmetosis.

Mr B: what the hell is that? Systemic blah blah

Me: well I am afraid it is a disease with no cure. It is systemic and auto immune so it messes with every organ and it has a number of problems. It seems you may have had this for a long time., those mouth sores of yours are not related to tooth paste allergies. It has remained quiet but it has done some damage already.

Mr B: I have one question. When do I get out of here? You said you will only keep me till you have your diagnosis.

Me: I knew that would be it, just a few more minutes and then you are outa here.

Mr B: music to my ears.

Me: where is Mr K?

Mr B: he has been suffering with his bowels recently. Probably the gourmet food here, huh?

Me: oh ya, guess I will see him later. (But I was thinking already, Mr Khumalo came in with an eye problem too that was a query scleritis and now he was having bowel problems, not the first time either. I had to share this with Dr Raghavjee.)

My day was almost done but I had to go and speak to the newcomers. I had to nip this in the bud now. Yet as I walked into casualty I saw Karen putting up an IV line. There was Kurt doing an LP, I just felt a sudden tinge of guilt. I was supposed to be down here. The only reason I could go home a bit early every day and have a proper lunch was because of their cover.

I wussed out and went over and showed them a few tricks of the trade here in South Africa.

We put the IV line and took the bloods from the line at the same time.

Then we got the patient to sit up and did the LP. I used some local anesthetic and alcohol swabs as our sterile agent. (As that is all we had.)

We had done twenty minutes or more work in less than ten. But there was still a lot more to do in casualty. There always was, all the patients from OPD now were in casualty. It was buzzing. I took my cue; it was time to leave before I get roped in to do more work. There is always someone who needs help.

I remember my first days as an intern. I started of in pediatric out patients. How we tried to save every kid that came in flat. Oh the detailed notes I used to write. The way we used to take time to work patients up.

We never left before five and we were there everyday before eight. On call we were up, practically up the whole night.

We were so full of verve and enthusiasm. However I never had a social life and I came home ate and slept. I guess my job was my life and vice versa. As time went by we all just changed slowly. We still did our best but we learnt to work faster. We learnt when to say no, when to go home. It just came naturally. You find methods to help you cope.

I have noticed the same thing with the first year interns. They came in just like us, jumping over each other to do CPR but very rarely did the patient make it. I guess I don't know whether it was experience or complacency that had set in. this was the doctor I was now. I would come to work. I would do my best. But when it was time to go home, I would.

Well I should, but I look to my watch, its 17h45.

I rush home, shower and change, get something to eat. I still have to meet Stevie.

I drive in to Frankies. It's already passed eight. I am already tired.

Stevie: what is up my man?

Me: (Stevie is already on the booze train.) howzit man?
Stevie: thanks for coming man.
Me: no prob man.
Stevie: you want something to drink.
Me: I will just have some passion fruit and lemonade thanks, so whats up?
Stevie: the girl I was going to spend the rest of my life with broke up with me bro.
Me: why what happened?
Stevie: she freaked out with the whole HIV thing.
Me: what do you mean?
Stevie: well I told her what happened. She never thought about it, till it happened. She was also sick for a while. She had bronchitis. She blamed me; she said I gave it to her from the hospital.
Me: well that is possible.
Stevie: hey whose side are you on?
Me: well yours of course, man. I guess . . . I dunno.
Stevie: what up? Tell me what you thinking. I can see that look in your eye when the wheels in your head have been turning.
Me: well maybe she is not the one for you Steve. I mean you guys have been together since last year and most of the time you fight anyway. You could never tell her you love her. Remember how she used to get when you were on call, phoning every couple of minutes.
Stevie: ya I remember.

Me: some, well most people don't get what comes with the job and title of Doctor. I don't think she did or will.
Stevie: ya, you are right.
Me: I think you should take it easy. On the booze I mean, its back to work tomorrow.
Stevie: ya, you right again.
Me: well you know I am always right.
Stevie: thanks again for being there man. I have a lot of different friends you know but you are true friend, through the thick and thin. I always seem to be in some kind of social crisis, yet you always seem so calm.
Me: well I owe you too. Remember O&G last year.
Stevie: as I said forget about that man.

It was Obstetrics and it was my second block. I was only into my third call. It was an all weekend. On from Friday 08H00 till 12h00 on Saturday. Then you go home sleep and you are back on Sunday 08h00 till Monday 12h00. The bad part was that I was sick with the flu. It was clear early on, there was no way I was gonna make it through this. My partner for this week end was a guy who studied at Tukkies I barely knew, Steven Hendriks Farel. No way was I going to get any help there.

Normally what we used to do was cover the admitting area, woman coming in labor or what they thought was labor. Then there was the labor ward for women who are in labor. Add to that the gynecology emergency area. Of course there was high care area, for the more problematic cases and post delivery ward.

Covering these many places were four doctors on the floor. Two interns, a medical officer, a registrar. There were at least two nurses at each station and a consultant at home. Suffice to say if you had time to go pee, you were doing well.

Now you can get lucky. By lucky I mean less than 10 caesars over 24 hours. However in this facility that rarely ever happens. We have a record of 21 in one day. Yes 21.

A Caesar takes 2 people out, an intern and the reg. so the work load can build up if it is busy. Of course there is no time to be sick.

The funny thing is when at hospital, the nurses and patients often wonder where is the doctor when you page or try to call. In this scenario, the doctor is running around like a headless chicken trying to sort out each problem that arises.

If it's not a 14 year old who has per vaginal bleeding at 32 weeks of her pregnancy in the admitting area, then it's a "normal delivery" of mother who has suddenly bled to hemoglobin of 5.0 in the post delivery area.

In between all this there is high care with an eclamptic having seizures and the sisters don't know what to do.

So Friday is nightmare, I sleep for four hours uninterrupted, and Steve covers a lot of the above. And he does not even tell me. Everyone knows you are sick. They can see that but what can you do. You have to carry on. Till you need ICU.

Sunday was just as bad, and again Steve covers for me. I notice it this time. On the Monday round there was 12 caesars, I assisted in 4. Steve did the rest. There were some major problems in high care, yet he was there again.

He never said anything either.

From that time on we became friends and I knew this was one of the few good guys.

I asked him about it once. He down played it and said as a doctor we often forget how shit it feels to be sick. And he knew I would do the same. But would I, would anyone, I don't know.

It's funny how honest, good people never take credit and thus are never really recognized except by a small few who really know.

At the heart of it when you are on call, it is figuratively like being in trenches of some war when it is crazy busy, your humanity and who you really are shines through.

And that was Steve. I try my best to remain loyal to a good man, my friend.

Now he was in the eye of the storm. I could see the ARV's and his emotional upheavals had taken his toll on him. He did not have much support either.

I find it strange that generally in the Indian communities especially, the family continuum is a special life trait.

Our parents generally are there for us on every level from birth till their own death. We, as children out of love are there for them too. I hope we are.

When Steve graduated his dad said good luck son, but now that you can earn your own money, you live your life. I have done my bit.

At least his Dad helped pay for his studies, some students are not that lucky. However, in Stevies case that was his first degree, Bcom which he hated. His second degree, his dad did not help at all, he is still paying for it. When you study medicine it might take years to pay back a student loan. His mum and dad divorced much earlier and she remarried and had other children. He did not speak much of his mum. But I knew he missed his dad, if not on any other level than an emotional one. I knew I was lucky, as not only did my parents pay for my studies, I still lived at home. My parents still took care of a lot of my needs But in that is a toss up, of a loss of freedom too. I was saving though financially or supposed to be anyway.

Stevie had family but no one he could really talk to. I am not sure if that was cultural too, as Indians we are always in each others business. Whites are a bit more lax that way, sometimes too lax. Blacks are also becoming more westernized. People may even feel isolated. It was obvious to me Stevie was having some issues. This was a reason I knew I would be a doctor. You just see something there. Inside this person, there was pain. To everyone else it is mundane, inconspicuous but to me it was obvious.

Stevie: I love my job, I am good at it, but this thing scared the hell out of me man.

Me: yeah I know.

Stevie: you know when she said I was positive, everything around me just faded. It was like being dead.

Me: Imagine how the patients feel.

Stevie: I never thought of it like that. I know people just took it for granted that his patient slept around, now he is HIV positive. I don't really see it that way anymore. Before I saw patients as objects.

Me: yeah I know what you mean. I felt the same way till I met Mr B and Mr K, its different when something about a patient resonates with you.

Stevie: you are right. I just try to do my best. It's often not enough and I am just so tired and frustrated at the system that often I give up on patients before I begin.

Me: my GP told me once when I became a doctor, "treat everyone like family, your mother, father, brother and sister.

Then you know you will be doing your best". But when I look at any queue and call, where there is anything from 20-100 mothers, fathers, brothers and sisters, I just know if I work this methodically I will be here till I die or go insane.

Stevie: that's it exactly. I mean I know I am doctor and I have a responsibility but I am not willing to kill myself over that man.

Me: sure I get you, and listen to me carefully when I say this; there is no need to feel guilty about self preservation. If we don't have that instinct then we are not even animals anymore.

Stevie: ya, no, you are so right ma man.

We sat in silence for a while. Then Stevie said its best if we leave early as it was back to the grind stone tomorrow.

He never got back together with his girlfriend. I knew he missed her a lot. That night also brought clarity and peace to me Clarity, to have some appreciation for having these nosy parents in my life. Peace, knowing at least I could be there for my friend too, as I owed him.

16

It is a brand new day for everyone except those like my brother who are depressed. He goes to work. He does his thing then he comes home and mopes about. I remember those days, when he was just so depressed even reruns of Seinfeld could not pick him up.

Traumatic moments are embedded in your mind forever. You remember the words people used. You remember the things they say. What they wore on that day, the smell in the air. It is crazy the way the mind is programmed. Every good day, the best meal you tasted, the awesome events that were, all just vague memories.

But the true shocking sad ones you can recall with crystal clarity.

My brother was many things. The one thing I knew he was. He was his own man. The time came for confrontation and after Christine said she was going on holiday with her parents for a week end, to her not coming back a month later. I was confounded how he waited so long.

He went over to see Christine's dad. He was ignored night after night. Till eventually he went to her dad's work place. Then the court order was given and he was not allowed over there.

My parents never said a word to him. They talked about the usual subjects and topics. Total denial of his obvious plight.

My father was silent on the subject and totally indifferent.

I came in and brought new perspective to the subject. I told him to write a letter and get it to the mother. A mother can tell true love. She would tell him the truth.

I have no idea what it must be like. I know he thought the worst, so did I.

Was she shipped of some where with some distant family?

Where would her parents send her and for how long?

My brother loved her. It was not puppy dog love or that lustful love. It was real for them. The real thing. Whatever that is, I don't know.

It's different for everyone. Only you know it.

He knew that his love for her was true and that nothing would change that. Not time nor distance. I know all this as I spoke to him about it at length and you see it in their actions, words.

We had a strange relationship. I mean sure we hit and wrestled with each other as all brothers do.

But after all we had been through we were close.

We were able to talk for hours on end about important matters to us. I hate to say it but sometimes I would even liken us to girls. Discussing feelings and what not. I believe the reason was when it came down to it; we were all we had to fulfill this need.

So we talked and talked, about things that were important to us. As time went on though, I noticed a distance developing.

It was not obvious but it was like the way a crack develops on the wall and slowly it widens and grows without you even noticing it. Till suddenly its too late and there is a huge problem that is almost beyond repair.

So it happened. It was autumn. It was a pretty normal day. I woke up late. I was on holiday. I had some breakfast and vegetated in front of the TV the whole day. Mum woke up and cooked my favorites. She made some nice chicken karhai and roti with some carrot atchar.

Dad came home in the afternoon. We went for our Maghrib Salaah. Then my brother came home. He just sat at the dinner table with the look a raining heavy weight has before throwing his first punch.

We sat down for dinner.

Akbar: so dad, I did not know you were friends with the Christine's Dad.

Dad: what do you mean, Akbar?

Akbar: as you know but have ignored quite obviously. Christine is missing. It has been close to three months.

Dad: of course we know, but all pain passes son.

Akbar: what do you know about pain?

Mum: watch your tone Akbar.

Dad: the way you feel for this girl will fade with time and you will love again, trust me, I am your father, I will only want what is best for you.

Akbar: what about what I want?

Mum: you don't know what you want beta?

Akbar: oh is that so, how do you know what I want?

Dad: hey, I said watch your tone son.

Mum: that is because I am your mother, a mother always knows.

That is why I have set an arrangement with Aunty Jameela's niece from Durban. She is a doctor; she is one year younger than you. She is very pretty. You will be happy in no time.

Akbar: I will never be happy without Christine, I love her. She is the only one for me.

Dad: son your love should only be in making Allah happy, and with this Christine you will not do that.

Akbar: how do you know that? How do you know what the future holds?

Dad: I know this path has brought you sadness. I mean where she is now, Akbar: Gone. For good you hope.

This is when the profanity kicked in from both sides which I have edited out but I sat quietly till my brother's trump card was revealed.

Akbar: I have unfortunately for you discovered your version. of what is all good and noble. Lies and deceit.

Dad: what do you mean?

Akbar: I have no idea what pact you formed with Christine's parents but I have tried for the last couple weeks to get some information about her, anything. I tried the house. At first I was afraid to knock on the door. But as time went on my desperation has pushed me further and further. I tried her father at home, at work whenever wherever. Then her mother. Finally when face to face contact never worked. I wrote a letter to her mother. At the end of it, all I asked was if she could just tell me, why they would do this to us?

She replied to me today.

He opens an envelope and places on the table. He gets up and walks out.

All it says in the middle of the page is ASK YOUR FATHER, HE KNOWS.

Akbar moved out of the house. I never felt the same way about chicken karhai. I have to admit I was shocked my dad would stoop that low, but I got it. Why he would do it? It was just fear.

I know it was difficult for my brother. The lies and deception had cut him up deep. Yet it also strengthened his resolve.

He could not let her go. I used to visit him when I was down from Johannesburg. He would talk of her like she was in the other room.

The times they held hands in the study room at varsity. Having ice cream and chocolate sauce at the Wimpy. The long strolls on the campus grounds. The letters over the holidays and messages through the night. Stolen glances in class, the longing stares and subdued smiles.

In time he came around. We had suppers at home together. Wounds healed but scars remained.

My Dad never said what really transpired but we found out later on.

She was to disappear. It was the only way. She was sent to the Free State to her aunt and then it was off to London. She was going to live with family there, and start a new life for herself as her mum and step dad would also be emigrating soon.

Although he got over my fathers planned involvement, there was a change in his demeanor that concerned all of us. It was somber, and sobering at the same time. He was not the Akbar that we all knew.

So it came as no surprise when he got a job in Joburg and he moved there. We saw even less of him then.

I just hoped he found some peace there, in the city of gold.

Away from everything.

17

It was the weekend baby. It was the big movie date. Now I know this sounds really dumb but this is a big deal. I mean Islamically we are not allowed to date. We are not allowed to be alone with a girl/women, anyone who we can one day, marry. So that just leaves your immediate family. I mean you can marry your cousin, I know it sounds a bit sick but trust me, it happens. Not that often though now, but we do often marry distant relatives, it strengthens the family, ya ya, similar to the days gone of where royalty married royalty.

Its not as bad it sounds.

So we were here at the movies, well with other family members. Oh yeah, we are not supposed to be at the movies either but we all do some wrong, right? The real problem was that no matter how hard you try, the inquisitive mind is always drawn to wrong like a dog to a bone. We just have to see what all the fuss is about, but where some of us have that grounding that keeps us stable, others cant help but get lost in that maze forever. It is the same in every religion but Islam over all is stricter still, no booze, no drugs, no adultery; it has kept the vast majority of us Muslims in check. We do wrong, we all do. We know it too. But we should all try and do more good than evil, right?

So the aunties and uncles were around to make sure that no funky business occurs. Yeah right, like that will ever happen, OK maybe . . . I am here.

Call me Casimnova, slamo(muslim slang joke.) In South Africa due to our rich segregated past we have slang for all types slamo-muslim charo-indian vito-white braino-colored and pekyo-black. I know it is crazy.

I had been trying to come up with a strategy to make this work out, in my favor of course. This family date I mean.

Now the key is that I end up sitting next to Anya. And oh was she in fine form today.

She wore a beautiful white skirt that was layered in some way, don't ask me I know nothing about ladies fashion, but it looked awesome. She had blue neatly cut denim top over a t-shirt by guess with some weird but fascinating sequence.

Of course it was Khatija who came up to me first.

Khatija: slmz Ali.
Me: hey there. Slmz
Khathija: you surprise me again; I like that brown leather jacket on you, its so rough rider.
Me; You know that is a condom brand right.
Khatija: you have a sick mind.
Me: I know.
Khatija: so what you been up to?
Me: agh just work and stuff, you know how it is.
Khatija: no I don't, so tell me about your job.
Me: you wanna know about my job.
Kahtija: yeah why is that so surprising.
Me: well no one ever asks that, everyone knows what a doctor does.
Khatija: we all know but I am sure doctors have problems like everyone else.
Me: that is interesting.
Hey look its Anya and Jojo.
Khatija: and Taahir. They came together?

Now this was ominous. It meant that either he called or they called. If it was him it was genius, if it was them I was just plain screwed. First call of action find out! who called who?

Jojo:	slmz couz, howzit. Howzit khatija.
Anya:	slmz everyone.
Taahir;	slmz people.
Me:	slmz. Howzit. You guys come together.
Jojo:	no we just met now, fighting over the same parking spot huh Taahir.
	Ok, relief. I am still in the running.
Me:	so how was the week, Anya?
Anya:	oh it was very relaxed.
Me:	I wish I could have a relaxed week, just once.
Anya:	varsity life is the best.
Me:	you don't have to tell me twice sister.
Taahir:	so what you guys wanna see, today. I am up for anything.
Me:	Suck up. He has opened pandoras box. We will now watch some soppy female rom com.
Khatija:	oh there is this really nice comedy with Jennifer Aniston and Drew Barrymore, its called "hes not that into you."
Jojo:	oh yeah I heard of it, supposedly it's pretty good.
Taahir:	yeah, I am up for it you Ali.
Ali:	sure, why not I mean we are out numbered here anyway.
Anya:	that is really sweet of you guys. Normally I would end up watching some action movie back home.
Taahir:	oh not here, we are true gentleman.

This guy was a true player. I was a faker. Maybe he was the real deal. If he was I was toast. He was way out of my league. All I had was an analytical brain. I had no experience in the field. I was dead.

Taahir insisted on paying for the tickets. A master stroke as chicks love guys who pay. I got the cokes and popcorn, no one even noticed that. The grown ups came over and checked in on us like we were ten or younger.

Aunty Sara:	you kids behave now. Thank you again Taahir for paying for the girls. That was really sweet of you.
Uncle Ayub:	we will meet you all at home after the movie. Aunty Sara is preparing her famous grilled prawns.

Now came the crucial part. I had to sit, next to her but how.

We cut the tickets and we were on our way in. I stayed next to her the whole way on but Taahir was in front of her.

And so as we sat down Khatija went in first, then Jojo then Taahir, then her, then me.

It was not perfect but I was in with a chance.

Me: so you miss home much.
Anya: um ya but its nice to go on these adventures. See the world.
Me: yeah that must be nice.
Taahir: would you like to tell me about that problem you were having with your stats assignment.
Me: and just like that I was gone.

They talked about a whole lot of variable mumbo jumbo, some x and y shit, and here I was bored out of my mind.

Anya: I need to go to the bathroom.

And she left.

Taahir: so what are your intentions?
Me: what do you mean?
Taahir: do you like her?

Jojo could not stop laughing. Luckily the shorts came on and Khatija could not hear.

Me: yeah, I like her but I don't know her yet.
Taahir: fair enough. Well let's see what happens. She is something, huh!

The shorts were over and the movie was just starting. Anya came back in a little into the beginning. The funny thing was she did not take her seat, she asked me to scoot in. I could not see the disappointment on Taahir's face, maybe he just gave up.

The movie experience was a complete success. Ali 1—Taahir 0.

I joked with her through out the movie. I joked about the movie, which was not that bad. I just love the way she laughed. It was light and warm. It was not loud and it was completely feminine. That's one of the things I really like about her. Her laugh and smile. I mean sure she was beautiful but she was a girly girl. They were a rare breed nowadays. Most girls were becoming more man like by the minute. I know everyone has a type but I have to say, I get lost in girls smile and infectious laughter. The softness of a womans voice and tentative glances.

She even put her head on my shoulder just before the movie ended. Taahir saw, he would have to concede soon. But he did not seem to care much. Weird.

We came out.

We talked about the movie for a while, how guys and girls look into signs and make up signs etc. it was fun and fascinating.

Anya however stated that people just need to be more open and honest and not so false and cynical. They should just explain how they feel. I could not help but notice her look longingly at me when she said that. It was crazy but it looked like for the first time in a long while I had a chance. A real chance.

We jumped in our respective cars and headed out for supper. During my drive I could not help but think to myself, could this be it?

I have had the odd flirtation and near miss, but this was different. The feeling inside me was different.

In school I was a nerd. Well I played sports but I was not the famous or most popular kid.

I had my group of friends and we hung out, we had fun. But I never got up to any mischief. I heard the stories from other guys and their wild week ends. I guess since I went to an all boy's school, I did not have much of a chance of finding love.

I spent a lot of time with my big brother and his friends and girl friends were older, and well out of my league.

So believe it or not I went through high school without a single "date" or kiss, nothing. I went to Islamic socials. Sure there were girls there, I even spoke to a couple but nothing ever came of it. Anyway I did not like any of them.

University was something else altogether. It was unbelievable. I was in a place where there were really no rules. It was an interesting and dangerous time.

I had all this responsibility. All these new people. The first year I made a lot of friends. Yet the closest of them was my chem101 lab partner Jane Suttcliff. We were paired up according to alphabetic letters of our surnames.

At first it was nervous and clumsy, the interactions. We warily adjusted to working with a new person. I was shocked as to how friendly and open she was. Generally people for some reason are very cautious around different ethnicities. People don't like different. They like the same. Jane however was different she asked questions all the time. She was fearless and sincere.

Soon our chemistry got better both in and out of class. (A little goofy laugh after that comment.)

She kept nagging for us to go out and do something. I was not too sure how to take it. It was risky. I had seen first hand where this could lead. My brother was in his own mess. I also felt guilty. My parents sent me here for a reason and what was I doing with that privilege.

Then there was that other side of me that said to hell with it just do it.

I remember my first date with her.

I was used to people staring at us especially other Indian Muslim students.

It was a look that said why the hell are you two together?

Eventually we just did not care. We got on like a deck of cards. We laughed, we had things in common and we were both weird in our own way. We knew that.

My friends at the time. My friends now. They all said go for it. They knew that these things were rare. What it was, or would become I never knew?

That first date was amazing. I lied to my uncle Aftab (my caretaker in Joburg) said I was studying at the library on a Saturday night. (Like he did not know, he was cool). We went out for supper. She wore denim jeans with some silver patterns on it that sparkled like the sun shining on water. She had a bright red top and for some reason, I also wore a red shirt and my blue denim jeans.

I always remember what people wear, how sherlock holmes/joan rivers of me.

I brought some red roses, 8 in total, the number of months I had known her. The evening played out dinner and a movie.

As I drove to her place we parked in the yard and she asked me if we could talk for a while in the car.

Jane: I had a lovely night.
Me: me too.
Jane: there is something I have to tell you.
Me: oh yeah.
Jane: but before I do, there is something I must do first.

She grabbed my neck and pulled me in, our lips just touched, my eyes were closed but I felt a cord strung in my heart. I felt like someone blew a firework in my mind.

The next minute I opened my eyes; she was smiling and looking out the window. I was in shock but I was amazed at her bravery and verve.

I just sat there smiling like a man who had just been fed his favourite meal.

So this was what it was like, WOW!

Jane: I just had to . . .
Me: I am glad you did.
Jane: I knew you would not make the first move.
Me: you were right about that.
Jane: the past eight months have been great.
Me: tell me about it. The best of my life.
      I leaned in to kiss her again.
Jane: I am moving to Australia.
Me: what?
Jane: my dad has been thinking about it for a while and it just kind
      of happened now.
Me: when are you leaving?
Jane: end of the year.
Me: ok
Jane: are you angry?
Me: no, not yet.
Jane: I just had to fulfill this before I left. You have been my best
      friend and I like you a lot. I just don't know what will happen
      once I leave.
Me: yeah, I guess this is the worst timing ever.
Jane: yip.

Jane moved later that year. I wrote to her and she wrote back. But our puppy dog love would not survive distance. More than that, I think I was grateful. I don't think I could have put my family through another one. She was still someone I thought about once in a while and smile. We all have those people in our memories. They are the symphonies of triumph and joy.

I met other girls and became close friends with a couple. I was rejected by quite a few. I mean a lot. The word got out I had hooked up with a vito, so my name was dead in the slamo cherry circle. It did suck, since that one small romance ruined a lot of my other chances. But I have no regrets as Jane and I had a real connection.

For some reason Anya felt different too. I felt a connection there.

We got to the dinner table and something strange happened. Anya went and sat next to Taahir. It was eerie. I was next to her and she purposely went and sat next to Taahir, why?

I ended up next to Uncle Ayub. We talked about the wallowing efforts of Bafana Bafana and moved on to the plummeting value of the rand. I was thoroughly entertained. (Sarcasm)

I could not help but notice how Anya and Taahir were talking and laughing. I was pissed.

Just when you think you are in. what the hell is this?

Supper was done and I was so livid that I thought of leaving directly after. That was until something even more unexpected happened?

Anya: listen after this we going to sneak out and go for a real Saturday night party.

Me: Two questions, who is we and how the hell are you going to get permission to go to a party.

Anya: we is you and me, and I will only answer the second question once I am in your car, meet round back of the house by the bougainvillea at 00h00.

Me: what the hell, that's in two and half hours.

Anya: I will be very disappointed if you are not there Ali.

Me: ill be there at 00h00 mam.

She gives me her flawless smile and I melt.

Anya: you better be. Its not often I can get out and Jojo will cover for us.

18

Now don't get me wrong, I do not do this sort of thing at all. This would be a first for me. I guess I could see now why man was in the mess he was in. its all eves fault I tell you. She sucker punched Adam into it.

I could now see clearly what all the fuss around woman was. As a man once enthralled and seduced by their beauty and charisma will do whatever it takes to keep them happy.

As in my case, point taken. I am standing by this bush and my watch reads 00h15. While contemplating how much longer I will wait for Anya, I hear a psst from nearby.

Anya: thought I wasn't gonna show huh.
Me: nah, I knew you would. (Then again maybe not)
Anya: ok so Jessica is having this party, its up in Hayfields area, you up to it right but I need to be back before five, Uncle Ayub is usually up for Fajr already.
Me: sure no problem. (Anything to see you smile again).
Anya: oh Ali, you are the best.
Me: I know, I was born with it.
Anya: born with what.
Me: style baby, style.
Anya: mmm and modesty too I see.

The drive was relatively short; it was less than fifteen minutes. The roads were quiet. I put some nice chilled music on. A particular song on my cd caught Anya ear, Erase and rewind by the Cardigans. She laughed and said she used to love this song. I still do I said. We teased each other and we both agreed that this was by far the most spontaneous thing we had ever done.

For me, this was the riskiest and most idiotic thing I had done since being in Maritzburg. As they say don't shit where you eat, but I was breaking rule number UNO, I was messing around in my back yard. I kep thinking if Dad found out i was dead, but for her i would risk it.

However, after arriving at the party, Anya disappeared to the bathroom. I realized I was relatively safe. I could not see a single familiar face and although I was now well onto my twenties, these kids were mostly just entering university or still in high school. As my "charo" buddies would say it was pure "honkie" or "Vito" jol. Honkie was a derogatory word for whites like white trash is. I cannot verify nor understand its origin and meaning. But call a white person it and they get as pissed, as Indians being called coolies and blacks niggers etc.

Although apartheid was all but dead and some may argue, the reverse was happening with affirmative action. There was still that scent of it around. It was like we moved a rotting carcass that was lying around for a couple of decades. The smell was dissipating with time and every year it got less and less.

We were the first generation post apartheid, everyone was still weary so Indians just stuck with Indians and so too the other races. Things were changing slowly. Very slowly.

Unfortunately the time you were brought up in, is generally where you stay for the rest of your life. As far as race/ethnicity identification goes. It takes a lot for an individual to change generations of inbred and family trained beliefs. But it can and has been done. Look at my brother.

I was one of a handful of people of color at this party. You could count us, two black guys and their two black girlfriends, I assumed. Then there was this other Indian guy. He was tall and lanky. He was drinking coke so I assumed he was Muslim too, although one can never tell. The rest of the fifty odd people were all white.

The music was loud mainly Rave, dance, house music. The braais were on and the pool was full, girls in bikinis and boys in shorts. It was like I was in a movie or a series about teenagers I had watched. It was initially exhilarating just observing but soon it became boring. I was not here to drink alcohol, I would not be eating or swimming and I could not dance, especially not to rave music.

That's when it dawned on me. What the hell was I doing here?

I knew no one and the crowd seemed like it was by invite only which I was not. And where the hell was Anya.

After about an hour of being through every area and walking around the place like a blind man without his guide dog I find her.

She was in one of the bedrooms smoking MJ with a couple of select guys and girls.

Anya: Ali where have you been I was looking for you.
Ali:　I was just outside. Where have you been?

The others in the room giggle.

Anya:　this is my friend Ali, he is a doctor, so if anyone passes out we have someone who can resuscitate right here.
　　　　This is Mike, Dewald, Susan, Kate and Madel. And this is our host Jessica.

I greet everyone and sit down on the bed.

Mike: glad you are here, bro, now I can go all out.

More giggles from everyone.

Me:　　nice place you have here Jessica.
Jess:　　thanks.
Dewald: ya bro, you want some or are you gonna get tested at the hospital or some shit.

Now this was your typical high school behaviour. It was a dare. It was a test. Now I don't care what people say about peer pressure. It is real and it sucks. It was simple, I turn this down and I am out of the group. I smoke and I am in. Had this happened a few years ago, I am sure I would have smoked. Now I did not come here to get high. I was an adult and I was here to impress but not do anything against my own

145

values, even if my values are messed up tonight. And I did not want to get high.

> Me: no thanks, got to keep my urine clean for the next test.
> Susan: do they really test you at the hospital.
> Me: no not really, but they should.
> Kate: you naughty boy.

With this little interlude I had been myself and still saved face. But I did not like this place or situation. Sure it was just dagga, kids getting high, getting drunk having a good time, each to his own I guess. But my reason was a girl that was a chameleon. She was your bona fide shape shifter. Much better than me, at quickly changing into a new environment. She must have a lot experience.

So an hour later of discussing topics like, is it better to dip or not dip your toast? And what kind of drugs I can organize from the hospital? Oh yeah and my favourite topic, whether there really is life out there?

I was ready to leave. My watch said 03h17. I was used to being up all night but this was pretty exhausting.

Anya then introduced me to Ridwan (the only other Indian dude here) and she whispers in my ear something about a surprise.

She heads of to the bathroom and here I am, with Ridwan while he is smoking a joint.

> Ridwan: howzit man.
> Me: howzit goin?
> Ridwan: you want a drag.
> Me: No I am cool.(this guy was definitely high.)
> Ridwan: So I see you with Anya. She is a real boiling hot coal of fire,
>   isn't she?(talking loud and dramatically)
> Me: oh yeah. You know her from university.
> Ridwan: yeah her has only been here a while but her fits right in. her
>   is a lot of fun to be around.
> Me: You mean she.
> Ridwan: yeah her.
> Me: OK
> Ridwan: watch out though, her has quite a bite. Better play it cool.
> Me: so are you guy's good friends.

Ridwan: yeah guess you could say that.

Me: what do you mean?

Ridwan: uh nothing. Her is one crazy chic and speak of the devil . . .

There she was in a crimson red tank top and the tightest skinny jeans I have ever seen with matching scarlet red stilettos. She walks up to me slow and nonchalantly. She gives that full million dollar smile that carves through all my inhibitions. She flicks her hair to the side. She grabs me by the arm and whispers in my ear, "surprised". I mumble something like "Wow, you are stunning, but the truth is I feel like am dreaming."

Every guy has at least one. There is this girl, not a super model or anything but someone unattainable. You know it will never happen. But it does not hurt to day dream. You just let your mind run for a second, everyday. Yet every once in a while, some lucky schmuck has this dance with an angel. Tonight it was me.

Anya: you have to be a strong man to be with me.

Me: oh yeah, I think I can handle that. (At this stage if she said she wanted the moon I would have it got it for her).

Anya: so bet you have never had a night like this before.

Me: me ya/no, this is what I do, Mademoiselle. ya/no typical South African reply meaning yes with a bit of no.

Anya: don't do the French thing, it does not suit you.

Me: yes mam got you.

Anya: oh I like that mam thing.

Me: whatever you say mam.

Anya: so its almost four, better be getting back soon. One last dance with me for the road.

Me: well technically this will be our first dance and I don't dance that well at all.

Anya: oh come on, for me. I will show you how, just watch and follow.

Me: (how could I resist those puppy dog eyes, and like men every where I was sold, putty in her hands) OK let's go.

Anya: let me ask the DJ to play a special song for us.

Me: um ya. I will be right here.

As I walk over to the dance floor, I hear this booming baseline and straight away I know the song, erase and rewind by the cardigans. She floats like a butterfly and seductively stings me like a bee. The dancing part was not natural from my side but I was competent. I just swayed my hips and clapped my hands now and then; I have watched Hitch so I was OK. She was awesome, the way she moved her hips and her hands, legs that were everywhere. She moved around me like a ghost and all eyes were on her mesmerized. All I could think was, she is with me suckers.

She said her goodbyes and the drive back was mixed with giggles and strained awkward glances.

Me: I had fun, thank you for that crazy evening.
Anya: oh Ali this is just the beginning.
Me: of what?
Anya: you will see . . .
Me: hey guess we are here now. Don't get caught on the way in now.
Anya: I wont, speak to you soon.
Me: will do.

She leaned towards me kissed me on the cheek and she was gone. It was more than I expected. It was a crazy evening. Something I have not done and probably would not have done. It was fun, but on the drive home I felt guilty. It was the kind of guilty a diabetic would feel after eating some chocolate cake. The guilty feeling you have when you lie to someone over the phone about something petty. It lingers for a while but evaporates quickly.

Mum and dad were asleep. I lay in bed for a while thinking of her look, her smell, the way she moved.

I drifted of from dream into reality, or reality into a dream as I fell asleep.

19

Now we had a few problems in the ward. Mr Botha's SLE was acting up. Something I remember vaguely from a lecture with Prof Paterson. I was in the back row, talking about how South Africa was going to win the world cup of cricket. I remember it because Jason, an avid aussie supporter was irritating the shit out of me.

So yeah I guess my lupus knowledge sucked, to make matters worse Rags (Dr Raghavjee) man was out sick. I read through my handy oxford handbook of medicine, and began some basic treatments, much to Mr Botha's pleasure. And I retired to an early lunch, while the cat is away the mouse will play.

As internship was winding down I was feeling more confident. I had this whole medicine thing down. Even though I had my working diagnosis on Mr Khumalo; it was an inflammatory bowel disease. I had a hunch but eyes, lungs and bowels meant something, and I was going to get to the bottom of this.

It all starts with the history they say. They, meaning people who do research, and never spend more than a day at any hospital in the last year. They, meaning people in first class settings where everyone including nurses and patients listen to you, understand your language and take it seriously.

In reality most doctors spend a couple minutes on a history, making a diagnosis in the first sixty seconds. The funny thing is majority of the time I think we get it right. However that is when the patients tell the truth which is also not that often. As House says all patients lie, times every beer he says he drank by 3. Case and point, to get into hospital Mr Khumalo said his eyes were troubling him for the last year, on admission he said it was a couple days. He also said he was having difficulty passing stool, more constipation, and some diarrhea. He never once told me there was blood coming out.

I don't know why, but like doctors. Patients are intricate, they are human. Some lie to get into hospital, some lie to stay out. I have had a patient in my family medicine that feigned mental illness and epilepsy by taking meds to cause seizures just to get a grant from the government to support his family.

So we go through this history as quick as possible, often missing terribly important clues. Sometimes you can blame the doctor, others are on the patient. We all have our lay out. Things we know to ask, a Q and A checklists to tick off. The difference comes in the listening, understanding and interpretation of it all. It is said that 90% of diagnosis can be made on the history alone. If it is so high why don't we spend more time on it. Why are we always ordering more investigations, more tests? I cannot answer that. Well I can in a way. Money. Money. Money.

Medicine has become what everything else has become. It is business. It is about making money. Not everyone but most. We are all slaves to it one way or another. The system requires it.

Take nothing away from a through physical examination. Prof Rabinowitz always told us that. He was a surgeon, of course. There is a connection when you touch another human's body. This person gives you the right to do an exam on their body. And trust me as doctors we hate seeing people in pain especially when it is us causing it. But we have to feel, we have to add the body to the skeleton of our history. This too has decreased a lot with time. Not as much as before. What now, with the advanced CT scans and MRI machines. Soon we will be able to see inside the body without touching it.

Yet whenever I practice my clinical skills and I find something obvious, I feel good. Its like I know what this is, I can help you. Be it an acute abdomen or a wheezy chest. It is simple to pick up and quick but it goes a long way. Just the touch of the stethoscope on the patient's chest, when their eyes fall on yours, hoping you can tell them what it is that is wrong.

My grandmother passed away a couple of years ago. She lived well in to her seventies, and suffered with her heart disease and high blood pressure and diabetes.

The thing was though no matter how sick she was, the relationship she had with her GP was such that the moment he walked, examined and said that she was going to be OK, she was a 100% better. The trust she had defied logic, and she often really did just get better. Now as a doctor I could see why.

Sometimes not often but especially on my round, I notice some patients waiting for me. They smile, they even look better, "ow Dokotela am I right now?" They seem to be better the moment the doctor sees them and gives them that diagnosis, and medication.

I love that feeling, of helping someone. I used to love it even more before the fatigue and monotony of it all. I don't know why but most days it does just feel like a job. Like any other job, something you have to do. But on others it is like a dream fulfilled.

Here in the bush in Africa as they say. We have HIV and PTB that overrides everting else. No matter which department from dermatology to Obs and gynae it is a key question. Have you tested for HIV? And most patients, if you notice closely hesitate at this question. They will answer yes or no but they will never tell you the second part till you ask. And what was the result of that test? They take an even longer time to answer this question. It has to do with the stigma and nature of transfer of the virus. But there is something else there. I often think its fear of the known, or inevitability or the feelings associated with any chronic incurable disease. I have to agree with them too. The thing is when you know the status and the low cd4 counts you often think to yourself what can really be done at this late stage. You also give up, sometimes wrongly. It is like diabetes or hypertension or smoking, eventually they will get you, time is on the diseases side.

We don't have any long term studies. We don't have many answers when it comes to HIV. I mean sure we are making progress, the way a snail does on a cold winter's night. But we are not there. Hell for all our glorious cures in medicine, we still have not cured the common cold or the flu. HIV is here to stay and it has damaged us on so many levels.

We have lost a complete generation to it. If we are honest and hard on ourselves then is there is much we should have done to change the dramatic impact of this disease on sub Saharan Africa. If we are positive

151

and easy on our selves, the progress is statistically significant with ARVs and prevention from to mother child transmission improving. The policies on paper look good but I can tell you as a doctor in casualty late on into the night, patients are dying I don't know if it is slowing down. I hope it is.

Add to HIV, its terrible twin brother TB. Oh TB, you got us man. We have not had much success with you either. First it was a killer, and then it became resistant, now we have MDR and finally XDR. It just keeps getting worse. TB has not just killed patients I know, it's killed other doctors. A fellow registrar in pediatrics contracted it from a patient. She was treated, turned out to be MDR, had to stop work, developed TB meningitis and died.

So the stroy goes.

I know on the page it does not mean much. To see someone cough and cough, worse still wither away is shocking.

However believe or not we all still have hope, we all are trying to make that little bit of a difference. We know these years in the trenches are critical. These years will define us as nation. And when our children look back at the devastation, they will stand proud that hopefully we would have done some good.

So here I was preparing for my ward round with the Rag man, it was going to be a long day as I was also on call. Yet I still wore a smile on my face from the weekend. And we were planning a get together, the youngsters on Saturday. Of course I would be post call but hey I should be OK, hopefully.

The ward round runs as it does with critical analysis and theory to complement the cases. However I had a special revelation with Mr Khumalo. As we reach him I tell the rag man the history, the exam, and my working diagnosis of Ulcerative colitis. My first and I am sure one of the rare cases, we have seen apart from the usual HIV, HIV associated diseases and PTB.

And then with one question he cuts me down. Did you do the PR?

I envisage Dr Rabinowitz saying if you don't put your finger in, you should put your foot in.

No I reply. He looks at me with disdain and says well do it now.

I do, and I feel it. Its hard and its there. It's something I missed, fatally.

The rag man just stares at me. He does not have to say anything. I know what he is thinking. How could I miss something so obvious? All this time Mr Khumalo was here, I never thought of it and now on his first round back . . .

I felt sick, and so I should.

20

The thing about your parents is like children they grow on you with time. You love them immediately more because you have to, but later on you love them because you want to. I know it's an opposites yet same same thing. As a child you see them as Gods, Mum and dad, the movie stars of my life. They are all you know. They are your first teachers. They are your role models for life, whether you believe it or not. Parts of them are imprinted onto your psyche and though you hate to admit they are apart of you no matter where you go or what you do.

My dad, as a child, he was what any child needed. He was strict. He was simple. He was fair, I suppose just like his old man. I did not know my grandpa that well. He died when I was six. I remember him vaguely as a kind man.

My dad was a religious man. He was bound by the book. He read all his prayers five times a day. He read his Quran everyday. He was a Hafez of the Quran. A protector of the Quran, he had by hearted the entire Quran. He was a simple man. He was a simple businessman, and provided well enough for all our needs

He never asked for much yet demanded a great deal. He was respected by everyone in the family and in the community. I don't know why but my early memories of dad were very vague. I have seen pictures of the way we used play cricket and soccer out in the backyard. My mum and aunts have told me stories of how he used to just spend time with me as a child and read me like a story book. But the apple of my father's eyes was his big son, Akbar.

They were inseparable. They did everything together, went everywhere and agreed on everything. I know parents say they love all their children equally. It's probably true. I never felt less loved or had any feelings of jealousy or anger. I knew I was loved. And anyway I had mum.

After years of being a shop owner, he was now finally doing well His father was a businessman too, who had a small shop. He sold your everyday requirements. Milk and bread, and the daily paper. He lived within his means, and became staunchly religious in his later life. My dad was an only child and his mother died young. She had some lung disease that no one knew. She died when my dad was seven. It had a major impact on his life, I am sure. My granddad never remarried and dutifully took care of his only child. My dad had the best that his father could afford.

It is an interesting observation that most people as they get older start thinking of death and their life. Most either turn to God, or their deep beliefs in an afterlife and try to repent. Some become more melancholic and fall into a deep desperation, something they must do or say to find salvation.

The thing is my dad was brought up right for his generation. He understood what was right and wrong. He followed the black and white. I have to admit I admired and hated him at times for that.

As time goes on though especially our generation, I hate to admit it; we have changed things a lot. We live with different mind sets. We do what suits us as far as right and wrong go. We find a way to argue ourselves out of doing what is right.

We know what we should do. We know we should not listen to music, or waste time watching movies. But we do. We carry on doing wrong as long we do a bit of right at the same time. And I guess that is the state of all religion. We cannot abstain from having sex before marriage, majority of us, for some reason. It is strange that this notion, a hundred plus years ago, was the norm, Most marriages were arranged and most people would never consider adultery as the norm. Now we need condoms to protect us from killer viruses, disease and pregnancy. Our pleasures and vices have become so strong that we find a way to legalize all negative behaviors in our combined subconscious. Are we progressing or regressing socially?

Not my dad though, he lived by the book. And as it often happens, he was tested. (A number of times) and he showed patience.

My dad as a child worked hard and grew up in Durban, in the then Indian only brickfield area. He studied hard and his father saved up all his money for my dad to study, but he never did. He used the money to go into business as he could not afford the fees of university.

This was a common practice in them days. So my dad opened a shop and joined the world of small business enterprises.

He never told us too much about his upbringing All he said was that we should be grateful that our forefathers came to South Africa.

Yet he still had to fulfill half of his belief which can only be done by getting married.

I am often asked the question by my co-workers, why do Muslims marry so young? I can say for me, from my dad, it's not just because of sexual desires etc. We do it to as it is what is right for us. We hold the belief that getting married young is virtuous and right. A man has responsibilities and focus now and so too a wife. I mean sure you can sleep overnight with a person and do not see anything wrong with it. Yet in the same breath how can you judge someone who has married young, and judge his/her way of life.

How can you look down upon a man who has two wives? Provided he takes care of each equally and sees to their needs by the law of god and country.

Is there anything wrong in this?

Some women spend many years of their lives as the other woman, the girlfriend while the man enjoys his wife and has no real responsibility to this other woman.

In many countries you may spend years with this guy who says he loves you. You move in with him, share your life, financially, emotionally and physically entwined. And one day you have a fight, and since you are not married or anything, he ups and leaves.

So yes I agree with my religion that one should find a partner real sharp and settle down. But that's just me. And I am like everyone full of ironies and ambiguities. But I do wish I could have a love like my dad has for my mum.

He saw her at the hospital while visiting a friend. She was studying to be a nurse. She was as my dad often put it, Cinderella in waiting for her prince charming. She had a kind demeanor and was honest, warm. She was very young when they got married.

156

My dad saw her a couple times. Then he came with a family friend and asked to meet her family. He met her family and proposed and she said yes. Her family was happy. He was well known and liked by everyone. Well that is how I think it probably went down.

My mum fell pregnant within a year and her studying was cut short. It was a difficult choice and something she later missed but never regretted. She dropped out of nursing as a job and took up nursing us, her family.

She like most mothers always put her family first. She loved my father, that was obvious, but she always added it took years of practice. Many people think that Muslim women are subservient. However this is far from the truth. My mum always had the final say on a number of quite pertinent issues even though my dad wore the pants in the house. I noticed things often went her way. You keep your ears open when the grown ups spoke.

My mum often said when she married my dad she never knew him. She liked the look of him; she knew he was a good man. Yet it took time to get to know him. However the more time she spent, the more she fell in love with him. I guess in a way, it is like dating except you already know the end point. As you are, already at that end point. Most people know anyway after a couple of meetings whether they like someone or not. Whether they can see themselves with this person or not. Sure it is risky but so is all of life. I can say the statistics I have seen on Muslim marriages speak for themselves.

My dad worked hard and was often out when we were kids. Like most dads he was providing the best of us, yet somehow it did alienate us from him. We did not spend enough quality time together.

My mum on the other hand was always available. She would listen to our dumb school stories, helped us with homework. She never missed a beat. She was wonder woman.

So my parent set up house and we were happy. We all had our day's ups and downs like all families but we were happy. Unfortunately though a lot that takes place in an Indian community is about reputation and how you are seen and perceived by others.

It is sad but that's just an inherent problem that we all have. Indians I mean and others. It does not matter how you feel on the inside as long as the outside is all hunky dory. A lot of the problems stemmed from peoples perceptions, but there was a true sadness for my parents when

Akbar chose to love Christine, despite their obvious contempt of the notion.

I could see my brother's happiness on one side when he was with her and I saw my parent's sadness when he was with her too. It was strange and unfamiliar like someone had died when she disappeared. For Akbar it was a devastating blow but for my parents, they assumed he would get over her but he never did.

He slowly drifted away farther and farther away like the way a ripple moves from the center. He first moved away from home, then he got a job in Joburg and he disappeared. Sure he came home every once in a while but he never was the same Akbar.

I always asked myself, could anyone love someone that much?

Can you just love one person?

Forever?

We all spoke to him. We all tried. We did the usual things at first. It was me, my family, cousins and friends. We told him about other fish in the sea etc. we told he should move on. We told him she probably moved on. But no matter what he said, he never flinched. All he said was she was out there and that he would find her someday.

Mum and dad did not say much after that evening. They avoided the conversation subject of her altogether. Of course they all forgave but did not forget.

It was the same thing that happened when Akbar was younger. He never wanted to be an accountant but because of the relationship he developed with Christine in high school. My dad decided he would not study away from home. I don't know if he regretted that decision.

That is why they say be careful of your actions as Karma is a b . . . because of that move the wheels were set in motion. The two of them grew even closer. They were stuck in the same town, on the same campus, doing similar courses. And no one bothered about their illicit relationship till it was too late.

In a way though my father will never admit it, he helped them.

And then, his lies to protect Akbar, further deepened Akbar's resolve to find Christine.

It reminds me of the time when Akbar was in high school. As I said earlier he worshiped the ground my father walked on. For some reason my father did not like Akbar's one friend, Segrin. He was a non Muslim. Sure he was into some bad behaviour. He messed around with a daisy gun shooting at dogs and the birds that flew by. He got into his dads booze and smoked. But my dad had this look on his face whenever he came around. It was one of fear and disgust that this was Akbar's choice of a best friend. Segrin was a big belching lad that got into a couple fights at school.

My father always wanted us to have Muslim friends. And somehow Segrin became my brother's best friend in high school. Sure my brother had other friends, some Muslim some not, but he did not understand why dad would disapprove when he was just a friend. Segrin was someone that made him laugh and that never forced him into anything.

However Segrin had a troubled home that was well known in town. He was a good guy though in my opinion. Honestly, he had his bad points but he was hilarious to be around. He never took anything too seriously and I could see why my brother would need that. When everything we had at home was serious then.

His parents got divorced and he moved with his mum to Johannesburg. I don't know why but Akbar blamed Dad for messing up his life then, as teenagers often do. It was just after that, Akbar started hanging out with Christine.

It was one of those things that slowly changed and shaped their relationship.

My dad like all parents had an idea of what he wanted for us. He had a plan but each man has his own plan. My brother's plan did not correlate with my fathers plan. Sure every night we heard the same story from dad. You kids don't know how lucky you are. In my day we never had it this easy. Meat on the table every day. Television in the house, and on all the time. Children listening to crazy types of music. Going out with friends, with your expensive designer wear and this is how you repay me. I had to work for what I have. I never had a mother to wash and iron my clothes. I never had a mother to cook my food.

Initially we would all just listen. But as the years went on we started talking back. I don't know why we did that. In your teenage years it is true, you have all these raging hormones in your blood stream and just like dodgems at the fair you want to ram everyone and everything.

The saying your parents are perfect as they are, till you are old enough to judge them, comes to mind.

Then you say stupid things like, Is it my problem you had to wash your clothes or eat a lot of veggies? Is it my problem you listened to a radio while everyone else had a TV?

And this would just serve to anger my dad even more.

The other thing was my dad always wanted one of his sons to be a Hafez. To be a Hafez is a huge deal and responsibility. It requires the by hearting of the entire Quran all 30 chapters 830 some odd pages. Imagine trying to by heart that. The fact that it is done by kids of 5-6 years old is a miracle in itself. The responsibility comes in later to remember and read the Quran everyday till you die. Yu have to remember it all forever. He also wanted us to learn Arabic.

It was Akbar first who let him down on both fronts. He started it and went to the 5th chapter but stopped after that. He could not go any further. He said it was difficult with school and extra curricular activities.

The extra curricular activities at high school were soccer and cricket depending on the season. Both of which my brother Akbar was very good at. He was in the first team for soccer and in the second team for cricket. He had real talent and with hard work and extra tutelage, perhaps he could have become a professional.

At the time though it would never have happened. It is difficult for an Indian to follow their passion for sport. It is difficult to tell your parents that you are going to follow this dream. The problem is with sport there is no certainty. An injury can rule you out for life and as I said anything can happen in sport. Parents in general have a problem letting their children follow anything that has no end goal, even if you have talent. Add an Indian family to that and you wonder why we are all doctors, lawyers or accountants. Our parents and most of us choose safety and security over chance and luck.

But the truth is like Hashim Amla, it is possible if you are willing to believe in your own talent and have the support required from your family and friends. My brother unfortunately never had that. He finished of his matric with six distinctions and an exemption pass, and his cricketing career slowly ebbed away. He played socially for a club but as time studies and his social turmoil picked up. He became one of us, a couch critic.

I was never as good at sport as my brother. I played soccer socially and dabbled in cricket, squash and tennis. As for my Hafez classes, well I tried for a year or so, but never was committed to it.

I went to Madressa as every Muslim child should and does. After school from pre school till grade eight I was at Madressa. We learned the Quran and special Duas and prayers and the proper way of life. The correct or should I say good behaviour or Ahlaaq of a Muslim man and woman. Initially boys and girls are together and then as time moves on we are separate.

People always go on about the segregation of sexes in Islam. Initially I found it strange and yeah I am a hypocrite I don't follow it. But if you think about it and rationalize, it makes sense. How do you pray to god when there is this hot young sexy mama next to you? Man is man and that is how he will always be. We are visual and highly sexual in nature. It makes sense to try as much as possible to protect woman. Protect them in the sense that only once you are married can you enjoy their fruits? And once you are married you are committed and have a responsibility to them.

Sure women and men are completely different and as we grow older especially in our early teens hormones are raging and we know what happens. So yeah it helps to keep us separate for a while. I don't mean totally separate but I mean we should not be left alone to our own devices till we are mature enough to make proper commitments.

Sure you can visit a girl at home with her parents if you like her, but you should only take that next step with the hope and promise of a future. The amount of adultery in the last hundred years and single parents, unwanted pregnancies seem to be on the increase.

But in the end I should take my own advice and follow my father's footsteps.

He has been with and loved one woman his entire life. He saw my mother and made a call, and stood by it. He was just in awe of her vitality and beauty. Even after all these years I catch him watching my mum do something mundane like wash dishes and he sits there in awe.

I know as a modern person reading this, you will be like, say what? But just think about for a second, after a couple meetings with someone you know whether you like this person or not. And trust me anyone who can spend hours with all your family at the same time, and try to get on with everyone and remain themselves cannot be all that bad. It really is like a thick novel condensed into a page. You know what you going to get faster this way.

You may spend years with a man and he may never really commit to you. I know of friends with boyfriends and girlfriends for months, years, no end in sight. Money and time spend on each other, sometimes even children but there is no formal arrangement.

Yet what if you have to commit first all the way? And you have to prove your love for this person.

Women need men and men need woman. But it does not mean you have to sleep with a number of people before you find the one. The one is anyone you choose to love. How is it that most of us find someone that was there all along that we just missed? They were always there yet we did not see them. It's because there is a number of people in life you can get attached to for different reasons but that formal commitment from both parties in front of God and witnesses, that is what seals the deal.

Its funny but generally no matter what your religion, culture and upbringing, when some one says, I am married, you back of. Your mind says this person is taken and you accept that. However when someone says I am single, or I have a boyfriend or girlfriend. You just believe you still have a chance.

Sure you can argue it both ways like anything. But as I was taught, live and let live. To you, your way, and to us ours. The key is not to judge or enforce any of your own views. And let people make their own informed choices and views. I guess in that case I am the pot calling the kettle . . . , well you know.

21

It was a mild, fine day. I was up early, well reasonably early. I had my morning crap and I was relieved. Ready for the day.

Now most people, well hygienic people I am sure can relate to this. We are run by our bowels and bladders and one of the most important things for me is to off load in a quiet comfortable known toilet. This is usually home or a families place. Public toilets in general are the equivalent of being gutted with a knife. They can do you physical harm on a number of levels. I just leave a public bathroom feeling dirtier then when I went in.

First there is the smell. I know I don't shit roses but hey I don't like smelling the shit of the dozen or so people before me. A mixture of all the worst of the bowels in the world, which is what, is available at any local hospital. Then there is the sight, something much worse then your worst horror movie. Sometimes you wonder whether a two year old just used the toilet before you. Whatever happened to cleanliness is next to godliness?

How can you use a toilet and not flush? Men peeing all over the floor. I get standing and peeing, but then you just put it back in your underwear. Ironically you then proceed to wash your hands. What about the other guy or gal? No wonder STI's are so high.

It's like a sick joke that is never funny. You walk into the toilet, the pan is down. You have two choices shit in your pants or open it. And you do, and then you shit in your pants.

And why is it that you are always so desperate to get to a toilet and you always find the most disgusting one.

Sure you come out relieved and then when you turn you find two leafs of toilet paper. Gods cruel humor, one for the front and on for the back I suppose. All we have to use is water to clean our private parts which means majority of us, in non Islamic countries have to be careful where we go. And come now, how healthy can dry paper be for your ass. In majority of the Middle east countries there is a hose to wash out your special areas, which also leave a mess of water everywhere. (well I hope its water.). Yet it is still better than plain old sandpaper.

And trust me you can pick up "shit" with shit in the pan splashing all over.

So yes when I wake up in the morning I am hoping it's a brown letter day and I can fill that post box right up. I try to get it all every morning with my all bran flakes. Alas like lots of Americans out there I think I suffer from IBS. Irritable bowel syndrome, it means what it says. And on any given day you never know what you gonna get. Sure like most doctors I have delayed seeking medical help and self medicated. Some days are good and some are bad. And believe me I have taken and given a lot of shit in my life, especially since the last three years of medical school. And now during internship it is an absolute hindrance to normal work.

And no one understands or gets it. It's a funny joke, but it's a real disease and it stinks. But everyone has some cross they have to bear right.

And today is a an even more glorious day as both my long term local friendly learned patients Mr Botha and Mr Khumalo are ready for discharge. They are stable and they are going home. I told them two days ago and its all they have been talking about ever since.

However both will have to return soon. Mr B has a follow up with Rheumatology. Mr |K has a date with a surgeon for de-bulking of his colon cancer.

My family medicine block is coming to an end and once I get through this week in the wards, all that will be left is my month in casualty. I can't wait.

Mr Botha is spending the weekend at the coast with his friends and Mr Khuamlo is going to his sister's place at a farm just passed Hilton.

I was also looking forward to a weekend date if you can call it that.

We had a few weekends of group activities, a braai where Anya and I barely had two seconds alone. Then there was a mid week soccer game where I was invited to watch at Uncle Ayub's big screen television. It was a Man U vs Barca champion's league game. It was a brilliant game but I could not concentrate. All I could see was Anya and Taahir talking and laughing on the couch opposite me. It made me jealous and angry. This was new to me, feelings that I have never had before. I was going crazy and I promised myself that was it. We had one crazy night and I had fun and gained some sort of weird experience but that was it. I was not going to call her. She was not going to call me. Right.

Wrong. After two weeks two days, 16 hours, 32 minutes and 8 no 9 seconds she calls me, the nerve, like I was waiting for her.

Anya: slmz
Me: wslmz.
Anya: Missed me.
Me: huh
Anya: I was thinking of you and that night and I was wondering if you up for another night out . . . with me . . . please!
Me: ok, what do you have planned?
Anya: I was thinking a drive to Durban.
Me: what?
Anya: come on Ali where is your sense of adventure?
Me: what do you wanna do there?
Anya: oh I have some ideas. So it will be exactly like last time, I will call you and then we meet half hour later by the tree out back ok.
Me: oookkk, but I gotta think about it.
Anya: see you Saturday night then, slmz
Me: wslmz.

Boy did I show her whose boss. I just laid my cards out there. I told her all those feelings that have been boiling up over the last couple days. Well I felt much better now that it was all out. And I had a night out to look forward to.

As far as my chronic patients go, it was all good. The ward was practically running itself. The rag man and I had worked up Mr

Khumalo for the surgical boys. Mr B was fully worked up for Rheum and all the other patients were stable.

The only patient that needed some attention was Mr Pillay. He was going for a Cholecystectomy.

He had a mild lower respiratory tract infection together with some chronic lung disease from his smoking exploits as a young man.

So yes we had to get him sorted for the dopers or anesthetists as well.

If he did not get the all clear, he would not have surgery.

You see the dopers dope. That is what they do. They are the drug masters, pain relievers and they can make your op, a dream or a nightmare literally. It seems easy enough but trust me I did some time in doping. It is a horrible feeling when things go wrong. Most people expect to die because of operative complications but as dopers know, drugs kill and they can do so very insidiously.

The removers, the pluggers and the replacers (RPR's) are cut from another piece of cloth completely. The surgeons either take pieces of you out, and put things in or plug holes that are placed there by families and friends. Very common pass time in South Africa.

OF ALL THE SPECIALITIES A SURGEON IS AND SHOULD BE THE MOST RESPECTED.

I write that in bold as it suits the surgeons nature. But really kudos to them, they are the craziest yet they are hardest working and solid doctors there are. There is very rarely any bullshit when it comes to the the RPR's. They say it like it is and manage concisely and immediately. I respect them. But I could never be one of them. Surgery is not just a passion or a calling, it's not a lifestyle. It is you and you are it, like the mixture of gases all there invisible, but one.

And then there were the thinkers, the medical dudes, and my kind of guys. In the end I guess it did come down to your personality type and that's what makes us who we are to some extent anyway.

So Mr Khumalo and Mr Pillay was in need of some rpr. The day of doping and removing was not far now, and we had to get him there safely. They was almost there too, and this would be a lovely way to go for me. Try and do some good for a teacher, someone who gave his life teaching others.

Mr Khuamlo told me that he was the son of a poor worker on a farm. His fathers dream was for his son to study and succeed. And after many years of sweat and toil he did.

He studied and when his dad died during a political riot in Durban. He completed his studies and became a teacher, working in smaller rural schools. He said it was fulfilling giving back. He promised his dad that he would never get involved in politics and he didn't.

And so he married and lived out his years with his wife near Dundee, teaching and enjoying the beauty of the midlands. That was till he retired three years ago, then his wife died a year and a half ago. Now here he was with chronic renal failure, and colorectal cancer.

He was ready for death or should I say prepared, living on borrowed time as he put it. Yet all I knew was I had to keep him alive cure him. And that is what I believe we were going to do.

That morning was a quick working round as the rag man had some appointment in the afternoon. The ward was done quick and effectively.

I was even early for my Friday prayers for a change. The Molana's topic was about death and suddenly the calm was gone and I had this air of concern.

I hurried of to the hospital afterward and Mr Khumalo was gone with his family, but Mr Botha was still there.

His family had not come to pick him up. There he was in the corner of the ward looking out the window at the moving trees in the distance.

It was an early day finish for me and I should be leaving to go home, but something made me want to go up and talk to him.

I finally after two years of internship and real medicine was feeling something different. It had taken a while. It was a much less stressful environment, and I had grown to learn know and understand a little bit more about my patients other then their specific pathologies.

It was a good feeling. I liked it.

I walked up to Mr Botha.

Me: what is up Mr B?
Mr B: no I am OK, Doogie.

Anyway what are you still doing here on a Friday afternoon, go out and live your life my young friend.

Me: ahh I have got a few minutes thought I would just share half a
       lunch bar and talk some non sense.
Mr B: you know I am a sucker for lunch bar.

Me: so what happened to the friend?

Mr B: mother in law not well in Joburg. He had to go over there.

Me: Ok.

Mr B: you know my wife and I always went out for supper every Friday night. Even after we had kids, it was our thing. I always had a steak and she always ordered fish. Oh how I miss her now.

Me: I am sure you do.

Mr   B; You know she died on a Friday. Did I ever tell you how?

I sat down because I wanted to. I always found Mr B's stories interesting and thought provoking.

Mr B: It was July and winter had set in. I was working that morning in the farm. Busy trying to sort out something, which does not matter now nor did it then. Oh it was cold, yet Moira always came out with my coffee and some Ouma rusks. Sometimes when I close my eyes in the morning I see her walking toward me, always with a big smile and warm hands.

That was a day like any other. My daughter was ready for school by half seven and she was looking forward to her weekend with Aunty Pat in Joburg and a visit to gold reef city.

Moira and I were looking forward to a weekend alone and we had our booking for supper. It was beautiful sunset. We freshened up and headed of to one of the few restaurants in the area. The only restaurant we frequented.

It was a lovely evening, quiet, intimate and everlasting. You take those moments of silence for granted, yet it is in these moments that meaning of life is spent.

I sometimes even smell her perfume. Dream of her, and the stupid things she would say or do. The way I always made fun of her.

I saw them on the way home. It struck me as something to worry about. Yet somehow convinced myself it would not be an issue. I grew up in Zulu land. Of course I was a product of an apartheid government, my father followed the rules but as an adult I knew he was not a fair man. He never went against the stream. He followed and did as he was told. He was like most of the whites in South Africa at the time. They were happy with the high chair they sat on. They never saw any one else but for the ants that crawled on the floor.

But ants need to live too and they can carry a heavy weight. They also bite and it does hurt.

I saw the three black men standing outside on the road. I thought this is it. Since 94 we heard of crime and saw it in the papers and news. Yet you never think it can and will happen to you.

The land was my fathers and before that his fathers and before that, well I never thought of that. I don't know.

When the Nkosi came telling me that this was his land and that I had to move before something would happen I laughed. In the early hours of that morning when the barn was on fire and I ran out with my gun, I knew it was too late.

Most of the harvest that year was burnt and I started shooting like a farmer with reckless abandon. We were just too isolated and un-beknown to us, we had no real support from our workers who had been with us for years.

They were boys not even in their twenties, but they shot back.

It all happened so quickly, one minute I was filled with anger and rage. The next I saw what had transpired, I was shot and so too was my wife who was just behind me.

In that minute of madness I had lost everything, I saw blood on my torso and I reached toward her and my eyes closed.

When I reopened them I was in a hospital.

And I was told that my wife was dead and all my possessions and farm burned. I never even got to tell her I loved her, not one last time.

I just took everything for granted. I collected my insurance and my daughter and left.

Yet I always knew I would die here in South Africa as this is my home too.

It was when Mr B said that, I became afraid. It was a tragic story and it stirred something in me.

It just means a lot more when you care about someone and you hear a story like that. I mean sure usually it would be like a minute steak, one or two turns and that's it.

However Mr B's story was like a lamb spit braai, slowly turning and the spices like thoughts flowing deeper and deeper.

For a man to lose so much, yet still have no hatred but love for life concerned me. But today was the first time I heard him speak of death.

And I felt angry. I did not know why but I was angry. Not at the story. Not even at Mr B I just had this feeling of anger.

I had experience with crime. Most people have. It is a true test of courage and character to note how one deals with it. The loss or the emptiness is the difficulty that we are all faced with afterward. How does one fill that void? And with what?

Mr B had lived a full life but the pieces of his puzzle were falling into place now.

I had always and probably should have always kept my interactions with my patients purely professional. It is so difficult though. I don't think there is another profession where one gets to deal with the mind body and soul of their product, so to speak.

It is frivolous to think that we only touch the surface of a human being and cure them when the truth is so damning. We are multi-leveled and highly complex organisms. And sure most disease is superficial and like the boil, once popped it should heal and most of the time does.

However there are other diseases with highly evolved pathologies that have years since their onset. They are linked to your genes and your makeup as a human being. And we will never fully understand them or you, completely.

So we get a diagnosis and think we can cure or manage. And hey we do. Don't get me wrong, we do. But cure people of all their problems, I don't think we do that. We are kidding ourselves if we do.

It's just like using a light vacuum cleaner on a tarnished carpet, we get the surface dirt but not much more. The rest stays, goes deeper and festers.

And so even though Mr B was on treatment now, his outcome was poor. I listened to him. I heard him and his story, gave him a light punch on the shoulder and left for home.

22

Akbar had a successful time in Joburg. He was a big hit at work. He had made new friends at work. He was playing action cricket again. He even sounded more vivacious on the phone when I spoke to him. A couple weeks went by that way.

I was very close to my brother. It was not just the age group and our linked social pasts. We had a bond, one that only another brother or sister would understand.

So when Akbar told me one day out of the blue that he had a lead on her, naturally I was afraid for him.

He hired this private investigator and he was spending an exuberant amount of money trying to locate his lost love. It had been a just over 18 months now since the disappearance of Christine.

I was younger but I was a realist. I was a Virgo. My brother was a dreamer, a Pisces man. Of course I do not believe in any of that astrology hocus pocus, but it was strange. It was my brother's belief after all this time that she was still out there. She was waiting for him to find her, set her free. And they would live happily ever after or something like that.

He had a location in the United Kingdom. It was serendipitous that at the same time he was going to work there for his company for a couple weeks. I called him a few days before he left.

Me: Akbar slmz bro. whatsup?
Akbar: wslmz. How you doin?

171

Me: so packed and ready to go yet.
Akbar: yip, so to what do I owe this pleasure, three separate calls today, mum, dad and you.
Me: I guess we are all just worried about you bro. we have not seen you in such a long while and now you are leaving again. You just keep moving further and further away.
Akbar: Ok hold up. I know where this is going. Save me the lectures and the speeches bro.
Me: we are all worried about you.
Akbar: so you are all in on it then. I bet you tomorrow mum will get sick and then dad will call me, and tell me to come home. Well this is bull shit man.
Me: take it easy bro. I am just talking to you here.

We want you to be happy. But we all know your motives for going over there. You can't spend your whole life chasing after this girl. You just can't.

Akbar: well I guess it's a matter of life priorities then. Is it not?

You have the things that you think are important today in your life. But they will change according to necessity. You will find somethings are naturally more important than others. You don't know why, but to you they are. And Christine is that for me.

Me: Ok so you find her then what?
Akbar: first I find her and then I talk to her.
Me: what if she forgot about you. She may be married with children now for all you know.
Akbar: she may be, or she may be waiting for me.
Me: are you not a little bit deluded in thinking that two years on she is just waiting for you. Why would she not just have come back?
Akbar: maybe she can't, she needs to believe. I know she will when she sees me.
Me: you are a successful accountant. You can have any one. There are so many other woman out there.

Akbar: but I found the one for me. She is my Juliet and that is not going to change.

Me: well good luck bro. By the way, you know Juliet dies.

Akbar: thanks man, thanks for the 2 cents.

Me: I will be here when you get back. Go find her and see, but remember I don't think I understand you. No one in the family does but I love you. I know that you know that I don't support this. But if it's something you need to do then do it. As you know mum will get sick tomorrow and you will leave. Then she will really get sick. You are not winning any brownie points there.

Akbar: yeah I know but I have to do this. I have to know for sure. I can't move on without knowing. And I know no one gets it but thanks for the call bro. its good to know you all care so much.

Two days later he left for London and we did not hear from him for a week. We loved him, we cared but after that trip. When he came back he was even more reclusive and he became a true hermit.

He worked in London for a couple weeks. He followed leads I suppose but when he came back. He spoke less and less to everyone, even us his immediate family.

I don't know why that teen love for him was so strong and resilient. It was like the south Easter in Cape Town, iced cold but always on time and present.

They both loved Shakespeare and Romeo and Juliette was their favourite play from school days. Their attachment was embedded deep in my brother's cerebrum like walking and talking.

Christine, well I was never truly sure how she felt. I knew she loved him then, but two years is a while and a lot can change for any individual.

I admired his love for her and his dedication. It was interesting that in this day and age we live in, that this kind of love was at all possible.

Then he came back home for Eid, Our relationship had strained over the year but you are always close to your siblings. They are generally your first port of call after your parents.

They are your true links to the past and the static stars in your future. To have a sibling is to have a shadow. Someone who has seen you at your worst and lowest low and they still love you.

The fact that my brother and I despite being three years apart, our social scene was the same. We spent a lot of time together and we genuinely enjoyed each others company.

Now as young adults we respected each other and we were still close. But the one thing that I never understood even now was how he could have fallen so low, over a girl.

"Frailty thy name is woman", and men fell for them every time, so what does that say about men. From the beginning of time, they will always be our Achilles heel. The funny thing is when you are so lost in love like my brother was; it does not matter to you, the person involved at all.

You are in your own little bubble and that is where you stay till it bursts.

And it always does. It has to, right?

On |Eid day, when he sat down and he said I need to talk to you bro, with that childish smirk on his face. I knew straight away he was back. Akbar was back and I was relieved.

For the first time in a long time Akbar was Akbar. The bubble had burst. The penny dropped. The mist had lifted and he was standing in the middle of an island alone, and it was time to come home.

He told me, he searched for her. Through out the United Kingdom he searched for her for weeks. In between work and this crazy wild goose chase, he began spending money on some cheap yellow page PI's. The traveling far and wide and wasting money was crazy. One morning he just had enough.

He thought he found her more than once but she always was two steps ahead. It was obvious and clear, that she did not want to be found.

Then one of his PI's said he got more than just pictures, he had a location and a name, Cindy. Her entire identity was changed. It was the first time he could see her, he had a lead, a strong lead.

And so he did. He found her. He looked on from afar. She had seemed happy so he did not go up to her. She was with another man He just walked away. But later he hated himself. How would he know if he did not at least look into her eyes? How would he know without a single word?

174

So this time he promised he would go up to her. He timed it well enough. There she was and she was alone this time. But she was at the station, and she was moving fast. He ran after her, screaming her name. She must have heard him but she carried on her way.

He saw her getting on to a train. He ran up to it just as the doors closed.

He said their eyes met for a couple seconds.

He looked at her eyes and her eyes met his.

And he saw her eyes say NO. And he left.

It was all he needed to know.

And after that he decided to come home.

But he was not completely over her yet.

A few weeks later mum hit him with the round about question. He had moved closer to home, working in Durbs on a project for a couple weeks. He had his own apartment from the company. He was doing well now, financially speaking. And he was home most week ends, which was good. He was no more his down and dopey self. He was not even that man on a mission any more. He was almost himself. Self assured, witty, charismatic and poised. It was Akbar of old and we all loved it.

Mum: So son, my friend Zahida, was querying about you the other day.

We knew where this was going straight away. Even Akbar knew it, he had this smirk on his face. It was playful and willing, the kind your pup has when he is busy biting your hand.

Akbar: oh yeah, so what were her queries about?
Mum: she has a daughter who is a lawyer working in Johannesburg.
Akbar: oh yeah we could always use someone with a knowledge of the law in the family.
Mum: anyway she was saying that she is a nice homely girl.
Akbar: you know how I love homely girls.
Mum: she is three years younger than you, starting her career. You are set in yours. She is very beautiful and has a calm pleasant demeanor.
Akbar: God knows I could use someone with a calm demeanor.

Mum: she is a good Muslim girl. (GMG)
             Even mum had this GMG thing down.
Akbar: I am pretty happy at the minute Ma. But I don't think I am
             quite ready for that yet.

The irony was that later in the week mum got a post card in the mail for Akbar. It was blank, but on the cover it had face with a frown, the opposite of the smiley face, and a hand waving goodbye. I did not know what the hell to make of it. But it was from London.

When Akbar saw it, he looked at it for about a half hour and then he just looked at mum and said, what was that girl's name? the GMG.

And mum jumped up and hugged him and even Dad managed a broad smile.

Mum: Her name is Naima.

And that was that.

Mum: oh ya and Ali some weird white Russian woman called on your cell phone while you were in the shower. She said she got her problem checked out and it is Ok now. I thought it was a prank call but I wrote her name down in case she was a patient, some weird Russian name. She said I must thank you and she told me you a good boy, I was so proud of you beta, my sons doing so much good.

I just smiled. And said, yes mummy.

23

I was already late for my date. Or whatever this relationship was? I was getting a bit frustrated with this entire hide and seek: cat and mouse game. I knew what age I lived in. People who like each other never actually say they like each other. I would call, leave messages on her phone and get replies a day later sometimes two days later. Most of the time I was so busy, I did not even notice, that her replies, were pretty friend like.

An example, my sms:

Hey there gorgeous, so what have you been up to, have not heard from you in a while, was hoping we could hook up this weekend. Thinking of Durbs. Hope you free, slmz

Her sms:

Ok, will let you know by Saturday, have some stuff I got to take care of.

And there it was. All her messages were icy. And why do people always say they have stuff. They gotta take care of. Surely after you have been close friends with someone for a couple of years, even months you can say what you up to. I mean we are all not working for the CIA here.

Ok we had only known each other for a couple weeks but unless she was planning a surprise for me or doing something behind my back, I found it all very strange.

It got me wondering about what my dad had said about pretty girls. While I was at varsity my dad said that I will see the most beautiful girls and every boy would want them. And they knew that and they would most of the time milk it for all its worth. Like the blond bombshell in the crime thriller that the hero knows is bad news he takes his chances anyway. And of course she leads to his down fall but she is killed too and he forgives her.

Beautiful women will always be showered with attention, today tomorrow forever and people(not just men) do whatever they ask and more. Who would not take advantage of that?

"like dogs chasing that car we men always go for the biggest loudest lorry and we would never catch it, and those of us that did, had no idea what to do with it."

The weekend would arrive and on Friday like she said I would receive nothing, not a call not a message, not even a damn post it.

So I would be at home moping and then every once in a while I would get a message meet me at such and such a place, always different people, same music, same drugs and alcohol.

I don't drink, I don't smoke but still I went to be mesmerized by the scent and beauty of a woman. What a loser?

But here I was again on a Saturday afternoon waiting for a save me message and there it was, from my boys.

We were going to watch some classic movies like Forrest Gump, Braveheart and sixth sense at my fiends place in Durbs. I know what you thinking, that's the story I tell mum and dad. This weekend we are of to the coast.

As Jack says in a few good men(which we were not), to my parents: "You cant handle the truth." And it is better this way, my dad would skin my ass if he knew.

Jameel was down again and Stevies friend Bruce had a pad available. It was his dads timeshare at one of these fancy hotels and we all had a place to stay.

It was funny how these things take place in a couple of minutes. Having no commitments, huh. When my parents plan a weekend a way they do it a couple months in advance. It was crazy that when you are young you just do and it's Ok. Why can't life always have some lightning strike every now and then?

So we meet up at the hotel.

Unfortunately since I was the only one not in the south coast vicinity already, I drove down alone. I was told to get the meat and some extra stuff to eat. They trusted my meat selection and extra snacks selection too.

Jameel was picked up by Kubin who was already starting to get drunk. Stevie and Bruce were at the hotel in the casino area when I arrived trying to pick up older woman. Why was I here? I had nothing better to do and being out with the guys was just fun. It was amusing listening to their hyped stories and made up romances. It was a far cry from my mundane weekends.

These guys made me laugh; they made me realize not everything is life and death. They were my gin and tonic,.

Of course I never did anything wrong(by my standards), but I observed the frailties that indulging in alcohol can have. They always made fun of me the tea drinker and teetotaler in the group. But they respected me and I can honestly say they accepted me as I was, more so than my parents and family did.

I arrived at the hotel at 7:30 pm, it was glitzy and garish. It was definitely a timeshare, something I could never afford on an interns salary. Maybe some day though. The setting was beautiful, the sun had just set over the lagoon and the night had begun.

My timing was perfect. The fire under the grill had reached the fever pitch. Now was the time to braai, the rest of the world barbeque, but in SA we braai, it's not an art but it sure as hell could be. I took it very seriously, my meat had to satisfy each person I served. And every person likes their meat done a certain way. It was the reason why I was always chosen to braai. I did not mind it though.

Standing round a braai stand with your mates with a cool breeze at your back and a cold can of coke (in my case) in your hand was how time should be spent. I loved these moments. Guys talking absolute nonsense. A good game of English premier league soccer on in the background. The best part was that there was still a whole evening of shenanigans to look forward to.

In about an hour everyone had arrived, all still sober, this was impressive. Stevie was filling me in on what to expect with the dreaded Community service. Jameel was telling us about this new hot chick he was supposedly dating. And at the same time Kubin was talking about getting strippers again. Bruce however was the most worrying of the lot. He was postulating a fail safe way of always winning on the roulette table. He was adamant that if we each put two hundred down we could walk away tomorrow morning with a thousand each in our pockets.

Now this got every ones ears perked up for some reason. It was haraam or forbidden for me yet the irony was here I was in a hotel with nothing to do really but something wrong. But still it was wrong and I knew that, yet it fascinated me how intelligent people always rationalize their wrong doing, including me.

So now we were all engrossed on how we were going to win thousands of rands tonight. Typical boys weekend out I thought.

Kubin liked his meat rare, very rare. His was done first. Stevie liked his meat a different way every time, as such he was braaing his own meat. Jameel was a chops boy and he liked his burnt. I know, he liked biting through the bone. Bruce was too busy working out mathematically how we were going to win. He just was just happy with anything, as long as it was cooked.

Meat had to be perfect for me, same every time medium to well, cooked with taste.

It did not take us long to enjoy our meal and like the carnivores we were, we devoured our meat piece by piece. Yet we were satisfied once our bellies were full. And Man United and the Sharks won. Stevie prophesized that tonight was our night. He could feel it. Kubin believed it too, but I think he was mildly drunk now. He said he had a good vibe.

The plan was intricate and too complex for a Saturday night. I had no idea what Bruce was saying but he was a maths whiz so we all just went along with it. We were all probably suffering from hyperglycemia and in some euphoric state. Bruce collected the money, which totaled R1500. Some how he convinced us all to part with R300 of our hard earned money. I gave it, but knew I would not ask for it back or take any of the winnings. I was just here for the company and the experience/s.

It was like the weekend with the boys or Anya was an escape for me from a life I barely knew and tolerated. This danger of bordering on the edge of a cliff at high speed in a far from road worthy vehicle excited me. It kept me sane.

We started our first round of roulette, a game I had heard of, but not played till tonight. It seemed easy enough, it was a bit of maths but all I could see was pure luck. Gambling is gambling and it's wrong because you always lose, in the end. Money that is not earned is like a wave it just comes in and then goes out.

Bruce seemed confident enough; he had given in our money for some plastic pink colored chips. Pink. He furiously starts by putting these things all over the place in between the numbers on some numbers.

Half an hour later we were one thousand rand down. Jameel was bored and was eyeing some of the girls walking around. Stevie was getting drunk with Kubin who was already talking about all the problems in his life. He was in stage 3 already.

I have never been drunk nor will I ever be. But my years in varsity around students and being a doctor in casualty on Saturday nights around drunk patients, I would say I have a good idea of what happens.

Stage 1— (I will just have one or two drinks tonight) early drinking, light joking and pleasant conversations, early flirtation with the opposite sex.
Stage 2— (this is my last one) soft punches to surrounding people and reminiscing of glorious events in the past. More than playful remarks to uninterested females/males.
Stage 3— (ordering for others) vociferous, powerful bad singing to old classics, and removal of items of clothing, pushing and tugging of the opposite sex, re affirming belief by repeatedly saying I am Ok, I am Ok.
Stage 4— (I feel/am sick) morose and sad, recounting every mistake ever made, especially in relationships. Then somnolent and abusive, wanting to fight with inanimate objects.
Stage 5— comatose.

The first time Bruce came to us and said boys I have some good news and some bad news. Which would you like first? And we all looked at him with that duh look that parents get from their teenagers often.

Good news: I won three hundred bucks.
Bad news: I lost one thousand two hundred bucks.

So when he said, "guys, I have worked it out, I know now how to win, I just need two hundred more from everyone."
I gave him the duh look.
Stevie and Kubin both now well on their way to stage four gave him whatever money they had left which was eight bucks.

Jameel was smooth talking some girls that looked like they were still in high school.

That was when I received the sms:

"hey there, heard you in durbs, from Jojo, sneaking out for an early morning swim, are you game? I am in durbs too Anya

I think to myself, typical. We have a policy now, of bro's before ho's on a boys weekend out. But looking around me I don't think I would be missed much this morning. My watch read 01h45 already.

We had played cards and lost, roulette was a bust and we were just about two men down already.

Bruce was intent on winning something, even if it meant losing everything, again.

Jameel who had earlier gone on about this new girl in his life was intent on getting into trouble with some seriously young looking lasses. Overlooking them were their brothers, I was pretty sure of that.

Stevie and Kubin, well they were out, already, pretty early for them. Things must be really bad.

So I replied:

How early?

Two minutes later:

Meet you at Addington, in front of Milkys at 03h30, sunrise will be beautiful. Looking forward to seeing you.

And with that last sentence my resolve and indisposition melted like a mushy marshmallow in between Marie biscuits.

Woman. They know just how, what and when to get us. And get us they do.

I was off. To see her again, and I was smiling, for how long I did not know.

It was quiet and dangerous. I knew my parents would not approve but I was compelled to see her.

The drive was smooth and comfortable. I love driving on empty highways. Everything just seems so peaceful and placid. I drive up to the beach front. It is a Saturday night and there is a buzz in the air but I only have eyes for one.

And there she was, surrounded by groups of boys and girls. I make her out straight away, flowing brown hair, larger than life smile and soft brown eyes that haunt you. I flock to her without a care in the world at three thirty in the morning.

She introduces me to everyone as her friend. It is a bit weird, I try to act cool but inside I am just confused.

We all start on a slow walk down to the surf. I start wondering if I am the real serf now. I want to get her alone but I just can't. I need to talk to her and settle this today, now. Being in the dark is killing me.

Supposedly these were friends of hers from facebook, most from here and some from overseas. They were talking about the different type of sea sides they have seen, and the way the sun was so awesome. Within an hour I was bored and contemplating leaving, except that the sun was rising and it was beautiful.

I have seen the sunrise on call often but not like this. It was the dawn of a new day. The radiance and subtle power of this star was so unassuming. The background of the ocean was terrific and there it was, a moment in time. The company was not right so I took a walk on the pier by myself.

I watched as a quarter became a half and just as the suns lips left the ocean floor, I felt a tap on my shoulder. It was her. She grabbed me and pulled me in. we kissed long and slow, till I was breathless and shell shocked.

She just held her hand in mine and rested her head on my chest. Neither of us said anything. We stood for a while. I just smiled and watched as the suns rays sparkled on the waves like a million lights

Then she just turned to me, looked at her watch and phone, and said she had to go. And just like a song you hear on the radio, the words that were playing with the song are now fading in your mind.

She was gone.

On my drive back I kept thinking, this is definitely not how friends interact. I was concerned, but still there were no alarm bells ringing and if she called me now to come back, I would have.

I got back to the pad with everyone still fast asleep so I decided to get some shut eye too.

When I woke up with tooth paste up my ass that hurt like a third degree burn and my right side burns shaved off, I figured the guys knew I had left. I had broken the rule of bros first, and I was being punished or pranked on. Either way I did not care. I had a moment that I will never forget.

I could not believe the time after the shower. Daylight was disappearing. I adjusting my shaped beard and hosing my burning backside. I hated the feeling but the weekend was just about over.

We had our second braai done by old Stevie boy. Everything was pretty much raw. The boys had to take stock of the weekend.

Stevie-drunken stupor =awesome weekend

Kubin-drunken stupor =awesome weekend

Jameel-made out with a 16 year old, thereafter was beaten up by her bother. He had the blue eye to prove it. His back stop was me, who was not present. Thus he got his revenge with some old but painful tricks=awesome weekend

Bruce-lost everything on roulette not once but twice=crap weekend.

Me-shared my first kiss with Anya=awesome weekend.

Thus it was only Bruce who had a bad weekend. As we were about to leave he asked for one last chance to redeem himself.

We gave in as he was one of the guys. We all put a hundred bucks and put it down on some numbers we thought would win. I called 17 Anyas birth date and would you believe it, we won. It was pandemonium.

Of course the guys went hysterical and security came over and told us to politely shut up. They later realized we did not care, it was just sheer luck but it was still great story.

I donated my money to Bruce as it was his father's time share and who knows how much he really lost that night.

The guys were just happy that we came out with some money in the end.

Bruce-won at roulette for the first time=awesome weekend.

24

It was my last month as an intern, and I was out of the wards and in casualty. It was a bitter sweet departure. I would miss my patients especially Mr Botha and Mr Khumalo.

But like most doctors, most notably interns, in public practice, we just keep moving on and around. It was interesting though, that we lose patients and move on. I think that is also in part why doctors are a bit callous or come off as cold at times. We just don't spend enough time with one patient, except perhaps for specific GP's and other specific private practice doctors.

I pass Dlamini in the corridor, after the usual morning meeting. I have to admit I was practically a zombie in that meeting. I heard the good morning and the thank you for coming, now go back to your working stations. That was it. I just felt tired. I suppose it was that time of year. Almost there, but not quiet at the end of another year. I was like a comrades runner in his last marathon.

Dlamini, hits me with a soft fist, and a thanks for leaving him with a decent ward. I ask him how my ex patients are doing, and he tells me something that makes me shiver.

Mr Khumalo has colorectal cancer and he came back with symptoms of complete obstruction after his week end at home. He needs urgent surgery but according to his blood results he is no shape to go under that knife.

And he is refusing surgery anyway.

Then Mr Botha's renal picture has worsened and he requires dialysis. He has a second problem. He is not agreeable to it. He wants to go home. He wants to die.

I realize then.

I just have to go back and speak to my patients. The only problem is, they are no more my patients.

My duties now are in casualty. I have to go there, be there. And if I am not there, the gateway and queue to the hospital just grows and grows.

In our hospital, casualty is like a pit. An animal pit. Scary, weird and wild. You see everything and anything. You are on your toes from arrival till departure. It is the worst place to work; it is the best place to work. The experience is priceless but the load overwhelming.

I walked in like a panther on the prowl, walked up to the files lying on the table. It read 48, how is it that there are 48 patients waiting at 08h30 in the morning already. No red or yellow cases yet, but then again the sisters doing triage do often get it wrong.

My first case in casualty is a five year old girl with her mother. Her name is Precious Vukani. I ask the mother in my broken Zulu, what is the problem today? Her reply sends an electric shock all through my body.

My daughter was raped yesterday.

I call in a Pediatrician straight away and I start working on the history.

You hear about it. You read it in the paper. But I tell you what, seeing it in the skin is something else. As I said it's a jungle out there, this is Africa and there are predators everywhere. The true sadness and pain is that, it's the young that suffer time and time again. It just makes me sick. It makes me angry.

So here was the story, mother is unmarried living in an informal settlement. No father, he left. Precious and mum live in a shack.(an informal settlement.) The history is pretty plain, mother and boyfriend Vusi have fight. She tells him to leave and never come back. He storms off only to come back and rape the innocent child.

Well that is the mother's story anyway.

This was done yesterday and as often happens, the lack of insight and intelligence or perhaps level of education is always working against us. The mother sees that the child was sexually abused. She is 19 herself. She proceeds to bathe the child, already changed the clothes and washed the previous clothes. She brings in her child today with the police to open a case file. Unfortunately most of the evidence is already lost.

Dr Stevens comes down with his intern Dr Marais. We all take the patient and her mother to a private room. We open the special rape case kit and get to work.

Dr Stevens was nice enough to let us go through the kit with her. She goes on to tell me, this is her seventh one this year. Seven too many, if you ask me. Rape is an abhorable act. The worst crime possible. Not to make it alright any time but it is one thing to rape a woman but a child is just something on another level altogether. How does a man rape a 6 year old child? What makes a man do that? What kind of man does that? All these questions and no answers.

And there it was a six year old child with bruised and chafed inner thighs. Tears of the labia majora and minora tells this child was definitely sexually assaulted, soft slow tender tears moving on her skin like raindrops on a windshield.

I work my way through the rape kit collecting evidence being professional, it's a bit too much for Dr Marais, she is also like me just holding it in.

You know the feeling, you feel that deep sunken heave in your heart, so much pain that it even drowns out the screams.

I see the tears welling up in her eyes as she excuses herself and Dr Stevens helps me finish up.

We collect what we can; collect the evidence hoping and praying it is enough to place the scum of the earth in jail where they belong. If that is even sufficient punishment? I do not know.

We fill in all the forms, do all the blood work. Despite the entire acute trauma this child has faced, she now has a new enemy. HIV.

Her initial tests are negative but she could still be in the window period. Her mum is also negative. This is the part that really gets to me.

Imagine the worst abuse you can traumatize a child with and it's only a doorway to a lifelong disease with no cure.

And we still have not even touched the emotional trauma that will plague the rest of this child's life.

I do my job, try and remain professional but I am angry at my fellow countryman, a man, a human being who is out there on the prowl.

Dr Stevens tells me not to worry and that she will take care of the admission and the social worker. I nod thank her for building my experience.

She shrugs her shoulders and tells me this was my first but will not be my last. It's an unfortunate truth that this exists, and moreover this is common.

My luck that my first patient throws me in, at the deep end. The day just got better and better from there.

Three pregnant woman, all with miscarriages. The first 22 the next 21 and the last 16.

It is amazing how young patients in Africa are living adult lives. They are pregnant young, sexually active younger. Most without jobs, some without parents. All living of grants, on the taxpayers dime. On the on hand I see the need for social grants, on the other I see how they are abused.

The youngest I have dealt with personally was a 14 year old girl. She delivered a healthy 2.3 kg baby. The next year she would be attending grade 8. A baby with a baby. And no parents to help, and to add insult to injury, sick old grandparents too.

But more common than that was the lack of contraception and high risk sexual behavior in the youth(by youth I mean 12-19) raising rates of HIV and other sexually transmitted infections. And the other minor thing, pregnancy.

Then you have these young scared school girls running to traditional healers to get rid of unwanted babies. Others run away from home unable to live with the shame. Or worse throw the babies away, down toilets, in the bin.(sick, I know but it does happen)

Many of the miscarriages are failed or successful abortions. It is also quite common. The funny thing is I rarely see boyfriends or fathers at the hospital. I always thought perhaps this was a cultural thing but I was told it is not. Most of the time, they are just too busy with work and other things. I have to give it to them though, black woman are strong, very strong. Well excuse me, all women. They can endure the worst of hardships.

As men we are strong but I really do believe we could not deal with half the stuff women go through.

And so these women with problematic miscarriages had to have Dilatations and curettage or a D&C, not a pleasant procedure. But a required one nonetheless.

Luckily I just hook em and book em. One of the few perks of working in casualty. Work up, diagnose and refer.

The worst cases are those young girls 16 and younger who fall pregnant. Then they come to the hospital 5 months later requesting abortions.

I remember when I was in O&G; I had a girl who had three abortions. On counseling her on proper contraceptive methods, she said her boyfriend would never allow it. She just could not and would not be able negotiate condoms, she suffered with migraines, and mistrusted all pills because they made her headache worse, and she did not want to consent to any surgical procedures. She was a nightmare patient. The worst kind, you give options and they close them.

There are also those patients who refuse to have HIV tests or have them and deny or ignore the results. It is what happens in the real world.

A couple years down the line you meet the same patients in medical wards with end stage HIV and PTB, there is almost nothing you can do to save them.

Casualty is a mad house at times. You can see a runny nose and then a seizure, a stroke to an insect bite, and trust me you do. It is very rarely dead but the nice thing is you stabilize a patient then refer to the correct specialty.

But the best part was getting comfortable with emergency medicine, one og the most critical disciplines in medicine

I enjoyed the rush and the bustle but to be honest I missed the wards. In the wards you see a patient everyday. You build a little a relationship with them. You get to know them intricately and you see them get better and worse.

That reminded me I had to see how my two boys Mr Khuamlo and Mr Botha are doing?

I take a walk up to my ward. Well my old ward and meet Dlamini and Lithuli along the way. These guys are always so wound up and now they were running my ward. I was sure my patients would be OK, with these interns.

Me: hey dude, how are things?
Lithuli: ah not too bad. Learning a few pearls from Dr Raghavjee and Dr Okuvango.
Me: Dr Okuvango is teaching you.(maybe he is racist).

Lithuli: He is very knowledgeable but a tad too condescending for my liking. Dlamini:Yoh, that oke is frickin lazy bru.

Me: tell me about it. (At least that has not changed).

Lithuli; what is up with Stacy dude?

Me: what do you mean?

Lithuli: she knows I am on leave in November and she still gives me five calls. Its bull shit man.

Me: (ah finally someone else is cracking up too.)

Now it is a common fact that the worst job of all is trying to do a roster for a group of doctors. Everyone hates calls and everyone has requests. I used to do it but gave up. It was too difficult looking into peoples eyes and begging them to do certain calls. I gave the baton for that problem to Judy who than passed it on to Stacy. As you can see it a very sought after job.

Generally the person doing the roster and all her cronies get cool calls for a month maybe two, but that does not last long. Once one person sniffs a rat the news spreads like wild fire and then you are in big shit. So I devised a method of screwing one person over every month, and never repeating the screwee, me the screwer however never got screwed, one perk of doing the roster.

When going on leave however, the unwritten rule is that the person going on leave gets less calls then everyone else. This was what Lithuli was pissed of about and rightfully so. But unlike SuperM who did not mind, I don't think Stacy will get away with this one.

Me: you should take it up with her.

Lithuli: I did, she said there are too many of us on leave. I was the last to join this crap group and was the unfortunate odd man out.

Me: that sucks man. (Thank god it was not me) You seem a bit on edge man, that's not like you.

Lithuli: yeah I lost a couple patients in the ward.

Me: So, listen dude, hows my patients doing?

Litrhuli: which ones?

Me: Mr Botha and Mr Khumalo.

They are both dead man. Well one for real, the other went home to die.

Me: ya funny Lithuli.

Lithuli: no seriously man, Mr Botha died this morning, he refused dialysis and his potassium level killed him. Mr Khumalo signed RHT (refusing hospital treatment) this morning. I am so tired of watching people go out like this man.

Me: yeah was all I could whisper. I was in shock.

For a minute I could not move. All I could see was Mr Khumalo's face as he went of with his relatives on Friday and Mr Botha telling me to go off and have a great weekend.

I have lost and will lose patients.

But this was different; I felt like I had lost someone I knew. Someone that was supposed to be alive today.

For the first time in my internship I felt something, I felt genuine remorse.

Over my patients death. My patients.

At that moment I was paged to casualty, resus. And life carried on. I had to run to save someone else.

As it always does, carry on.

And so did death.

25

I have to tell you about my vacation leave now. I got to be positive, think of something positive after so much negative. It was my first holiday that I paid for and organized all on my own. Two of my buddies were supposed to come along but in the end it was just surety man, Jameel and I. Once you start working and you move to different parts of the country, even the world. It's difficult to keep in touch. Even with facebook and e-mail, try as we might, we end up close to those in our immediate vicinity. As studies have shown, you usually marry someone at work, at the office. Your friends change as does your environment around you.

We had always talked about it and after a year of internship I had saved enough money to do it. We were on our way to the UK, London and some parts of Europe.

The folks took some persuading but they knew nothing was gonna stop me.

My mind was made up, even it cost me an arm and a leg, and it did, but it was worth it. My leave was scheduled and I was ready for the time of my life.

London for 3 days and, 11 days for the rest of Europe. It was going to be epic.

The trip itself was my first time on a plane. It was daunting organizing each detail but exciting nonetheless. I could not wait to see it all but the exchange rate was killing me 13:1. I would have to be penny wise.

I did my last call in pediatrics and off I went. Luckily it was a quiet call, I got a full five hours uninterrupted sleep which is golden. Never heard of in paeds ward call, so I knew God was on my side.

Dad even drove me to Durban. Mum came as far as the house door. She kissed me goodbye, she said she would be better of at home, making dua I go and back home safely.

The drive to the airport was quiet long and winding. Dad finally broke the silence.

He gave me some advice.

Dad: son, don't go there and behave like an animal. I know you have all this excitement and testosterone, but have good clean fun. We have sent you because you have earned our trust. Don't break it now, Ok son. Have fun, remember you're Muslim and that Allah is watching you and you will be fine.

Me: In that drone like voice we all have, yes papa.

First stop was Durban airport, everything ran through smoothly. I would meet up with Jameel in Johannesburg.

Jameel's entire family came to see him off at the airport. The Indian family ties are tight. We love and hate goodbyes. We always have this affinity for our blood ties more so then other races. Sometimes it can be overbearing but as you get older, you realize that the love your family has for you is so great. They just cannot help sharing in every moment of yours. Be it the moments of joy and those of sadness.

Jameel's family was no different, His dad and mum were there. His two brothers and sister. His two aunts from his mother's side, and his uncle from his dad's side. Not to mention their respective spouses and children. (Just the usual charo airport goodbye.)

His uncle who lived in London for a year kept on drilling us with information. He was telling of all the places to eat.

Uncle Akram: now remember to go to little India, ask for medina palace, best tarkari in London. Anyone who knows anything about curries will tell you Aishas den near Kings cross is brilliant.

For some reason the food always ends up being a focal topic. Where to eat? What to eat? And then we reminisce about foods like we can actually taste them, while we talk of them.

It was a quick goodbye.(lasted a good half hour) Everyone wished us a good time. We wanted to be on time so we went through to the international departures, like birds everyone makes their way through to the nest, lounges on the other side.

You always feel slightly apprehensive when they look through your passport. They study it like Sherlock Holmes. I mean how long does it take. You just hope you don't have any problems.

The anticipation was building up, we had already started with the before trip photographs. We were drunk on the adrenaline rushing though our veins.

And then next stop, Heathrow airport.

Well there was that minor blip of a flight first.

For some reason I felt proud, of myself. I had fulfilled a dream. Well a couple of dreams. How many people can actually say that about their lives? I had worked, saved and used my money to travel.

The international lounge area was a mini shopping mall for foreigners that had pounds and dollars to spend. It was way too expensive for me, thank you very much.

Sure they had some nice stuff, if you did not know any better like the foreigners. But they could afford it what with the dollar at 8:1 and the pound at 13:1, and the euro at 10:1, personally I knew I would have to be as thrifty as camel with that last sip of water before a long journey.

So when I saw those lovely South African ornaments of elephants and lions. The hand made South African straw mats and hats. They were things I had seen before and I knew of places where they were much cheaper.

Luckily my mother had packed enough food to last me two days in the wilderness. Add my stash to Jameel's and we had enough for our entire holiday.

We had our padkos, some samoosas, some pies, a couple of chocolates, chips and some other snacks. In true charo style.

We spent some time walking around then I sat down with my book, House of God, almost finished reading it. My fellow Interns thought I would get a kick out of it and I did.

Before I knew it, it was time to leave and we were waiting in this long queue to get on the flight.

First problem en route. I sit down for a while then walk up to join Jameel. He was in the queue and I went off to the washroom just before. (I have heard horror stories of onboard toilets).

And this 100kg white man tells me to get to the back of the line wearing a suit and carrying his laptop. I look at him once then ignore.

But he keeps going at me. "Hey you Indians are always looking for shortcuts", in a very polished rich english accent. "I am not letting you cut in, it's the principle I say". Well he did not say "I say" but it fit in nicely with his overall personality. Then I say to him, "listen, if it saves you ten seconds to get on to the plane before me, then by all means go ahead of me, I was in the queue, I went to the bathroom and now I am back."

He gave me the click off the tongue noise of annoyance.

I went behind him and joined the queue from the back. Jameel just laughed, he found it quite amusing as did many other people.

People and queues, a recipe for fumes and flashes of fury.

The flight was fine. I watched movies and ate and drank. That is all you can do. The food was terrible, and boy was I grateful that mum packed something for me at that point.

My friend form the queue was getting smashed. Do not ask me why people do this and they get a bit abusive and loud with the air hostess.

I started making a mental list of all the things I wanted to do. Oh here we come Trafalgar square, Buckingham palace, Piccadily circus, British museum, London tower, eye of London, London dungeons, and Uncle Akram's, Little India of course.

So much to do, so little time. I closed my eyes with a feeling of uneasiness. I don't know whether it was the flight but I had the weirdest dream. I saw my brother and a woman together with a little baby, walking in the park. They seemed happy. Mum was there but not Dad. I opened my eyes feeling well rested and we had already landed.

Now for the fun and games. Off the plane, go through customs show face show passport, green light, red light. It was a time of minor tension again. I don't know why but I always look at everyone and think, is he a criminal mastermind that skipped bail, as they walk up with their passports.

But then I realized my name is Ali Sha, being a Muslim was not the flavor of the month. So I was expecting to be grilled, I mean lets face it Jameel and I could pass for Pakistanis, Iraqis. It was sad that for a few, we would all be victimized but that's the way the world works.

And sure enough we took the longest; he looked at me then at my photograph. He then took my passport and documents and went to another older guy. The older came over and looked at me. Jameel was taking just as long in the next booth. Finally he got a phone call and nodded. He then asked what I do.

Officer: You are too young to be a doctor, are you sure mate? Don't wanna change your story?

Me: no officer, I am a doctor. I can prove it too, you are suffering with an allergic conjunctivitis, your eyes are red, and you have a mild eczema on your arm. I hope you got some meds for that.

Officer: he looks at me and smiles "get out of here and have a nice trip."

Jameel followed soon after me and on a quick glance back I had the last laugh.

The Englishman that was going on about me cutting the queue and hassling staff on the plane was being taken away to a private area by police escort.

I wanted to wave goodbye but that would have looked a bit suspect.

We were in London and boy was Heathrow massive. We kept getting lost but we finally found our exit and there was Jameels Uncle Idrees waiting for us. I was glad that Jameel had some family here. They were our accommodation in London for a couple days before the contiki began and without them we probably would not have come. Accommodation is pretty expensive. I felt a bit bad for imposing myself, but as Muslims I know my family would have and will do the same. I planned on buying them a nice gift before I left.

It was only for a couple nights as we would be out most of the day. And it was just Uncle Idrees and Aunty Zubeida. Their only daughter Hafiza was at university. Jameel's uncle owned a small Tire business here just outside London.

The drive home was unforgettable. I don't know what it is about being in a foreign country and environment, but I just felt alive. It was all new and fresh. The traffic and atmosphere was like busy bees buzzing through the restless streets. It was awesome.

Jameel's uncle was talking in the background, and asking a whole bunch of questions but I was beside myself with excitement.

We finally reached his uncles place, an hour and five minutes later. And we had traveled a grand total of 49 km, believe it or not.

I underestimate how lucky we are with traffic back home.

The streets were narrower, and the houses were like cottages, tall and slender. They were sophisticated and aristocratic like everything in Britain. They reminded me of houses I had seen in story books as a child, like little red riding hood with the chimney, except this was real.

The neighbour hood from the looks of it was Indian. Nothing changes wherever you go in the world, the scientific rule holds. Like attracts like. Jameels Aunty Zubeida or Zuby as she liked to be called was warm and hospitable. She relished the company and her sincerity and kindness was evident in her luncheon spread.

There was just too much to eat, Aloo Ghorse, some Akhini, some parathas and grilled chicken. We were stuffed after the first course but in true Indian style we ate and tasted everything. I ended off with an angle grinder belch and my face was like a Ferrari. Everyone started smiling and uncle Idrees further lightened the mood with, Why fart and waste it? When you can burp and taste it.

The house was warm but the rooms were much smaller then ours in South Africa. The single bathroom was tiny and Jameel and I were sharing a room with single bed and a mattress. I insisted on sleeping on the mattress. Jameel did not put up much of a fight.

Uncle Idrees and Aunty Zubys daughter who was at varsity studying biochemistry was not at home, but from her pictures she was a baddam, a beautiful baddam.(If you rated chicks according to nuts the order would be Pista for pistachio almond or baddam, cashew, then peanut). I choose nuts because come on woman are nuts sometimes, or most of the time, right? She was in her final year and would be coming in for the last week end of our trip. We would then have to vacate her room and call the lounge our sleeping place.

I did not mind. I was just grateful we had a pad to come back to every night, and it was for all intense purposes free.

I had myself a hot shower and instead of being tired and weary, I was wired and ready to go. Jameel on the other hand was knackered, and he wanted to sleep in, and shake of his jet lag.

I decided to explore, with my directions from uncle Idrees I was out and about. We were on the outskirts of London, but the underground tubes run everywhere.

It truly is a terrific transport system. Kudos to the English and whats more is it works and it's always on time.

I was off to the British museum, as I knew Jameel would not be into that much. It was the largest museum I had ever seen or been too. To cover it all in one day would be impossible, so I just drifted around soaking the atmosphere, with all the tourists.

I enjoyed the vast history that the museum holds and it covers every civilization, and their contribution to the world. The cultures and beliefs, I was in awe but it was information overload. I took a walk in one of London's many gardens, and watched the famous black taxis and red buses drive by.

The gardens were peaceful and serene, and whats even more is that they were well kept without litter, well I lie I saw a couple of pieces.

I stopped in at a bistro for some coffee and donuts. I watched the different cultures and listened to the foreign languages as time passed by in the bat of an eye lid. Before I knew it my first day in London was over. I could not believe it.

Even though I was dog tired, I was happy that I did not waste a moment. I caught the tube back; I followed the maps, not bad I say. And I was back at my London pad in no time. I closed my eyes and had a strange dream that I was standing with a whip making lions do tricks at the circus.

The sun was just peeping in behind the curtains, I could not believe it, I was waking up in London.

Aunty Zuby was a very warm host, and her cooking skills were commendable. For breakfast we had some pancakes and some Chai, with samoosa's and gulgullahs of course.

Today Jameel and I would spend the day together. However tomorrow he had family to visit and I would be on my own.

So we decided to do all the things that we both would like to cover.

First was the red bus tour. It was well known that you could not come to London and miss the big red lorry.

Jameel and I were just listening and chilling out. Any morning when you wake up and you know that you do not have to go into work is a good morning. But when you wake up, and you are on holiday in Europe. That is something else altogether.

Mr Hibbard:	and to your right is our famous art gallery founded in . . .
Jameel:	what is that statue? Is it not Sir Nelson?
Mr Hibbard:	well I was going to come to that.
Me:	Jameel, how cool is this, sunshine, an iced cold coke, a soft breeze. Here we are on a bus driving through Trafalgar square.
Jameel:	the poor schmucks we left behind. They have no idea what they are missing.
Me:	there is just so much history here. One of the most powerful nations of the world, past and present.
Jameel:	I know. There is just so much to do, kind of a bummer I won't be able to see all of it. But then again I have not seen my mum's side of the family in a long time.
Mr Hibbard:	and here is Hyde Park. And coming up next is the famous Buckingham palace.
Americans:	is it true that one can actually go into Buckingham palace?
Mr Hibbard:	well yes part of it.

And there it was good old Buckingham palace and the famous guards with their big black fluffy hats and red attire. There was always a crowd outside these gates. Yet even the tourists seemed prim and proper, here in Britain.

We made our way through the bustling streets of London, sight after sight.

Jameel:	did you know Piccadily circus was a place?
Me:	I thought it was like a circus where people performed.
Jameel:	dumbass. Well my idea was something like that too.
Me:	hey look, whats coming up, it's Big Ben.

We went passed the famous 10 downing street and even popped pass Westminster abbey.

A couple hours later we had been through most of the important sightseeing areas in London. It was cool that we had seen just about everything we wanted to and more, it was all in day too.

And then there was the London eye. We decided to jump of there and take a ride around.

It was a serene view, just as we reached the zenith, the clouds cleared and the sun shone through.

It was breath taking. I have to admit, it was a beautiful fixture to have in this stunning city that honestly has to be on any tourists to do list.

Sure it was just views. But along the famous Thames and the silence with 360 degree views, I thoroughly enjoyed it and had enough photos to prove it.

Jameel on the hand was trying to chat up some of the local lasses without much luck.

Jameel: hey there good looking, how would you like to show a foreigner around town.

Female 1: bite me!

Jameel: tell me where and I could do that for you.

Female 2: take a hike you Paki!

Jameel: I am actually South African but thanks for the compliment.

The next lot of girls.

Jameel: hi there, can I get you ladies a coke or something.(he means the drink)

Female 3: I don't do coke; only weed and I don't date or go out with people who don't eat meat.

Jameel: oh I eat meat alright, I love meat.

Female 4: you think you are funny sicko, Martin, Martin; this Indian guy is irritating us.

From the sight of Martin my first instinct was to run, but I stood with my knees shaking, next to my buddy. After all what is backstop for?

Jameel: hi Martin, can I get you some fish and chips.
Martin: listen you Paki, you are begging me to whip your ass.
Jameel: look no harm done, we are from South Africa, and we are
         just trying to mingle in with the locals.
Martin: I hate the Boks. Thus I hate you.
Jameel: I don't play for the springboks but will pass on the message.
Martin: oh we have a comedian, here.

Now when it comes to Jameel, his shortcomings were his love of the chase and the catch. And he loves cornering himself and those with him.

At this minute that was me.

Right now we were cornered, and my idea of fun was not getting into a brawl in front of the London eye next to Mcdonalds.

So I came up with something I saw in a movie once.

Me: listen how about we just leave, no harm done here.
Martin: no one is going anywhere.
Me: (as I expected) OK I have a proposal, one punch each and
         then we leave.
Martin: you must be joking.
Me: oh my god, look its the cops. And then I kicked him in the
         balls, turned to Jameel and we ran like crazy.

So I had kicked a young man who was probably an aspiring body builder. Thereafter I ran away, all in a days work.

Jameel thought it was hilarious. I told him that was our first and last fight in London. And that was his first and last attempt to try and pick up chicks here.

Of course deep down I knew, I was wrong on both accounts.

Next up on the agenda, and lastly today was the London dungeons. It was just what we needed, something to scare us shitless.

The queue was the longest so far and we had to wait a good half hour, still it was not so bad.

Jameel amused himself talking to two young girls, one with a strong Irish accent, the other a young Indian beauty of note(a pista for sure). They were 18 and 19 respectively. Funnily enough, they were quite accommodating and actually indulged his one liners and stories.

Jameel: this is my friend Ali.
Girl 1: hi I am Sharon and this is my friend from London Bilqis.
Me: hi there, nice to meet you both.
Sharon: so where about in South Africa, are you guys from.
Jameel: oh you know South Africa.
Sharon: my mum has family there.
Me: we are from Kwazulu natal, Maritzburg; it's close to Durban
        on the east coast.
Bilqis: I would love to travel there.
Jameel: so you born here in England then.
Bilqis: yes, my father was originally from India, Kashmir actually.
        He came with his father when he was 10.

So we had some common ground, and since there was a discount for groups of four and more; we joined forces.

Jameel turns to me on entry and says shotgun on the Kashmiri Kebab. Why he always names woman after food I will never know?

So once again I was wing man.

Sharon was very nice; she laughed at all my jokes and even grabbed me through the scary thrills of jack the ripper.

I must admit I even jumped with fright a couple of times. Sharon was Irish as I had guessed; she was from Dublin and was here on holiday as well. They were studying in Dublin together, they were room mates.

We talked and chatted through an eerier maze and smoke filled great London fires. It was history lesson with theatrics and a real twist. Interesting, entertaining and fun at the same time. It did not hurt to have girls clinging to you either.

We got on well but before you know it, the London dungeons were done.

They were staying with family on the opposite end of our pad. We were in the north of London, they were in the south. We had a nice time this afternoon, laughs and giggles, reminded me of a school excursion. But we had to go home and so did the ladies.

We exchanged e-mails, facebook contacts etc, but I knew it was just an afternoon thing.

Jameel on the other hand was in love.

Jameel: dude I am in love.

Me: dude, she is 19, we are 25.

Jameel: so age is just a number, right.

Me: so they say.

Jameel: I am going to call her tonight.

Me: dude we have a couple days here, come on now, don't leave me in the lurch like this man. But from the look in his eye I knew he was gone.

The problem with young love is like everything nowadays, we want it fast, here and now. We want better connections, we want lasting love and wealth without the hard work and difficult times. And when things do not turn out the way we like, the first bump in the road, we jump ship.

We made our way home on the tubes. They were once again quick, efficient and not too expensive.

Aunty Zuby had prepared supper for us and boy was I grateful. I must admit, when it comes to family we always are there for each other.

I had never met Jameels family before, let alone his Uncle and Aunty in London. Yet they treated me like their own. Without their hospitality and warmth, this trip would have been a bust. Now it really was something special. We were going to split costs and B&B's four ways initially, but since everyone else bailed, Jameel assured me that we did not have to worry. We would have a place to stay at his uncles. Family is family, right.

But food and drink were a real bonus. And boy could this Aunty cook. Her chops were tops, the rice was savory and soft, it was smooth in your mouth like a soft piece of feta cheese. The chows were spiced to perfection and with the addition of the salty Dhey, it was perfect.

By the end of the night I was stuffed and it had been a good day.

Tomorrow the Contiki tour began

I left a special Parcel for Aunty Zuby the last day before we left, something I knew she would love, for the kitchen.

26

Europe really is something else. It is old yet it is new. It had its tradition yet it is always reinventing itself, oh and the culture of each country. The smell of the cities, architecture, foods and the people. It is something one can only experience by traveling there.

I went on Contiki and our tour operator wisely said on our first day to forget about all the travel books and where other people said you must go, this is your experience so live it. Do what ever you want to do.

I kept a journal, but to be honest it was not worth it, too much to write, too many thoughts. At this point in my life like most young adults I was curious, I was interested to see the beginning of civilization and where we all in one way or another were founded and then colonized.

To go through each experience would be too tedious but I will touch on my highlights of the journey.

Amsterdam, what a high!

Too corny, I know, but it was.

It has its own rules and its own way of doing things which is contrary to all I have been taught Islamically. It was really interesting though.

Different strokes for different folks. However one cannot miss all the wind mills and clogs, Mary J, and prostitution. The latter I only observed, I swear.

Red light district at night is scary but during the day it is just weird.

The canals and walk ways are scenic, beautiful and calm.

The tulips are now firmly my favourite flower.

Anne Frank s museum was an eye opener and the use of public transport and bicycles were amazing.

The people are friendly enough, and I could converse well with my broken Afrikaans. But the Netherlands was all a blur and before I knew it, we were on to the next country. You just get the mood and texture of a place and then its time to move on.

I did not go clubbing, nor did I chase any dragons or butterflies for that matter. All the same I still enjoyed myself and some may call this clean and boring. But it was my holiday and I thoroughly enjoyed how I spent my time there. I cant say the same for Jameel though.

We moved through into Germany and Munich, more beer at the Hofs and steak(which i could not partake in but was told it was good) Munich is a beautiful city. Speeding along the autobahns, and although the consumer stores were very expensive, the people were friendly and warm, contrary to popular belief. The cuckoo clocks and home of the Benz and BMW did not disappoint.

We drove into Austria and went white water rafting close to Innsbruck. The water was freezing but the excitement of the rapids was enough to push your blood to boiling point.

All the way I kept thinking of home and how much Akbar would have enjoyed it.

Jameel was on the hunt to hook with a European chick but I have to admit unlike all the movies and shows you watch, most of the people we met along the way were quite reserved. Everyone was busy and had their agendas. I mean I guess we all would be. Imagine your interaction with a tourist when you are in your hometown and have stuff you gotta do.

Jameel tried his usual one liners on the german girls which was hilarious to watch.

They were generally wary of us. And they kept their distance even more so when they found out we were Muslim.

Italy was glorious; the people were bronzed and always fashionable, even when just strolling out on the streets. Rome was ancient, bustling and the history, architecture and Art were amazing. Some people in the tour had their history books and had a good knowledge of the eras of art. I just stared at the Trevi fountain, the Moses and enjoyed it in that moment.

Despite the rumors circulating amongst the guys, Italian girls were really the Holy Grail. And so they remained, you could not even find one alone, to strike up a conversation with. The men on the other hand would whistle and hit on every female in the group. Of course the American gals swooned as they whispered and whistled at them.

Rome was so busy and bustling and with sites like the Colosseum and Vatican City. They were so close by one another, you could only stand and marvel. To think from this tiny country we have spaghetti and pizza, and all the many fashion labels and styles. And how can I forget the Pantheon, one of the oldest buildings still standing on Earth and it is better built and kept than some buildings built only yesterday.

The Colosseum really is spectacular; you just stand there and imagine what it must have been like in the days of Cesar.

Vatican City is an adventure all on its own. Don't let me get started on the amount of history and arts and culture available for ones mind to feast on.

I know nothing about history or art but I could admire the extra ordinary feats that man had done then.

The Sistine chapel, wow!, you can spend the entire day in silence in that hall and still it might not be enough.

I was dumbstruck at Michelangelo's genius and complexities and I cannot fully appreciate this fine art.

The popes, some that came before are honored and buried there. The entire city stands alone like some sort of medieval play set in a time long long ago.

Then there are the walks where one can get lost in the cities streets, but you always find your way back and there is always a café filled with the airomas of pure cappuccinos and espressos. I mean the pure original caffe latte, none of this instant stuff.

The parks are beautiful and so peaceful and the walk up to the knight's templar park is breathtaking with the secret keyhole vision of St Peters Basilica.

Rome was one of the highlights for me, it is place that everyone should visit to behold the beauties of the past and on passing a Ferrari car park, the powers of the future.

Then there was Venice, just the construction of this city must be a civil engineers nightmare or dream. The Churches and buildings again are from another time altogether and not a vehicle in site. Only boats and waterways.

The festivities are wondrous to behold and just siting on the outside of a café soaking up the sun, is liberating.

The glassworks and Venetian cotton ware, blinds, art work, are a basis for all the fashion, arts and crafts today.

Florence was a delightful town, which rounded up the Italian tour. You cannot go to Italy and miss out on the David or so all the females on the bus made us believe.

The Tuscan town houses and the stretch of wine farms out there really are spectacular. The weather seemed to be kind to us with day after day of sunshine, but according to the locals that is how it was every year in summer.

Once again the churches and ancient architecture was breathtaking.

The town itself was like a village peaceful and calm tucked away in a quiet spot.

Everyone knew everyone and smaller groups formed but we all got on pretty well. Everyone was always happy happy bouncy bouncy, even me, I guess it was expected. I mean come on we were all on holiday on Contiki seeing Europe in all its summer splendor, what was there not to be happy about?

The girls all formed one big shopping crew, in our spare time while the guys played and watched sport.

I guess it really did not matter where you are from, some things just don't change.

We pedaled through the Swiss Alps. We even mono railed up to one of the mountains, the view was something else, we were looking through Gods window and even though there was snow all around and the temperature was—5 degrees celcius, I was on a piece of heaven on earth.

It was so quiet and serene and when the wind blew you could here God whisper. It was a moment in the trip I could not forget, mainly because I love views and quiet moments to be introspective.

We played with some snow balls and had some hot cocoa, and then we were back on the bus.

Switzerland was all about the precision and the price. The swiss watches opened up everyone's wallets and the so too the swiss army knives and clothing.

It really was a charming country and so clean and perfect.

And then there I stood looking up at the Eifel tower. What a sight!

Took the elevator up and looking into the distance on the Eifel tower roof, I suddenly felt so small and insignificant.

In Paris the city of love, our journey started at the Louvre. The Mona Lisa up close and personal, and Madonna of the rocks, and wow the Last Supper.

There are just no words. You gotta see it for yourself.

You could spend a week in the Louvre and it might not be enough.

Then there is Notre Dame Cathedral which boasts some of the most enigmatic architecture ever constructed.

And what is Paris without a walk down Champs Elysee and the majestic dome. It is something spectacular to see the HQ's of Louis Vuitton and sit down with a coffee for fifty bucks on a veranda and watch time pass you by.

Truly enchanting city where everyone could be a model, they are so stylish and dressed to the tee.

Although I have to admit most of the French are quite aloof. Don't ever speak in English, that won't get you far, at least an attempt with some French works.

There are so many brands and fashion labels in Paris and at Galleries Laffayette.

The Contiki tour was coming to an end, and we only had two days in London left.

I know I sped through all these wonders like Usain bolts 100m sprint, but to be honest that is how the Contiki tour was, before you knew it, it was all done. All I had as proof was my photos and memories.

27

My plan for my last day in London was simple, tomorrow was all about shopping for presents. As you know when on holiday, there are a couple things that must be done. Eat and drink and be merry, for tomorrow, you return home and you better have presents.

Luckily for me the Notting hill carnival was on, so I would check that out as well. It should be fun. Unfortunately I would be on my own, as Jameel was out.

For him it was a day of visiting relatives.

I was on the tube again early in the morning, it was quite amazing how easily and confidently I was now navigating this city.

The Notting Hill carnival was awesome. There was live music and loads of little markets, and groups of interesting people to say the least. I was like a kid at candy shop. All the colors, and vibrant vigor of life. I felt alive. Today I felt alive. I was on my own and I was having the time of my life. I did not even feel lonely.

I had always been afraid of being on my own, walking alone with nothing but your own thoughts, traipsing along in your own pair of shoes. But at the same time it felt liberating to know that, yes I can do this.

I met some people along the way, Gunther from Germany. He was drunk on german beer and was going on about how the EU was the death of each countries own independence.

There was Candice from the US she was backpacking through Europe. Of course London was her first stop. She had three months to go where she liked, when she liked, now that is what I call a holiday, her parents allowed her a gap year. I never got the whole gap year thing then, but looking back now I wish I did have that option. Its just you are always busy with some aspect of your life and you never get to spend time with yourself, which in itself is brilliant. You have primary school, then your senior years, then suddenly its college and varsity. Before you know it you are 27, you have a job and you need to get married. What have you done for yourself on your own nothing? Nothing at all.

I don't know about growing up, but I liked meeting new people and never knowing exactly what the day held for me.

This was me in my element. I was saving the sunshine on my untainted skin. And then I saw her. At first it was like seeing an old friend, then your mind registers the information, and you stand there for a minute.

It was like when I had my first car accident. Time slowed down, I could see that I was going to smash into the car in front of me. Yet there was nothing I could do in time, and I just kind of waited for the impact.

She was wearing her denim jeans and did not look any different from the last time I saw her. She was eating an ice cream; it looked like vanilla, in a cone.

I could not stop myself from staring; I was about to turn around and run, acting like nothing happened.

But as it so happens when you stare at someone, they subconsciously know and they look up and smile.

However in our case there was no smile.

She looked at me up and down.

She began walking toward me.

I was rooted to the floor.

I knew what was going to happen. Or did I?

28

Christine now Cindy, and I got on well together. We were friends through my brother of and although I never told her to her face, I liked her. We got on, not like a house on fire, but a low flame. Since my brother and I were quite similar we shared common interests and we conversed well.

Now I know this is going to sound weird, but I have always been afraid of white people. I don't know whether it is a sub conscious setting form the days of apartheid but it is a strange feeling. I feel compelled into helping them making sure they are OK. It is crazy I know. But more than that I know I am not the only one. In South Africa more so than the rest of the world, it is like an unspoken belief that what the white man can do, has done what no one else can. Dating back to the heart of darkness and colonialism. You see a white man and you just assume he should be in charge and all is well.

Sure things have changed greatly, even I have a little bit, but I cant help feeling sometimes that a small part in my brain is going Yes Baas, Thank you Baas, like I am lesser being than them.

Well the Muslim thing is obvious. Like all religious sects your religion and your beliefs are yours, we respect that and you respect us. Right, well if only that were true, in today's world it seems everyone is trying to force you to think and believe in something, some of it is the truth, the rest lies. Clearing the dirt from the clean is getting very blurry.

One small problem is that in todays day and age with everything so interlinked and everyone in the world attached at the hip, there is no leave me alone.

We are not allowed to drink alcohol. We are not allowed to listen to music partake in any illicit relationships with the other sex. No drugs, no fornication. And trust me most of the big religions cover these obvious wrongs, but like any road sign, we see it and ignore it.

So yes I had broken a couple of rules. I was living in the gray too, my gray not the black and white.

How many people left in this world live in the black and white, I wonder.

I mean we all try to rationalize every single wrong thing we do.

We do it in different ways:

1— Oh I kissed a girl today but I did not sleep with her.-the lesser sin
2— I cheated on my wife but I still say all my daily prayers and do everything else right—the higher wrong.
3— at least I believe in God, he will forgive me for whatever, whenever—false sentiment.
4— i lie for a living but I am better than her, she sells her body for a living—above the other man

Yet every now and then when we see a cop next to speed limit road side we slow down. Just as something bad happens in our life, we slow down and then we remember him, God. Our sudden savior, answer for it all.

When its good who needs him, I did it all on my own baby. Now its bad. Need to start praying, need to stop this bad behavior, but then we sort it out and the freeway is ours again.

Free to sin with no consequence, at least for now anyway.

There she was wearing her jeans, a warm fleece jersey and blue scarf my brother gave her as a present some four years ago.

She looked the same, yet older, more worn, I could tell from her eyes. She did not want to runaway as I did. She moved slowly and purposely toward me. The air was still, it was stifling and I felt that fear rise up in my throat.

What to say, what to do?

And when she spoke I knew it was all OK, I sighed and suddenly we were talking like old times.

Suddenly I realize how sorry I felt for her, she was part of a fellowship. We shared good happy days and no one forgets anyone from the purple patches of their life.

There she was, her normally flowing brown hair wrapped up in some kind of a pony tail. She was wearing jeans, sneakers and a T-shirt. She smiled politely and whispered as she spoke:

She; so how are you Ali?
Me: I am OK, and you, how have you been? Is it Cindy or Christine
She: come on Ali you know me.

Awkward silence, which I hate. But I was not ready to leave yet and neither was she.

At the same time we both ask so what are you doing here?
And then a sudden you first.

Me: well I am on holiday, doing London as they say. You know its always been a dream of mine and now its happening. Actually on my way back this weekend, alas the holiday is over.
She: oh that sounds nice. I am so happy for you. Where have you been?
Me: oh all over. We started in London, then Paris, saw a bit of Amsterdam and Munich, then it was Rome and Venice, Florence, saw a bit of Switzerland and Austria too.
She: wow that's amazing you have seen more of Europe than I have in over 2 years.
She: so where you staying?
Me: Well I was staying with family but on Contiki now, will be staying my last night at the Royal hotel.
She: lucky you, fancy hotel.

Awkward silence again. And then she asked.

She: so how is he?
Me: he is good, carrying on, you know how it goes.

213

She: So did he tell you about seeing me.

Me: yup. He did. Listen I got to be honest with you. He has not gotten over you and I don't think he ever will and its not my place to say anything but you should have spoken to him. You should have. And you should have left out the post card. He is slowly drifting away now.

She: I have just been so twisted up inside for so long. I think of my duties to my family and the ones to myself. I have been living here with my brother and his wife and kids like a zombie for so long now. It has become a norm for me just to let each day pass. But I can't say I have been living. I just can't get over him either. I wish I could but I can't. But I fear my family will disown me if I ever go back.

I have just been so Deurmekaar for the last few months. Last night on my birthday I just closed my eyes and asked God to help me through this, but with you showing up here today. I dunno if it's quite clear what I should do.

Me: well I dunno either. I don't believe in signs and humans interpreting them are even worse. But I will say this, you have to make a choice and you should make it some time soon, before your whole life passes you by.

She: has Akbar made his choice?

Me: I would not know.

She: well you know him best, if you had to guess?

Me: well how well can you really know anyone? I think Akbar has followed his own path. I don't believe he will ever feel that kind of love he had for you with anyone else. I honestly don't know what he has decided. After he came back the last time I knew, something happened. And when he spoke it was if the starter in his engine was dead, the spark was gone.

His fire was put out. But he lives know in a place only he knows. I don't know if he will love again or get married, that you will have to ask him yourself. Personally though I don't think he will wait forever though.

She: I don't think I will ever get over him. He tortures me so much, in my dreams, thoughts. Oh Ali it is so nice to see a familiar face, though.
I had better get going.

Me: Yeah me too.

She: So one more day huh,

Me: Yip and then I'm going back to South Africa.

She: Wish I could join you?

Me: I look forward to it.

She: Someday.

29

I may have mentioned it or not, but I would have had a sister.
But she was never born.
She died in utero, around 20 weeks.
Azra, that's what my mum wanted to call her
My father was a man who rarely showed too much emotion. But I swear the pain and stress of that loss was something that changed him and our entire family forever.

From all the excitement of just finding out we would have a little sister in the house to a true tragedy.

I was ten and Akbar was thirteen. My mum was older and the risks were higher. But the car accident was shattering.

It was a drunk driver and mum was alone, unfortunately she and dad had a fight like couples do, earlier that day.

I know my father did blame himself for not being with mum at that moment.

She went out to buy groceries alone and did not make it home on time.

The other driver was prosecuted, got a couple years in jail and is out now.

Its hard to talk about as a family so we just don't.

But I will say it has changed us and molded each of us in a different way.

And as they say God is the best of planners.

The funny thing is it hurts in that moment, but you learn to move on and cope.

We are all individuals yet all the same, that is how it feels when you are in a family. We all had our roles, likes and dislikes, and we knew each other so well. So we did help each other through the pain in some way.

But there is no doubt mum and dad took it harder.

The family dynamic changed from then.

There was a crack, a chasm, a hole that could not be filled.

The void and despair was a catalyst.

We all began living our own separate lives like a schoolboy disheveled and lost on the first day of school; we marched around aimlessly for a while.

I focused on what was important to me as the years went on, my studies and I think Akbar did the same with Christine.

For mum she became quieter still.

Dad's grief was all internalized

He was always a religious man. After that he turned to his faith completely and I do believe that is what saved him, kept him sane.

Luckily I had my brother, we lived in a mixed ethnic and cultural neighborhood and although we never did anything stupid. We got up to our fair share of mischief or Musti as we call it.

My parents later thought it was our way of acting out etc etc. but the truth is we were just being boys.

It took years before they even noticed how fast Akbar and I had grown up.

Akbar and I, we just had fun. I followed my brother's lead. He was older and my role model, and even though he disliked me tagging along like a remora fish he let me partake in all his experiences.

We would visit his friends, play cards, smoke Hooka, watch movies and TV. Play some music and they would talk of girls and who had the best face and the biggest Boobs and most elegant body.

I was three years younger but I was happy at least I had my brother.

And I think deep down he was happy he had me,

This went on till she showed up at that Wimpy. And they kind of became friends and more since.

Akbar liked her. Then they were inseparable, two peas in a pod. Even thought they were different, the backgrounds were similar.

Christine had lost her sister young too and her brother was always doing his own thing, her father and mum were also quite closed off, from what she said. And as they grew up in a strict catholic household I can only assume what happened there. And so like all rebellious hormone ridden teenagers, her brother disappeared with his friends to England. And he never came back.

Christine hung out with us Indians which pissed of her Step dad to no end.

What can I say?

We were just kids having fun.

We never did drugs; we never fornicated, or even kissed girls.

Man I was too afraid to even talk girls at that stage, my brother was not though. Christine was different though, she was easy going. She did not see things in black and white.

But as we grew older and university came, we soon realized Christine and Akbar were now more than just friends. We all knew that Akbar and Christine had a mutual liking towards each other, but this had changed into something more.

That was till Christine's parents and our parents got involved and between them, they have tried to keep them apart.

Seeing Christine again however reminded me of my sister that could have been. A difficult time that we all go through as teens. She was a link to my past too. She was white but for all intense purposes she was family and she knew more about Akbar and me then most.

It's just that now with this whole Christine Saga, I do not know what to do.

I have this notion of going back and telling my brother everything and coaxing him on to coming and finding her, but the question is, will the past in the present only bring more pain and torture.

Is it best that he just move on with his life?

What would I want?

I would want to know. I know my brother and I know that he would want to know.

From her body language and the way she moved, the last thing I expected was to see her again.

Yet on my last day at the Royal Hotel as Jameel and I were packing up for the return trip back home there was tentative knock at the hotel room door.

And there she was, Christine.

Christine:	Hi Ali.
Me:	yeah, come in, how are you, you're soaked through, why didn't you carry an umbrella?
Christine:	you have no idea what it took for me to get here, but I am here now and I cannot stay long. Heya?
Jameel:	Hi there and who might this lovely be?
Me:	Jameel out, go for a walk or something.
Jameel:	OK then.
Me:	so whats up?
Christine:	I don't have a lot of time, but I have to ask you a huge favor?
Me:	yeah sure anything.
Christine:	I want you to give this to letter to your brother personally and promise me, that you won't tell anyone but him about seeing me.
Me;	sure no problem. (but this is a problem.)
Christine:	that is part one. I have a plan but I need your help.
Me:	ok . . . (trepidatiously)
Cindy:	I need your opinion on my plan
	We talked and I offered my advise.
Cindy:	thanks Ali, I know this will be hard for you.

Before I could say anything else there was a quick hug and Goodbye. She was gone.

And there I was with this letter in my hand.

I came on this holiday with no expectations. I wished to fulfill a childhood dream of seeing Europe and the Hub of the world.

I wished to get away from work and all the hectic crazy responsibilities of life and loss.

And here I was with this huge envelope in my hand and even though I chugged my backpack and pulled my heavy bag, this letter, was the heaviest thing I carried.

30

It was such a perfect day. The sun was out and skies were clear. I was saying goodbye to London. My first trip to Europe was over. I was readying myself for the plane back home. I had enjoyed myself, but in the same breath I had missed home.

It is funny how attached I found myself to the familiar faces and places. And it was not just the fact that I was going back to my little home town but that I would be back where I belong.

I think there are a lot of people that grapple with this problem their entire lives. Searching for a place where they can place their hat and let their hair down.

I am a South African. I grew up in Kwazulu Natal. I still knew where home was. After this Contiki and seeing the world a little bit I have realized how much I love my country for a whole lot of stupid reasons.

It's the people, the places, the Beach. The Howzits, the biltong, pap and chutney, to playing tata box at the café. It's the dissing of Bafana to the power of the Boks and the pride of the Proteas, and mostly the resilience of some of the most hard working people you can meet anywhere in our hospitals.

It's the Nandos, the Spur, the great weather, Nelson Mandela and my family.

When you are away from a place you have become accustomed too, initially you are afraid, scared, of the unknown.

I knew now though that I was not afraid, I could and would leave but I would always come back.

We got to the airport and once again the mad rush began. Boarding passes and checking in of bags, goodbyes and hellos, scenes from an airport. If you look closely enough you will see true humanity staring at you square in the eyes.

Jameel and I had a three hour wait, but we had the photos of the trip to look through and reminisce.

The world has so many physical treasures in it, and so much natural beauty, yet beneath it all there is something more precious. Meeting an old friend like Christine.

Passing through the photos I stared most at the ones of the people I had met along the way. New friends made. But these new friendships were transient.

Although I was not the type of person who would write to them everyday or even once a week, I knew we shared a special holiday. I probably won't see or hear from any of them again. Those few days on this holiday we all shared an experience together and I wont forget that and neither will they.

And there we were in a picture, all 20 of us, with big smiles and happy faces.

To the Australians and their jabberings about sheep, just kidding. They were actually the people I related too most, and that says something being on the same trip with other Indians and Jameel for that matter. The Aussies Mat, Sarah, Jim and Clark always had a positive attitude, a quick joke and an ever friendly demeanor.

The first time we were introduced all we spoke about was rugby and how brilliant John Smit was and the future of world Rugby. They loved sport and it was something that we all had in common. They were the most interested in Islam and why we did not drink alcohol or eat pork. From everyone they always acknowledged us and greeted without pause.

I liked them.

The Americans Steve Carla, Janis and Lee, Jamie and Burt, they came as a big group that knew each other well and stuck mainly to themselves.

I found them initially reserved when it came to us, but they were wary due the nature of the tension between Muslims and the west. Once they learned we were from South Africa and doctors, they spoke to us a little bit. As the trip wore on I think a barrier broke and at the end I could say we were friends. They were always the loudest and most excited of the group, with the most questions and answers. They geared everyone else up for partying. They were young couples who had the money and came for a European adventure and as such I am sure they had one.

They were always getting lost and they were the last to arrive and first to leave on their own adventures.

I would say they were goal orientated, and their goal was always to party.

I have never tasted alcohol, except in cough mixtures. I don't see the joy in it. The more people drink the louder they become and generally the more abusive and crazy. For the life of me I can't see the joy in being intoxicated, when most of the time drunk people regret their actions and words.

What I find even more amazing is how people tolerate behaviour while intoxicated?

I can't tell you how many accidents major and minor are caused by alcohol.

Even the wife beatings, I remember a woman in casualty tell me as I sutured her right cheek post abusive spat with hubby, "he did not mean it Doc, he was just drunk. You know how it is."

I just did not know what to say to this. They don't have control, and control of ones self is very important.

Somehow though being drunk, getting smashed is the highlight of every occasion.

How does one enjoy events if you can't remember them clearly?

Or if you say things you don't mean or never wanted to say?

Or worse still you put in jeopardy not only your own life but other peoples lives too?

I have personally been affected by this, perhaps that is why I am prejudice.

When you hurt someone physically or emotionally drunk or not, the victim is still in pain.

Yet like all dangerous things in this world it is still out there, and will always be 100% legal.

I like to think of it like any other drug, yet it does more general damage.

The Americans were sometimes embarrassing to themselves anyway when they were drunk, but I have to admit as in the movies they were always entertaining.

There were two Japanese girls traveling on their own, they never said much, but were a stark contrast to everyone else. They were quiet and respectful and loved sightseeing, this noted by the extra long time we spent waiting for them to complete their gigs of photos. I swear we spent an hour waiting for them to take a picture of the Eiffel with them in it from every angle.

They were the most punctual and were always right behind the group leader.

I can't say I got to know them much, but then again I did not attempt to get to know them on a more personal level.

Jameel did, and they avoided him like the plague thereafter. They also never drank alcohol and they kept a low profile but they were always there for everything.

The Canadians were similar to the Americans but they were more friendly and always were full of questions about South Africa and everything else. They were three female students Anna, Jean, Jemma and their two friends Harry and Tom.

Of course it became a thing when they first came on (started by the Americans) to ask where Dick was.

They were all in their early twenties and they were from rich families who decided they could go on the Contiki to further their experience of art and culture.

There were a few loners initially.

However they were not alone for too long, one turned out to be quite the ladies man.

Kevin was from New Zealand, he was the quiet brooding type, also on vacation, said he takes one this time every year. This was his third trip to Europe. He was a handsome 6 foot chisel faced broad shouldered muscular guy. Every girls dream or nightmare.

He was dashingly handsome and of course all the girls in the group were gaga over him, much to Jameels dismay.

Yet he was older then the rest of us, in fact at 36 he was the oldest person on the trip.

That did not stop Don Juan.

On day 1 he flirted with Anne and before you knew it these two were inseparable. They eventually started disappearing and reappearing.

We all knew what was going on there; the American couples even voiced their opinions openly as Anne was the youngest of the group at 21.

But she was an adult making informed decisions that was until we found out that DON was married.

I honestly don't know what the world has come to though in this regard. We sleep around like animals, just openly leaving our psyches to neglect and ruin. I don't know how you can go on holiday to a strange place as it is, and expect to just sleep around with strangers because that is what they are.

And guys lets face it, it is usually the woman who gets the raw end of the deal. Yet it has become a norm, even though it is evidently difficult to separate physical and emotional attachments.

Bianca the only lady from Brazil tried her utmost including all but walking up naked to an Italian man naked and saying, Hi would you like a free pass?

She was the party animal of the group, we would be having breakfast and there would be Bianca, short skirt boob tube obviously hung over and continually mumbling how that was the best night ever.

The truth however which we found out later was that she was dumped by her fiance and thus used her savings to come on this one time trip.

To be honest I often caught her crying when she was alone.

Once you spoke to her and got to know she was really nice. I had no idea what she was trying to achieve by sleeping with a guy who would leave before daylight hit.

It just did not make sense, and she seemed to be like that person who was really hurting on the inside but outwardly tried to come of as everything was OK.

She was the first to leave back home and she never even said goodbye to anyone.

Kevin or Don was always on the phone we never knew why, I don't think even our young naïve Anne would have expected this.

But on the second to last day, in the hotel, a beautiful red haired walks up to Kevin, and taps him from behind.

He turns around in utter bemusement still holding Anne's hand and receives the tightest back hand I had ever seen.

He had five red fingers strapped across his face like neon red paint.

Mrs Don then proceeds to say "this must be your business partner or is it your secretary or is she just a slut like the last one. Goodbye and good riddance Kevin. And you enjoy him while you can, which will probably the next five minutes."

It was the most extraordinary scene like something out of a movie. I had my suspicions but this was just too much.

And that was the end of Kevin, Anne and Bianca.

My company on the holiday I have saved for last, despite Jameel trying to hook up with some exotic European women, which we both knew was never going to happen.

There was Belinda, she actually grew up in South Africa and spoke fluent Afrikaans but now lived in London.

She spoke of South Africa fondly but she lived there only in the early 90's. She left when she was 14. She was my age and she was also fulfilling a dream of seeing Europe.

We took each country, city, and venue seriously. We savored each sight seen. I mean apart from costing me an arm and a leg, this might be the first and last time I would see all these far of places and meet all these wonderful people.

So we made the most of it. You can choose your excursions and miss and match the places you would like to see.

But Belinda and I we did it all, we hit it off on day 1 when she dropped her passport and I pick it up and noted that it had a South African flag on the outside.

I don't know what it is about meeting someone from your country or even better your city town neighborhood, there is an instant affiliation.

You feel like you know this person or you should, even though you don't.

Its weird but you just get an endorphin kick of knowing; hey I met someone from back home.

The fact that we were on tour together was just a plus.

She was nice. She reminded me of Jane, she was unassuming and sure of herself. She picked up on my sarcasm and sense of humor quite quickly and the fact that we spoke Afrikaans made it even better.

Anyway she was way out of my league. If you had to rate people which everyone does she would be 8-9/10 category. She was a Pista for sure. She was 5 foot 8 flawless smooth fair skin and light brown eyes to complement her pitch black hair.

As one of the first tasks was meeting everyone and we asked to swap places and I ended up next to her. But it was not a physical or hormonal thing, we just got on well together and had the same goals for this trip, to be in the moment.

Jameel teased me but I did not care, neither did she.

We were really just friends

But at the end of the trip when everyone exchanged e-mails etc I knew that this was goodbye and few if any of us would keep in touch.

Even Belinda, after what happened with my brother, I don't know, I just felt it would be prudent to throw all her details away. I came, I saw, I felt and now it was time to go home. I know she felt the same way.

Nonetheless looking down at the commemorative photo of the group here in the departures area I know we all shared this moment in time together and all the smiles we had will be there in that moment forever.

But thinking about it, it was just a moment that will fade with time.

And that is why I felt compelled to help Akbar and Christine, as some relationships will always mean more in this life. They are not superficial. They are not bound by time or place and only the people in that relationship know what it means to them, but to others just observing you cannot deny their deeper nature.

31

The first day I got back from my trip. I had this question of what to do and what to say? How to do this right?

I knew I would tell him, of that I was sure. But I was not sure exactly what I should say to him.

I knew Akbar very well and it was all in the detail. Dad was picking us up from the airport so there would be that uneasy silence as usual.

Akbar would only be down on the weekend so I could plan what to say to him very carefully when I would pick him up on my own.

Dad: Asalamu Alaykum son, so did you enjoy your European tour.

Me:　yes dad, how is everyone at home?

Dad: they are well, mum has cooked your favorites, and we have been busy with our preparations to go for Hajj.

Me:　oh yeah, so you guys definitely going now.

Dad: yes, we have saved enough.

Me:　wow dad that's awesome. So this will be hajj number 2.

Dad: If you did not go for this wasted money of a trip you could have come with us.

Me:　as I told you before I left dad, interns do not get off any time they want where I work, and it has always been a dream of mine to see Europe.

And not even five minutes and dad and I were at it again.

Jameel: finally got all my bags, so how are you Uncle Abdul.

Dad: I am Alhamdulillah and you Jameel, hope you boys remembered your Salaahs and did not get up to any mischief.

Jameel: we were as clean as whistles.

Dad: somehow I don't believe that.

On the drive home I kept thinking about Mum and Dad going for hajj again, this was big. It was huge. It is something every Muslim should do at least once in a lifetime if they can afford it. But the last time they did anything together this big was before the accident.

And affording it was always a problem. In South Africa for some reason it was bloody expensive. It was something like 100 000 rand a couple if you want to go comfortably. Not first class or anything, not even business class but decent hotels and no real hassles along the way.

Hajj is a pilgrimage; it's a journey of the mind, body and soul. To be honest with you I am a skeptic at best with all things in life.

But Hajj does change people, and it's always for the better. The one thing it is, in a word is, intense. Millions of Muslims worldwide go through Makkah and Medina annually but at this time of year there is always millions of people there. It's insane that a city can hold this influx of people and more than that, they are continually moving.

From one small area to the next, Medina to Makkah to Mina to Arafat, generation after generation has been there and done it.

Where else in the world do you get in our day and age, millions of people on a plain area of land in Arafat wearing the same two pieces of white cloth all in supplication to Almighty Allah,

It is quite amazing feat that I have to admit.

All these people making Tawaf, walking around the Kabah hour after hour, just reading Quran and glorifying the Lord, and all of it just for the pleasure of Allah.

I mean when was the last time anyone did anything just to please the Lord, no gain, no reward, nothing in it for you, I mean seriously sometimes it is at a physical and financial loss. I know all people of different faiths do good, but this is an important journey for Muslims.

Muslims do it year after year, and will keep doing so.

I know to the outsider it might seem lame, but we all know the importance of rituals and supplication when it comes to religion. Islam is the same.

Yet I have always been afraid of it, for some reason I don't feel religious enough to do it.

But family and friends have gone over and come back and told me it was life altering.

And now my parents would be heading off there.

I was happy for them. They were finally on their way.

On the drive home, I was smiling, just smiling for no particular reason.

Holidays can do that for you.

But I had some news of my own, a secret that would have to wait till the weekend, till big bro is here.

Akbar's flight was on time and he was in a good mood. Things were lining up well.

Me: Slmz bro, watzup?
Akbar: nothing wazup with you?
Me: nothing.
Akbar: so Europe huh, you dog.
Me: yeah it was something else.
Akbar: so what was the highlight?
Me: too many just too many.
Akbar: so meet any hot chicks along the way.
Me: a couple.

Once we were in the car,. I made my move. It was quiet. Akbar was waiting for me to start the car but I did not.

Akbar: So are we going home, or are you going to stare at the steering wheel?
Me: I met someone over there.
Akbar: oh yeah, were you awake and drug free?
Me: no I am being serious here dude.
Akbar: OK yeah so you met someone there, don't tell me you fell in love now.
Me: it was her.

Akbar: who?
Me: Christine.

There was silence for ten seconds, and then I could not get him to shut up.

Akbar: what was she doing there?
Me: I don't know; guess she is still living there with her brother.
Akbar: what did she say?
Me: oh nothing much, she just asked about you and what you up to?
Akbar: she asked about me.
Me: to be honest, she seemed the same but like a lost puppy.
Akbar: oh yeah, what makes you say that?
Me: well she misses you a lot, that's obvious, even after all this time.
        And that's why I felt I had to do this.
Akbar: you mean you were thinking of not telling me.
Me: no dumb ass. Of course I would and I did. But what you do with that information is up to you. And she gave me this to give you.

A couple minutes passed. While he stared at the letter now opened. I knew had played my part well.

Akbar: you know that feeling where you know you are going to do something no matter what. Even if it stupid. Even if it's crazy, well that's how I feel about her. I have tried to reason it out but I know there is something else there. I just love this woman and I am not complete without her and by this chance meeting you had with her . . .
Me: I was getting a feeling too now, the one that you feel when someone punches you in the stomach. What the hell will Dad do when he finds out the domino effect I have caused here?
Akbar: I love her.

Akbar got up and walked to the arrivals area.

My brothers not the sentimental type but he looked like he was about to cry.

There she was with her white shirt, white scarf and jeans waiting at the doors.

I swear I felt like I was watching a movie, it was slow motion, yet it happened in a split second.

Of course they had no eyes for me, only for each other.

They grabbed each other like the last box of smarties at the candy store and they were one happy couple again.

And their love and happiness was infectious and we were all gone, for those couple of minutes on cloud nine. They were in the bubble.

Akbar gave me the note, while we packed her bags in the car.

It only had a couple words.

"I will be at arrivals. If you will have me, I am yours, forever."

32

I love my job but hate where it is taking me. No matter how many times you try to turn a blind eye to it, you have to admit your job changes you. I know many doctors are disillusioned. Some of us believe we are doing the best we can. Others just do their own thing without a conscience. The big difference between us and most other professions is our currency is life and what is near miss today is a baby and mother dying tomorrow. A person losing their eyesight ten years down the line. It is always someones brother or sister mother or father, and you are there making life and death decisions.

When I first started I was wired, I could go through calls like an animal, searching for the next problem to solve. As time wore on and I realized that there were so many problems because everyone else had being dealing with this crap for the past 2,3,4,5,10 years, it dawned on me why everyone was so tired, figuratively and literally.

No resources that includes staff, the human resource the most important one, limited equipment, that sometimes is not even functional. I remember not having gloves at one time, in a hospital I know. Then there were no visors. The pharmacists are always out of basic meds. Some formal teaching, but we are adept at teaching ourselves and inventing new ways of settling old problems. And everyone especially the patient still expects the best. I don't blame them though, why should they not expect anything less.

And no one knows how the other feels. The reason is that we all just carry on. Even though it's probably getting worse, we all get paid, well enough. But patients are suffering. Then it's the next day and what can you do, strike, ya right, surely not when you are such an essential service.

So like the essential service of water, we keep flowing. Except instead of stopping for a while correcting all the problems with the pipes we continue on. In time the pipes are damaged, the water polluted and people are getting sick, and its too late to do anything but overhaul the whole system, and trust me, one can expect some casualties then too, if it ever happens.

But this is Africa they say, it was not built in the day or the night for that matter. It is still suffering from the wry smile of colonization. There is still infighting and a power struggle, and there always will be.

As a family Africa would suck, everyone wants to be big brother. No body shares anything at the supper table. And most of our greatest ideas and inventions are exported before we even get to use it.

The human resources were continually moving to greener pastures.

The bigger and better you are, the more you can bully and steal from everyone else. Till you are not stealing anymore, hell people are dying to give you stuff, even themselves.

It is difficult to make a decision of whether to stay or to go. I guess I would like to go but like playing soccer in your backyard or eating Mums mutton curry at Friday lunch, home is where the hearth is. We all know that. It just hurts us knowing that we could be more, so much better as a country, as a united world, but we continually let ourselves down.

I miss the days when our leaders stood for something, stood for us, maybe they will come around again, and maybe the tide is changing. It's up to us the collective to think and make these changes a reality though.

Life is short, way too short and we spend a lot of it sleeping in the dark. We are just too afraid to get out of that comfort zone and switch the light on and make changes. Changes that we know are needed, so sorely needed. It's scary to go against the wave of a comforter that is hugging your warm body, but like a winter's morning once you throw that blanket off and you are up, boy are you up?

You are ready for a new day and that's what we all need to do, wake up to our own new days.

I have not done it yet, I know that, I am still in my comfort zone. I don't know if I ever will, most people don't. They live their whole lives in that zone.

Some of us are born pioneers, others are sheep. To me it does matter that you stand for something though, and you lived a life you were happy with overall. Whatever that may be, as long as when you close eyes you can smile at the end.

I want to smile at the end.

I don't think money left in my account will accomplish this, or the latest sports car parked outside. I don't think a young sexy wife is going to do it either or famous accomplishments, that I will not hear of ever again.

In fact I still don't know what will do it for me?

But I am working on it and so should you?

The time is now, that is what our generation has come to believe instant everything. Instant satisfaction.

On our phones, we find music and cameras and videos and games. We have fast food everywhere. With the click of a button we can be transported across the worldwide web. I don't have a problem with any of this. I love it. Living in the here and now.

But I have to admit it is kind of an empty life. There is no fullness to it. Every minute is so fast that time filters through your fingers like sand.

And one forgets the bigger questions that our forefathers used to ask:

What about tomorrow?

And the day after that.

We get married then divorced, and wonder why our children are so messed up when their models of commitment and stability are us.

We have disease and death spreading like wildfire, yet we still cannot control our desires.

We sit at our tables with five course meals watching others die of starvation, without running water and food.

And as for the world we have started the flames of hell in our contained planet and now each year we just continue fanning the fire.

And then we lie to ourselves that we will soon be changing our ways.

The truth is we are so caught up in the moment that the future and what it brings does not matter.

Its not our problem, is it?, especially the fact that what someone does on the other side of the world, What does that have to do with me?

The funny thing is we forget how interconnected we all are, wired to the same mother board. Like the world markets when one big company goes down the knock on effect can be devastating.

It frightens me to think of where and what we will be 100 years from now.

I mean just look at the cell phone, what it was ten years ago and now. The computer, television and the media. Where will it all end?

Do we have the capacity to work together?

Can we share information with our brothers and sisters of this world?

Can we wish the same good for them as we ourselves have?

I do believe one thing though, with the capacity for self destruction that we possess, will we be able to use self restraint and not kill our fellow brother for the beauty of the few resources that may be left behind?

In a way we are coming full circle going back to Kane and Able. The sense of entitlement and power, it is what it is.

The last 100 years have been amazing. Two world wars and all the technological advancements. We are moving so fast now that we don't even stop for a break to take stock any more.

What next?

I don't know. Do we have the capacity to change, is it possible?

I believe it is. For a few. The few that can, will.

They will listen rather than talk.

They will do rather than say.

They will tell rather than order.

But they will leave you with all the facts and let you choose, your path.

The sad thing is how many of us are willing to take that path that requires so much sacrifice and pain in this world.

Very few.

In the end let's not kid ourselves, being good human beings may sound nice and easy but the truth is far from that.

It is impossible, yet at the same time, it is inherent in our nature.

All we have to do is choose.

We can be Adolf Hitlers or Nelson Mandelas.

We can choose how to live our lives with a conscience and an ideal that we know is true.

Everyone in any situation knows what the right and wrong thing to do is. We choose according to the beliefs that follow our actions which reward is greatest.

And so we come to it, is the reward here and now, greater than something bigger, better and later.

That is the choice you have to make.

33

It was a call like any other except it was quiet as I was doing an ortho call.

I had made swap with one of the interns on ortho.

The dodge man was on casualty cover as the senior and I found he was A.W.O.L as usual.

It was a well known fact that ortho cover was generally the quietest calls of all. I lucked out with this swap as Keith, an intern doing ortho really needed to be off this night and I knew this and took advantage of a good situation. I had to use my cell phone as a form of contact as the pagers were malfunctioning again.

My on call room was absolutely filthy, dirt all over the floor and the bed was wet from what I don't want to know. So I went to the extra anesthetic call area room, however there was no phone there, but I had my cell, they could reach me on that.

The hours passed by from 00h00 and I woke up at 6am and decided I would just pop in to casualty half asleep to see how it's going. I am awakened by Sister David, as I walk in to casualty and she says it has been chaos. It was 06h15.

Sister David tells me that an ortho patient died in casualty. It happened an hour or so ago. The patient was not assessed by a doctor and that no one could be reached.

At first I felt bad for whoever the sucker on ortho was, then it hit me I was on ortho call.

And when I said it aloud, I was on call.

All Sister David could say was check your phone.

I did not see a single message. I asked her to call it and she said it was going straight to voice mail, (oh shit Ali).

It was then I had that funny feeling in my tummy, and I think Sister David could see it.

I showed her my phone, it looked on and it had battery life and signal.

I switched it off for a minute then back on. And it began, six voice messages, it was insane.

I listened to all of them, first was Sister Davids reporting an emergency from casualty at 04h35, a second message from Sister Davids telling me it is urgent 05h05.

A third message where are you Dr Sha, it was the first time I heard a sister cry for help like that.

The fourth message was unbelievably Dr Raghavjee, all he said was, Dr Sha we are looking for you, I was called by the casualty intern, a patient you were called to see over an hour ago, had died.

I would later find out the patient was a GCS 8/15, and had femur fracture with a likely fat embolus, this patient needed an urgent ortho and ICU consult. But given his age and the severity of his injury his prognosis was poor. He probably would have not been an ICU referral but he should have at least been assessed.

The fifth message was mum telling me she was going to see Aunty Jubi this afternoon and she would not be at home.

The sixth message was Rags Dr Sha when you receive this message report to my office, it is a matter of urgency.

Then it hit me I was not in the ortho room, so they probably could not find me either. There were no pagers and my cell was on the blitz. (This old piece of junk cell phone, I needed a new phone).

At that moment I just felt like I was back in school.

We had to stay on weekends to support our schools rugby teams.

I didn't mind it too much although it was pretty boring.

So the Indian group well five of us, led by crazy old Shiraz decided to bunk.

I have no idea why I went with them; I mean there was peer pressure. I also just liked the dare, the thrill, of doing something crazy.

So there we were bunking a compulsory rugby game. To top it off after jumping through a toilet window and changing out of uniform, we then ran across two soccer fields one at a time, not to draw any attention to ourselves.

Once the deed had been done Shiraz wanted to push it to the max and we headed over to the mall to watch a movie.

The plan was that we would watch a movie, run back to the school, change back into uniform get signed of as present by the prefects and wait for our parents to pick us up.

However once we got to the mall an unforeseen problem arose. There like some nightmare waiting to pounce was Mrs Phelps, the maths teacher at our school. And worse still she took all of us for maths.

And there we were deers caught in the headlights with no where to run, all we could do was walk in to the nearest shop.

The nearest shop turned to be a video store and there we were looking at movies except there was on problem, this was a blue movie store.

Our luck Mrs Phelps walks in to hire a movie and just then the manager comes up to me and asks for ID.

And Mrs Phelps picks up on the commotion and busts all of us.

I would have asked her what she was doing there, but it might have been too much.

We were all hauled back to school and on top of bunking and the rest; we all were caught in a blue movie store which we had to explain to our parents.

I found it weird back then that we all admitted to the truth and Shiraz was on his last warning and was close to expulsion. At the time when the principal asked me if he coaxed us to come with, I just said No. I lied saying he did not instigate the matter.

Three long detentions and other school remedial work later I learned a lesson, don't lie or succumb to peer pressure.

But last night I do believe I did not hear the phone but I had this uneasy feeling that I should go and check casualty. Unlike being there earlier would have made a difference but I knew it was going to be an issue.

Now walking to see Dr Rags I had that feeling, a little bit of fear.

The steps were long and slow and suddenly I was at the door, there it was Chief Medical Officer Dr Raghavjeee.

239

I knock and walk in and to my surprise he seems pretty calm and cool.

Even on a normal round he goes ballistic so I had no idea what to expect.

Dr Rags: take a seat. I have a couple of questions to ask you and I want you tell me exactly what happened. We have an usual problem on our hands.

And I believe you already know what happened by now.

Me: yes.
Dr Rags: so what happened last night?
Me: I had my cell phone and even though it was on, I never received a single call. This morning when I switched it on and off. I received all the messages, When I went to casualty to see the patient, he had already coded.
          I was in the anesthetic room as the ortho room was dirty, and I guess no one knew. And the pagers were not working yesterday either.
Dr Rags: so that is why you never responded to Sister Davids call. I have made some calls and this is the first time, in any of the hospitals that we have had a problem with you.
Me: yes sir.
Dr Rags: the problem though is last night the sister and dr's in casualty were busy with two resuses at the same time and even though they could not get hold of you, they did try to get hold of your Senior Dr Okuvango and he did not respond either. In fact we have not heard from him yet . . . The problem is we have had complaints about him from sisters and other intern's alike. And he was the senior MO on for casualty. He should have been there, not just 2 casualty interns. You were on for ortho not casualty, correct.
Me: yes sir.
Dr Rags: So what do you have to say of him?
Me: (now I am in a catch 22 situation, I could tell the truth about dodge but was it my place professionally to snitch

on a co-worker, a senior at that. What would he do in my shoes? The other thing I know about Rags from the gossip that goes around is that he can read people and he can size you up quite quickly. In the end, it is best to stick with the truth, but I was no snitch.)

Me: I have had some problems with Dr Okuvango except that I cannot lie he is always available on his phone. I think it is more a personality clash. He does tell me what to do over the phone, and will come in if I have a real issue which is rare. Yet we have never had any thing happen like last night?

Dr Rags: and in the wards?

Me: he comes and checks up on me. But I do believe I have gained confidence in my own abilities although it would be nice to have some more support.

Dr Rags: so overall he does come to do his ward rounds and despite his tardiness on call, he is generally available.

Me: yes that's right.

Dr Rags: the patient last night was a 68 year old male found living on the street with a fall that seemed to have occurred at least 12 hours before he came in, GCS was low and vitals were not good so he had a poor prognosis but he should have been assessed and timeously treated. As far as your misconduct goes I will look into this swapping of duties as this is not acceptable. We will need a written statement to be handed at the hospital manager's office. It should state exactly what occurred last night from your side. And personally if I were you Dr Sha I would not cover for anyone. I would watch my own back and stick to the facts.

Me: yes sir.

And that was that.

On my way out though there he was Dr Okuvango, the dodge man. He did not seem too happy.

All he did was stare at me.

I went up to him. I was sure he already knew all that occurred but I had to tell him why I did not come out last night.

Me:	Dr Okuvango, I had a problem with my phone last night, it was not working even though it was on. Otherwise you know I would have been there.
Dr Okuvango.:	ok
Me:	I just came from Dr Raghavjees, I want you to know he asked me some questions about you but I told him only the truth.
Dr Okuvango:	I believe you.
Me:	it was strange, he did not seem too concerned.

And then I went of and did my ward round, went to the hospitals managers' office and wrote my statement.

The patient that died was a John Doe, no one came to see his body and thus nothing came of it.

Another stat, for the books.

Some days I know people are going to die and I feel nothing, I am not God and I can't bring back anybody that is meant to die, but I will do my best with the knowledge and resources I have to treat patients with the best care possible.

It was a series of events that lead to his death. A slip, a fall, couple hours before a passer by noticed him on the floor, swapped calls, no pager, my cell phone was out of order, the sisters could not find me, I was in another room, with no phone, and as we found out later Dodges wife was sick. May be these are the sequences that lead a man to death, I don't know.

Was he an ICU candidate? Would he have survived?

But I kept wondering was I responsible for this? No, not really.

Could I have done more? No, not really.

And that is the case with a lot of stress and worry that most of us have, it really is, a lot of the time, out of your hands.

AH, acceptance.

I exhaled and let it go.

34

The time of my life was passing me by and I had no idea. Youth is wasted on the young.

I have always understood that the universe and the Lord, God works in mysterious ways but I had no idea what would happen with my frivolous love life over a couple of weeks.

Anya and I had been having fun together whatever that is or whatever that meant.

That is how she explained our intrepid relationship.

She was gorgeous and fresh when I first met her but funnily enough that desire had changed slowly.

She was like a temptress and I was drawn like a worker bee to that sweet nectar.

The thing about beautiful and sexy woman like Anya is that when they flaunt it and they can and do, every man in the vicinity takes notice.

As woman go weak at the knees, men tend to stand up in more than one way.

And as I said girls like Anya can be with any man, not that I ever thought of it that way.

They say a lot of how you base your relationship is based on the social education and watching or observing closely for years of how, your parents interact or interacted.

Maybe that is why people who have been through a history of divorced parents and damaged close family relationships. They always have some extra baggage.

I have never been in love and I have seen it in movies, I have seen people in love and talked to people in love.

But what was it really, was it just a bunch hormones that are racing around that are hitting a button of euphoria?

And was that where I was now? Love or Lust?

All it took was seeing her one night at a braai and doing crazy ridiculous nonsense with her late at night.

We went to a couple get togethers and I met some weird and interesting people and after all this crap and that is exactly what it was, I was in love.

How did I know, I didn't. I just felt awesome. For now anyway.

I felt like I was happy doing all these wrong things with this girl.

I was sneaking around hiding from my parents but I thought I was having the time of my life.

I had been to the movies secretly; I did all the things I saw in every rom com out there. I stretched my arm out during He or She is just not that into you (looking back I should have paid more attention in that cinema). Was I just doing what I was taught through the media?

We held hands as we walked on the Durban beach front, and I even kissed her a couple times. But was this love really?

And the next time we did more than kiss but I was stopped just short of third base. All words and actions from movies

And through all of this I never picked up any signs.

I should have but that is what happens when you are doing something stupid, hindsight is 20/20.

The way you were brought up and I was brought up is different. And that is the problem with relationships, two individuals have to give up some of their individuality to co exist.

Generally in modern Islam you find someone you like and if you lucky they like you back and then you get family permission and you are engaged and quickly married.

That is how it was done before and how it should be done today.

That is exactly what my father believed, and he had lived a happy fulfilling married life.

Anya and I had become an item. Well that is what I thought, and she was going to be leaving for Canada soon.

I had thought about it for a while but I had to make my move.

I had become a master of the late night disappearing act. I knew like most once I became an adult and I earned my own money, I was an adult.

However I still lived at home, my dad's home, so under his roof was his rules.

I knew my dad would literally freak out if he knew what I was up to, so like all grown ups, I kept everything from him.

There were close calls, I got caught one morning and made up some issue a work. Dad bought it, he had no reason to suspect otherwise.

Obviously I knew what I was doing; heck this is my life, right. I should be able to make my own decisions and marry whoever I wanted.

I was not going to end up like Akbar; I was going to make it happen.

So that night we snuck out and once again we were meeting new people at one of her friends place. All in all this was close to our seventh secret meeting.

Again it was a pool party and again we were talking about random issues in a bed room.

Anya: I don't believe that you can live your entire life believing that you are happy with just one person.

Me: I disagree with that, I think you can. I mean I know you can have more than one partner and I know you can have love for more than one person.

But I also believe if you claim to love someone you can spend your entire life with them.

Tim: (pulls on his cigarette). You guys are going to deep into this topic of love man, I say just live and let live. Whatever floats your boat.

Jeniffer: oh yeah, well what if someone is floating on a boat and taking your girlfriend with them.

Jim: well that's different.

Jennifer: how so, maybe she has fallen for this new guy and his new boat is more exciting and different.

Jim: (pulls again) point taken.

Me: well yeah, that is the question though, are we talking real love here?

The one that requires more than just words.

Anya: love is when you know that no matter what this person will be there for you.

Me: and vice versa, for as long as you both shall live.

Anya: I do not know about that.

Me: what do you mean?

Anya: I don't know if in todays world and times two people can be together like that forever.

Me: Sure they can, love, is all about commitment, loyalty and respect.
         (I sound like my dad)

Anya: sounds like you talking about a dog.
         (Everyone laughs)

Me: well I don't believe you can say you love someone until you respect that person. And I know for sure you cannot love someone who you are not 100% committed to, and if you are not loyal to those you care for most. I guess you don't know what it means to have family.

Jim: That's the problem, most of our family units today are different anyway. No one knows what love is anymore. It is different for everyone, our idea of love is only what we think it should be like.

Me: (thus guy makes sense even though he may be high).

On our usual slow drive back home, something changed about the way I felt about Anya, I was not sure but I ignored it. I was in too deep and when I dropped her off and she kissed me goodnight I was right as rain.

I knew Anya was leaving soon so I had to make my move.

Before she disappeared into the darkness.

Me: Anya, I knew I liked you from the moment I met you. But now I know I feel something more for you and I know you are going to be leaving soon. I just have to know If these

feelings are mutual and if we can take this relationship to the
next level.

Anya: wow Ally I am so taken aback by all this, what do you mean
the next level?

Me: I would like you to meet my parents and perhaps I can meet
your dad before you go.
You know something just to say we are together.

Anya: Ally this is all so sudden, I have to think about, I will speak to
you at the walimah tomorrow.

The next day was a families get together day. It was a walimah for
my second cousin twice removed, a 45th connection, (a really distant
relative.) We were mainly there for the chow anyway.

The walimah is a gathering which includes a meal that the boy gives
to his family and his wifes, the day after he gets married.

It is more than customary in Islam and in South Africa; everyone
that has the means does it. It is also a time that the families can get
together and get to know each other better.

For me it was usually about meeting prospective mates as most
family functions were. Anya told me she would be here and it was
different this knowing I had someone at this walimah that I actually
cared about.

The theme of blue and white was nice and one could appreciate the
amount of effort the boys family had made.

Seating obliged for about two hundred people, I know what you
thinking but trust me I have seen bigger.

The procedure was formal,

A= Molana stood up and read a couple of verse from the Quraan
He would then go on to explain it to the people present and its
relevance today. Then he would make a Dua for the couple and
we would all feel happy for them.

B= usually some family member from the girls side goes on about
the lovely couple and the beautiful bride etc. this can take some
time, and usually is very entertaining to watch how people mess
this up.

C= someone from the boys side thanks everybody and then tells
everybody to eat.

This is of course is the highlight of the evening for most.

Yet for me the highlight was seeing Anya, she looked beautiful in a black custom made Abaya.

You see this is a hunting ground, the best hunting ground for partners.

The older generations introduce girls and boys etc and you can chat and get to know the person a bit.

I know how it sounds, lame, but it is actually quiet fun, well that is what I found, quick dating service.

And anything can happen.

And it's all above board, so you don't feel guilty afterwards.

I didn't need it any more since I was taken.

The meals at these functions are always great.

I initially was very optimistic but after years of seeing basically the same people and girls over and over, my enthusiasm has become some what subdued.

And there she was and I was smiling again.

Anya was glowing and full of laughter but yet again kind of distant.

I walked up to her with a smirk, with a secret only the two of us shared.

But the warmth I brought was met by a cold chill as Taahir came and stood next to her.

Taahir was wearing his cream and gold Nehru suit. He was decked out man.

He was here to impress too.

I was in my usual function apparel, Levi bootleg blue jeans blue shirt today and black coat.

I caught her alone on her way outside to the car, she had to fetch a pin where an aunties scarf who was coming loose.

Anya: well my South African experience is coming to an end.
Me: what do you mean?
Anya: well my dad called and he said he has some official business in the US and he would like me to come with him, and since I have never been I am very excited.
Me: so when will I see you again. (Sounding suddenly desperate)
Anya: no promises Ali, no promises.
Me: what the hell was this then?

248

Anya: well now that I am leaving I might as well let you in. you see
    Taahir and I had a friendly bet when I came over that first
    night. In the first movie we saw as a group, a wager was set. I
    cant tell you what I won but it was definitely worth it.

He maintained that South African Muslim guys are different and
they won't fall for a girl like me here.

He believed that there was no way I could woo a guy he hand
picked. He postulated based on your brothers track record, there was no
way you would mess up the family name,

Thus when he chose you, I knew it would be quite a challenge.

But I was up to it as I knew it would help on my thesis of cultural
loss in the western world.

Me: Through this whole speech of hers, my mind was just
    spinning, I had already shut off. I don't know at which
    point. For the first time I knew what it must feel like when
    you tell the patient, hey dude, you have cancer.

Anya: so you can consider yourself a social experiment, one that I
    had to endure although from all the guys along the way, I
    must say you were the quickest to fall by a mile. Yet I have
    to admit you were so kind and had such gentlemanly ways,
    I kinda liked you towards the end.

Me: So I was an experiment, part of a thesis project.

Anya: well look at this way, you will be in my thesis, but I can't
    use real names unless you want me too, just kidding Ali.

Taahir: chuckles and says did you tell him, as he walks in from a
    distance.

Me: you knew about this and you never told me.

Tahhir: come on Ali it was all just a big joke. You can see the funny
    side of it. A wager between friends. I have to do all her stats
    now for her thesis.

Anya: look if it makes you feel any better, you were not the only
    one. We also got Ridwan but he was not as brisk in his
    pursuit of me as you. He gave up early on.

Taahir: tapped me on the back and said no hard feelings. No one
    got hurt; at least you had a good time, you will not forget.

I mean what did that mean anyway, no hard feelings

I had feelings and they were hard to understand at this point. They were feelings of pain and anguish. And standing there with a cloak of depression all over me, I just kept wandering why?

I stood for a long time wishing I was dreaming and that this was all just a joke but it was not.

I could not answer the why?

Why do people, most of them in the world directly or indirectly hurt someone else? Why would you do that? Does it really make you feel better about yourself? I don't know.

Then it hit me.

Every one does wrong. Every religion, every sect and we all know that sometimes there is no why? Some times people just have no empathy.

I was making my way to my car. I was mentally getting ready for a good cry.

And then there was a tap on my shoulder, it was Fathima.

Fathima: I know what Anya and Taahir did. I think it's awful really. Look I only found out today. I know you just want to disappear now but remember what you have learned. And if you need a friend I am here. All experiences good or bad are still an experience.

Thanks, was all I could muster and then I was on my way.

It seemed so cruel. It was surreal, like something you would read in a book or watch in your weekly sitcom and be totally flabbergasted when one of your main characters is duped.

I was humbled by the experience.

You are probably thinking it seems so petty but just like when a Childs goldfish dies, you don't know the pain each individual is going through.

Empathy is walking in another mans shoes.

I had feelings which I followed and believed and though they may have been signs that these feelings were not reciprocated, I still believed that they were.

I was old school, or maybe I was just schooled.

I should have used my common sense and logic but emotions spin you out of control.

And so my first love broke my heart, how boring in context.

And I even let myself think it was because of this whole caste thing that it did not work. I know it had nothing to do with it, but we all find reasons to believe why somethings go wrong.

I did remember what Fathima told me, I would learn from this.

And in the end what is every lost love but a social experiment in what happens between 2 people. The findings were in, I had fallen hard. Her loss, right? (Trying to console myself)

And after a couple days of sulking and going through each encounter I had with her, a sadness brew inside of me.

I wanted to marry this woman. She had used me. I was her project.

I felt empty initially, numb, sure I functioned well, but I felt uneasy for a while anyway. A little less confident, in the skin I was in.

You laugh at others trials and tribulations, diagnosis HIV positive, you have cancer, there is no cure.

And when a girl plays you, it's the end of the world. Boo hoo!

One can only imagine what my patients feel. With the bad news they get.

True love I learned is not fickle and it is not without pain or tribulation.

My brother was teaching me that much.

As the week passed by, the anger dissipated and Anya was leaving.

She actually had the audacity to come see me. Jojo brought her home.

She came to say Goodbye, and there she was in a beautiful powder blue suit, jeans and sandals

It was a cloudy day and our veranda had some leaves rustling on the floor.

Luckily mum and dad were not home. Jojo knew they were going to a family function.

Anya: hey Ali. How you doing?
Me: let me say this once, loud clear and slow. I will never address you or see you in the same light ever again. Your callousness has hurt me irrevocably.

And henceforth I will not think of you fondly but as someone who hurt me. I thank you for the lesson. Taught and learnt, but at the same time I ask that you leave me the f.k alone.

I wish I had the balls to say this but I never would.

Me: instead I smiled and said see you around Anya

Slmz (peace be upon you) and safe journey home.
I GOT STUFF I GOTTA DO.
She called after me but I never looked back,
I closed the door on her.
That was the last I saw of her and the last I hope to see of her.
I learnt a lot about myself through that relationship (or whatever it was); I guess emotional pain does mold us.
The fairytale in my mind that I saw on television and read in books was very rare.
People would use and abuse. And they would do so for minimal gain.
I don't know what happened to the notion of honor and dignity.
It seemed strange that in the last couple of decades we have progressed so fast technologically and industrially.
Yet we have regressed over the fundamentals of human relation and the homes we live in are slowly being destroyed both internally and externally.
And so the moral and environmental decay has set in and continues to worsen.
This thesis of chemical love lasting was proven to be false for me.
And so it is, we all waste the one renewable resource we should not, time.
We carry on doing the things we know are not giving us joy today or tomorrow.
And I knew that in time I would heal. I would just have to do things the right way, next time

35

The after math of my lovely relationship deception was painful. Some people in the family knew(people I trusted I think) but luckily my mum and dad never found out about my bad behavior. I mean we all have little secrets. And my dad would have had a big I told you so speech. I thought about it for many hours. No one to share problems with and since Akbar was away I was struggling. I knew I had done wrong, was this punishment?

Was my dad right in the end?, just follow the path and you will be saved?

I don't know.

I mean this was sad. I was 25, this was my first experience with a girl/woman and it was all a farce. It was all staged. If I was in a movie I would hook up with someone lovely and this would just be a problem I resolved in 90 minutes. But this is real life and there is no lovely on the horizon.

And worst of all I had a sneaking suspicion that Taahir and Anya had hooked up, It was just tragic.

My so called love affair was dead like all the roses in the garden, and although I knew I would bud and see another summer. I knew it would take a while for me to be as gloriously in bloom as I was this year.

My brother Akbar and Christine on the other hand, they went from living like hermits to being the poster children for hallmark cards.

Everyone was happy for Akbar, if only everyone included me and me alone.

The first incident was the first time Akbar brought "her" as my father called Christine, home.

It was a complete mess, like trifle just one big jumbled up after meal that is always just too much to stomach.

My mother un beknown to Akbar had invited some visitors over.

It was just a pleasant lunch date, some nice mutton breyani with some soji for starters on a Sunday afternoon. The guests were my mother's friends from yoga class and a special guest was her Daughter Naima.

Naima was a baddam, she was extravagant, a qualified lawyer with special interest in corporate law. She was a mild mannered, soft spoken, listened rather than talked type of girl. She was a gmg, (good muslim girl).

And mum like any mother with a 29 year old unmarried son had her vampire fangs out and she was baying for blood.

Akbar and Christine, rocked up for our usual Sunday family get together.

Except mum and dad were only expecting Akbar.

And mums plans of hooking Akbar up was going to come short.

They were down from Joburg. Christine's family had disowned her, and they were planning on getting married. From what I gathered the Botha side of the family told them to get off their property. Since things were going so well, next stop was the Sha's residence.

Of course I came in mentally prepared for World War 3. I knew what the ramifications of my actions and siding would be, but I did not care.

After what happened with Anya I was using this phrase quite often, I don't care.

It was not in bad way, it was just to things over which I had no control.

Patient with type 2 diabetes comes in with a gr or glucose reading 27 for the eighth time this year after constant counseling on diet and compliance and the repercussions of his actions (with a nice complications of diabetes poster).

And what does he say, he forgot to take his insulin on a holiday for a week, well guess what my friend, I don't care.

HIV positive, 23 years old, 1 child, CD4 22, on the second line regimen, has been on it for a year now, CD4 not moving, viral load increasing number, and discussed compliance written in big all over file.

I DON'T CARE.

There is only so much you can do and so much you can take, and trust me everyone has their breaking point. I had reached mine.

And this Sunday I was prepared for anything, I had no idea, how it would go down but I was quietly confident and positive, it was my nature, yeah right!

I had never seen my brother happier and that can never be a bad thing.

I knew deep down somewhere in my heart, soul, gut whatever you want to call it that my brother was a good man. He had his sore points and sure he made mistakes but he was solid as a rock. From an outsider point of view there was nothing wrong.

He as an Indian Muslim man wanting to marry a white Christian woman. However it was social and cultural suicide.

It would bring great dishonor and embarrassment to the family if Christine did not convert, and still as a white woman, I am not sure how she will be accepted into our intricate and detailed world.

It was a tennis match that required both parties to play the game and be willing to change and live up to the challenger.

Whether my parents had it in them to live up to that challenge? I could not say.

Having guests at the house threw a spanner in the works already.

They approached the house and my heart had a little paroxysmal flutter as they came in.

I am sure Akbar had the same feeling, as for Christine, it looked like she was already in an uncompensated form of heart failure.

She looked like she was ready to hurl at any moment, and Akbar sensed it too, he stroked her back and looked into her eyes. And I am sure she knew, they would be OK if they stuck together.

It would be a battle.

"They may take our lives but they will never take our freedom", that is till dad comes in the picture, then I am with the English mate.

It was mum who saw them and as soon as she saw Christine, her facial features changed. It was like a slide in psychology tut, happy-sad, happy-sad, and happy-sad.

I was just waiting for dad to come out.

Mum: Slmz my boys are here, and I see you have brought your business associate, Akbar.

I gotta love my mother, already trying to sweep the dirt under the carpet.

Akbar: mum there is something I think we need to discuss as a family and since I am leaving for Joburg I think now would be a good time.

My mother's friend Zahida looked quite amused by the turn of events and wanted to stay for the juicy details.

You see no matter how much we try to deny it, most women (and some men) love gossip. They thrive in it like fungi in sucrose. They just continue to divide and spread that story like shit on toilet paper.

And no matter how much people deny it, the majority of us love it when other families are in the shitter.

We have some ego trip knowing that someone else has bigger problems than us. We don't want to help really; we just are satisfied knowing that their excess baggage is a whole lot more than mine.

I have no idea why but this actually makes us feel better. I think psychologically, for a brief while, you are relieved that you are not the only with major difficulties.

Aunty Zahida: oh we better get going then, Naima, you will have to meet Akbar another time. But while we are here we might as well introduce ourselves. Akbar I am your mums yoga partner, heard so much about you (with a wink in her eye) and this is my daughter Naima (slowly pushing her forward) she is also working in Joburg, you know doing corporate law in Sandton.

Akbar: nice to meet you both.

Dad: Akbar, what is she doing here?

Me: oh let it begin.

Akbar: I need to talk to you and mum in private, dad.

Dad: Akbar can you not see we have guests here, do not be rude. We are entertaining them and you bring people who are not invited.

Akbar: well if you are talking about Christine, if she is not invited then I am not invited, she is my guest.

Dad:	what the hell are you saying? Who is she anyway, she is not apart of this family.
Akbar:	well mum and dad, if you want to do it this way, then so be it. I have come to ask for your blessing but not your recommendations or judgments in me marrying the only woman I have and ever will love.
Me:	oh shit, I can't breathe, the atmosphere has changed, I must be in space, or in a nightmare. Pinch pinch no it's real, It's happening too fast.
Mum:	Aunty Zahida, how would you guys like to have some tea. Akbar, I think you and your father should discuss this some other time.
Akbar:	As dad used to say the past is over the future yet to come the present is a gift so don't waste it, huh dad.

Aunty Zahida and Naima just stood in silence as one does when watching heavyweight boxers slug it out. They were glued to their TV sets and so was I. Something was going to give, it had to.

Dad:	Akbar meet me in the the living room.
Me:	(won't be a living room for long!)

So Dad and Akbar went into the living room and Aunty Naima and Zahida went of with a juicy steak story to pass to everyone who has an ear this side of the South Pole.

Mum and I sat in silence watching a rerun of Kuch kuch hotha hai, a famous Indian movie starring Shah Rukh Khan. Christine was there too, in body anyway, sipping on tea, oh how Indian like. She seemed calm.

We got the part when Salman Khan is basically giving Kajol away and out stepped Akbar and dad.

After initial shouting, mainly from dad's side it seemed things had cooled down or so I thought.

You see as a Doctor you learn to pick up subtle clues in body language.

All I has was body language as they never, neither of them ever told was what was discussed.

I could see that Akbar's eyebrows were slightly lower than usual, a sign of worry/concern, his head was down when he walked in to the lounge and although he gave a nervous smile to Christine, I could tell things were bad.

Dad walked in hands in pockets also trying to hide something and announced it was time for Esha and we would go to mosque read Salaah and come home for supper, which Akbar and I did without question.

Salaah was compulsory five times a day for every Muslim but to be honest I am guilty of missing Salaah from time to time. But at home I never did.

Of course I try to read all, but its just some days at work I don't, it's not like there is a good reason either. I cannot blame work all the time. I am religious but just not enough.

But my dad rarely missed a Salaah. He was the epitome of what a Muslim should be.

It was amazing, how diligent he was, and when we were with him we dare not miss a Salaah either.

But I must say whenever I did read my Salaah; it was a time I did feel truly at peace. It was a kind of meditation and when you came out, you just felt lighter, a kind of clarity to your thought. I liked it and it was one of those things that we did together father and sons. There were not too many other things we did together now.

It was also amusing how despite everything we could still go for Salaah together. As it should be, like food or sleep, prayer should happen without distraction.

We came out and walked silently to the car and when we got home, I walked in and stopped on the porch while Akbar called to Christine. They would not be staying for supper.

Christine amazingly stopped and addressed my parents like Christine of old bold and to the point.

> Christine: I want you to know Mr and Mrs Sha, I do not know you but I would like to get to know you. And I love Akbar with all my heart, and will never be apart from him again. Whatever it takes we will be together. We just want your blessing and I hope we can one day be a family.

It must have been Kuch Kuch but I was sold.
Dad looked past her at the fly on the wall and mum looked worried.
With that Akbar and Christine left. I said and did nothing.

They carried on walking down the street to the car.

I know he said something to dad before he left, I called after him and dad grabbed me by the hand with a tear in his eye and just said leave him be, Ali.

It was not the first time I had to make one those life altering decision, I know Akbar knew I had no choice. It was about loyalties and sides, and right and wrong.

I knew what I should do but I respected and knew my father too well to know that if I did not listen I would lose him too; my brother would always forgive me. And I lived here, his house his rules.

So I watched Akbar walk away, and did nothing to stop him.

Into the dark of night breathing out thick smog into the cold air pulling in his black leather jacket close to his body, he walked off deep in thought and head down. He held out his hand and she grabbed it and held it tight.

At least he was not alone, he had a partner now.

And boy was she brave.

They were ready to sacrifice even more for each other.

36

And there I was, conflicted as my brother had left the game. It is difficult to get your emotions in check when life is so busy with work.

The year would soon be coming to an end.

I was back in casualty.

There was a double pneumonia in an HIV negative patient, that would need further work up.

A full on ST elevation MI or heart attack with one foot in the grave, in a 61 year old Indian father of 5.

And to add some flavor to the afternoon we had an assault brought in by the ambulance with a left hemopneumothorax and a cardiac tamponade that was taken straight up to theatre that required the consultants out for a thoracotomy.

The funny thing is as an intern now after 2 years, I could handle all this and more, constant calls to different cubicles, drips, bloods, procedures and stupid questions from patients, like a 22 year old asking if he can get a week off work, for a pinky finger laceration.

I was comfortable with the 8-6 run of the mill work now.

But what I could not stand is coming to a car that is broken into after a hard days work. My cheap thousand rand radio stolen. I go and ask the security guard that was supposed to be guarding the cars, what happened Baba? He looks at you, scratches his head and say UNGAAZ BAAS, UNGAAZ—meaning I am too lazy to care.

This is the chip in my chocolate cookie.

So I drove home without a side window and no radio.

And when I got home, I had more good news, Akbar had gotten married and I was not there.

I received the news was via email.

My only brother gets married and I was not even there to see it.

He even did it, following all the rules. And his friends pitched in. They got married a couple days after Akbars visit.

The photos were pretty good.

Dad forbid me from even thinking of going, and loosely stated he is no longer part of the family.

I felt sick, no I really felt sick and then I started having a fever and developing a sore throat, and my sinuses were completely plugged.

I was on call on this weekend Friday with Sunday call to come. My last weekend set as an intern.

I had no time to be sick.

So I took an advil cold and sinus and some flutex(First time I ever tried flutex), just to knock it out of my system.

BAD IDEA, dumb ass, as doctors we make terrible patients.

The first half hour I was awesome, at home on Saturday. I was flying on pseudoephedrine perhaps.

Then I came back down to earth with a thud, I was sick and I had some reaction to the medication and now I was paying the price.

First I had palpitations and then I had the drooling, just gobs of spit coming out of my mouth, then a rash, wheals all over my body.

And I realized then, it was likely an allergy to something in the flutex but I just wanted to lie in bed.

But I was on call tomorrow.

This was my worst nightmare.

In 2 years of working I had missed 10 days of work, never on a call day though.

This was bad; I had to make the call. I was already under the microscope with Dr Rags.

Or I had to find someone to cover my shift. You know what the sad part is when you are pushed in to a corner there is no one to help you.

Everyone I called was busy or had some plans.

There was not a single intern willing to cover me

I guess if I was put in the same position I probably would also make a plan and say NO.

Now I know what they say is true, Karma is a bitch.

I never covered anyone, I mean I did my bit, but nothing extra, I loved my job, but it was then I realized that the passion I had initially, that light was getting dimmer and dimmer.

I closed my eyes and it felt like 5 minutes but when the alarm went of and I opened them the clock read 06h30.

I had to get ready for work and I could barely move. I could get no one to cover me.

This was going to be the longest shift.

Luckily I was on with Stevie, I called him and told him what was up, he told me to stay at home but I could not. I had to go in. Our senior for the evening was Dr Okeyo, he was a new Med Reg, and it was then I realized it would not be okay, o.

He was straight out of community service.

He was from another hospital covering for dodge who had taken unpaid leave of absence.

So there were a couple problems on the ward round but nothing I could not handle. I had a headache and all my muscles and joints were sore.

I soldiered on till Jummah time when I went to read Salaah, after prayers I felt a bit stronger.

I knew one thing, it was viral and I just had to hydrate and keep popping Panados.

In the South African setting like most countries in the world during the weekdays you had triple the amount at stuff.

When the call starts on weekends though, things change, and with the staff downsized it gets hectic and tiring.

Add to that, a new senior, it was a recipe for disaster.

This is tragic when I say it, but for once I missed dodge man, even though he was never around at least he knew the system.

Dr Okeyo was on day 1 call 1 and it was going to be a long night.

I realized you don't always have to rely on yourself when you have friends and family.

Mum and dad came over with some food and drinks, which I was grateful for.

And boy did Stevie graph, graph in South Africa is slang for work and Stevie worked like a dog, he did the work of two people.

I mean we were covering the ER walk in 24 hours and I have to say thank Allah that was one of the quietest evenings of the year.

From 4pm to 11pm I had a couple trauma cases a diabetic ketoacidosis two asthma cases, two kids with GE and a fractured radius, and an incomplete abortion.

I turfed a couple out to ortho and gynae, and managed what I could.

It was not bad at all, most were straight referrals to the correct department.

In between all that were the usual snotty noses and sore throats that waited till the weekend to come in to the emergency department.(which always made me wonder how bored these people must be to come in on a Friday night.)

Then there were the usual social problems.

By social problems I mean house parties where people use each other as the bottles and food, hairs pulled here and there and bite marks everywhere.

Stevie sutured and dripped and pulled bloods, all I had to do was the paper works and the notes, and boy was I grateful. Our senior spent a lot of the evening walking and talking to all the other seniors.

Getting to know the place as such.

It took him the whole evening to get to know the place, so that in the early hours of the morning when a burns came in requiring resus and intubation and Stevie failed, our senior was busy calling anesthetics, the problem however was this patient was assessed by him a while back and he was not concerned about the minor burns in the nose.

That was the only casualty of the evening;

All I could muster in the morning hand over was I owe you one.

Stevie punched me on the shoulder and said yeah you do.

There was a day off and the nice thing was I could go home and sleep.

Sunday call was still to come; hopefully I would feel better by then.

The whole of Saturday I spent in bed.

And then it was Sunday and off to work again. It felt like I slept for an hour and I was back on call.

By the time I got through the ward round work on Sunday it was already midday.

You see after all the patients are admitted and they are now inpatients.

We have to check on them every morning and make sure they are improving so they can go home and we can admit more patients.

But someone has to be working up these sick inpatients. The consultant comes in and asks you questions you don't know the answers too and depending on how long your registrar has been there, he might not know either.

And then when everything is done you are left with a shit load of work to do.

So you can say the consultants the brain, pushing out all the executive functions, and the registrar is like the heart, making sure all is beating along smoothly.

The intern like the nursing staff is the blood, carrying forth the messages and doing the run around.

I must warn you though that if one of these components is out of sync, the repercussions are disastrous.

Now on our Friday call, we had a new heart, so blood was a bit damaged.

We over admitted. Although majority were legitimate this time.

There were no beds for the on coming team to work with.

So this fine Sunday morning post ward round we realize we have no beds.

Well we had 1 female and 1 male medical, which was basically zippo.

Now this might seem quite silly, but no beds means no more admissions which is a huge problem.

What do you with all the patients waiting to be admitted?

You can't let them lay in the ER the whole day and night, and this is finely balanced act that has to be perfected.

And this takes time and there is an art to it, I think.

As time goes on and you learn the art of pushing patients, you learn how to work with numbers and how to move patients around.

If they have to stay in hospital, the best way is to refer to another department, so you need to learn all their requirements for admission, and problems they have to admit.

Females are good movers to obs and gynae, elderly male and female always get internal med if you have it involved.

Any problem with bones is orthos, heart cardiology; chest is pulmonology, and so forth.

This is in a first world setting.

Here in south Africa you admit to adult male or female medical or surgical, paeds or O and G, and ortho if our hospital has an ortho department, \\if they aint pregnant and they have no fluid coming out of the vagina Obs and gynae is a hard push.

As interns we know this, and so do the registrars of every dept, there are hard pushes and soft pushes, for example a poorly controlled diabetic with hyperglycemia and acidosis is medical but find yourself with a septic diabetic foot you got a soft push to surgery.

But if you have a man with a diabetic foot as above in renal failure, now surgery has a soft push to medical.

Now this tug of war goes on day after day, and both department's give and take and once in a while things blow up like a bubble blown too big in your face.

On the whole, we shift around pretty well, and we try our best to keep as many beds available for intake.

I was not 100% yet physically and we still had this new registrar learning the system.

But what I knew by midday is that it was going to be a long day and night.

I had just finished all the ward work when I got a call from mum saying dad was not well.

The worst thing to have at work is personal problems cause if there is one thing doctors can't take is the inner war between family and work.

You hate to burden your patients and your colleagues but on the rare occasion when the two come together it can be very difficult.

A patient that is a family member, they say you must stay objective but it is difficult when the patient is your dad.

Mum: your father has been having some sharp pains in his chest all morning, from the time he came in after gardening out side.

Now I knew he had to have this checked out, but knowing my dad this was never going to happen.

Me: tell him to get to a hospital asap, if he has chest pain,(bad family history and hypertension, I would know) it is his heart and he needs to go in to a hospital as it is urgent, especially if it is worsening.

Of course dad would not listen to a doctor so I called Molana to talk him into going to the hospital, now all we could do is hope common sense prevailed.

As usual dad defied us, and he stayed home.

I had to let big brother know, and before I could even finish the story he was on his way, he had left Joburg and his lovely wife behind.

I wanted to leave too but I just felt guilty after what Stevie did for me this last call, I would really be taking advantage of this now.

I was in a real dilemma now.

What to do? What to do?

The problem was my dad was at home, it would be different if he was already at the hospital, and I doubt me going home was going to change that.

So I put it out of my mind and went down to the ER.

All the results were coming in and we had only one mover out.

So we had three beds to play with.

And as I walked down to help Stevie in er, I saw an ambulance roll in, a 56 year old man with a full on STEMI, his Ecg was positive for a heart attack and we started the protocol management but he went into asystole and that was it.

Despite everything half an hour later he was determined deceased, the reg called it and I have to admit we did all we could. We knew there was no chance he was going to make it.

It scared me to the core what if this was my dad?

So I spoke to Stevie and the reg and asked for an hour off to go and check on my dad. They were cool with it. At this point I could never repay Stevie anyway. So I raced home and found my dad lying in bed reading his just fifteen minutes prayer book. Mum next to him, wetting a face cloth and placing on his head.

I lost it.

For the first and last time in my life I swore my dad and he was shocked by it, he was speechless.

Dad are you f . . . ing mad?

You should be in a hospital unless you want to be in your kabr tomorrow.

I called the ambulance and they took him in, since we had medical aid he was taken straight to a private hospital.

I saw the monitors at least his ECG looked OK and he seemed to improve on the oxygen and morphine.

An hour and half later we learned my dad had unstable angina and he was going to need an angiogram.

His blood work indicated he had a NSTEMI.

His cardiac enzymes were not good.

I had to call Akbar, he was on the way.

I spoke to the cardiologist and quickly realized there was not much I could do, We would just have to wait for all the tests to be done.

He was being managed by one of the best cardiologists in the province, so I was at ease. Well a bit at ease anyway.

I had to get back. Akbar would come. I knew he would.

Back at the hospital while I was away, all our available beds were gone and we lost two more patients in the ER, a stroke and suicide who drank battery acid, quite common in SA.

The reg was busy putting in a CVP for a patient with diabetic ketoacidosis and Stevie was putting in a chest drain for a pneumothorax.

The ER was chaos and this was just minus one for two hours, I looked at the waiting patient stack, it was sitting at 37.

The feeling made me sick.

This was going to be an all nighter.

The admissions were a pneumonia probably TB that needed oxygen, in severe resp distress, then there was a chronic renal failure that may require dialysis and to top it off a young stroke came in the same time as a pulmonary embolus.

The fun had just begun.

So I began to push through the ER knowing that I was on my last call left this year and in medicine, once you get past internship, I hope it can only get better. And it always does, just when you hope things would simmer down, they just don't.

I had to do my best; I knew I would honor my dad this way.

He above all would recognize that.

Mum called and Akbar made it. She was relieved he was there, but by now about 30 family members were also there, all praying for dad.

37

We made it through the call, and I have to say I wrongly judged Dr Okeyo, he was not too bad. He pushed through the night with us and no one died in casualty/ER. He actually pulled out some good clinical skills and management on a few cases. Learned a few new tricks. The next morning he and Stevie even let me leave early. I was grateful.

I came back home post call, I did my ritual but left out the sleep part, I grabbed a red bull and went back to the hospital. Dad had has his Angiogram.

I hugged Akbar and congratulated him. But the mood was somber.

What a couple weeks!

It was crazy, Akbar married, Dad having a heart attack, but at least we all realized one thing, how we really needed each other now more than ever.

Dad had his angiogram done. He tolerated it well. Dad had some moderate blockages and he had a stent put in for a single vessel severe blockage.

He would be discharged fairly soon.

He only greeted Akbar and did not really want to see anyone. There was a congregation of 20 family members waiting too see if he was OK. I went and spoke to them and reassured everyone. Our immediate family just sat around Dad in silence, praying. He seemed numb. I know he probably was still in shock. He had a heart attack, his son Ali swore him and his other son Akbar got married without his permission.

My internship was coming to an end. I had 5 days left. It's great that I had grown as a doctor and what I know now compared to day 1 is quite spectacular.

But somehow I still feel empty.

My family life is zero, I did have a social life till I found out I was a social experiment and most of my friends are about to move on.

My last 2 days were in Casualty, then I had 2 days off to get down to my new job as a Community service (comm serv) Medical Officer. I was climbing the ladder.

The sad thing was all my buddies would be moving.

I knew I was heading to a rural area a couple hours drive from home somewhere on the natal coast.

Stevie was of to the Cape of Good Hope, Sam was going back to Johannesburg with Kubin who was going to "check it out too".

Jameel was staying put in Josies too.

So unfortunately the gangs home Kwazulu Natal was busted, perhaps we would meet up in Josies now, but it would be different. I was the only one who was staying behind.

How do years fly by?

It was bitter sweet; everyone had aspirations of specializing and doing stuff in the future. I was not sure yet.

I wanted to do something with my life. I just did not know what yet.

We all have this notion we will get married and have kids and life will be dandy, but it just does not work that way.

Especially from an Islamic background, I noted things were changing.

The western lifestyle had reached us too, divorce, marrying later and having children later were becoming more common now, add to that marrying out of religion, more appreciation of woman's rights. Whether that is good or bad depends on who is reading?

Tell this to my dad and you would have hours of conversation on your hands.

We are all too caught up in the world to know how much of life was passing us by. And that is the scary part.

Do what you love is what people say but what if all we love now is something that keeps us from God, family, and the more important things in life.

I wanted more, I knew that but how do you fill that void.

With love like my brother or God like my father or do you just leave it void and wait. Or do you just focus on work work work like me with a little bit of friends, family, God in between all of that.

I don't know, maybe I was just over analyzing it all and all I should do is just be in the moment but unfortunately that's not me and will never be me.

I live in moments, not a moment, always have, and probably always will.

So what next was the question?

The last couple days of internship were business as usual.

I had a lot of people come in for disability grants and it was depressing again. People with illness and the shadow of death hanging over them, trying to survive on a couple hundred bucks a month, and help their families in the process.

I saw patients with HIV with Kaposi sarcoma covering an entire limb, in constant pain, unable to walk. And the worst is looking at them knowing that the ARV medications you are giving is probably too late.

Then on the flip side I have this young 27 year old male just older than me, who has failed to adhere to 3 ARV regimens already and we now basically import medications, and he still does not seem to care, wasting tax dollars.

It worries me what the future holds with resistant variants out there, but I try not to think of the one or two lost, but of the thousands saved.

Some say it's too late, but at least we are doing something now, better late than never. South Africa in a lot of ways is like my family. The past is totally messed up and gone, it is too late to fix, maybe. And we are left with those problems that are not an overnight fix and we are just barely doing the right things or seeking the right advice to sort it all out. We will just do as we do and hope for the best. And we are what we are, a work in progress.

The diabetic clinic was even worse, lots of patients without limbs lost in the war of glucose overload. I guess maybe with education we could do more, but it is difficult to say, what you can eat on a low budget where your staples are carbo packed.

And you have no concept when the doctor says your diet is incorrect and we need to start giving you an injection twice a day, what do you do but just follow orders if you can. And if you have any idea how important it is, will you just follow orders?

Its not life and death situations that make doctors but the smaller problems in between that we need to seal before the crack widens. And we all realize preventative medicine is the future.

The sad truth is some patients are so disappointed with our medicine. They would rather seek traditional medicine.

And of they would go to see the sangomas or witch doctors and pay large amounts of money for hopeful cures that never seem to materialize. And then they show up at our ER in the early hours of the morning, the bucket next to the boot.

The reality is that for Africa as a whole change is slow. The taller trees are always the first to taste the rain and the shrubs will always be trodden on.

The tragedy is a deep hole which is so vast the pain of the world cannot fill it, the numbers of dead or dying are shocking and only few know the true statistics.

So my last day came and went without incident, there was the usual death certificates, two in the male ward and one in the female ward, and the usual buzz of people with overdoses and assault with a sjambock and knobkerrie, he died, not a good way to go. I had one emergency hypertensive patient come in that did not think tablets would help him. Then there were a couple of teenagers, street kids as they call them, two of them tried to commit suicide. Both were overdose cases of sniffing glue and other stuff. Luckily they were stable.

I went to the final hearing of the dodge man. He had a family emergency and and he had the documentation to prove it, although his lax work ethic would now be monitored.

I know I would not see him again or the regs or consultants for a year.

Come next year which was 2 days away I would be a medical officer, albeit comm serv officer but there would be no one to cover my ass, or help.

And so the next chapter of life is waiting to be read.

It was scary but what can you do, you just have to accept your responsibilities and move on as life does, nothing and no one is going to be there to molly coddle you along.

There was a hospital waiting for me along the coast where there were just 4 doctors that run an entire hospital.

The fear has left me, I know I should be OK after this baptism by fire, and I know the skills I have learned should serve me well, no matter what happens.

All the second year interns were getting anxious about their move for next year that was coming up. Everyone was excited and pensive at the same time.

38

Everyday comes with a day after.

Based on the guys who had been through comm. Serv, it was a year that will take you to your limits.

I mean of course it will, you work with two or if you lucky three doctors serving a community of 300 000 so it's like 100 000 patients per dr.

A year of knowledge, responsibility and deception had come to an end.

We live in a world full of lies and deception. It's so deep it's become normal, its part of what we do for work, for assignments, for your country,

And the people upholding the truth never seem to have a voice or be heard.

I was stuck here, in this time of our world.

My brother comes down and helps my dad after his heart attack, and he is told to go away till he sorts out his life.

That is the last conversation my brother has with my dad.

I don't know what to do any more.

It was the tenth of Muharram and the family was meeting up, to spend time together and exchange gifts.

Dad was doing much better now on his aspirin, crestor and beta blocker.

Only time would tell if he would stick to the cardiologists plan and cut down on his beloved ghee, this I thought as I watched him eat some more burfee.

Don't say it, I know I am a doctor, but to him I will always be a kid.

I was in the kitchen helping mum, when I saw a car I did not recognize pull up. And then I saw them.

Akbar came, he left her in the car.

He walked up like he was invited and everyone assumed he was.

That was until Dad saw him.

He was unequivocally told by my dad to get the hell out.

In front of everyone there

It was so embarrassing and filled my heart with melancholy.

But then for the first time ever, my mum stepped in, loud and bold.

This was shocking for everyone, including dad.

Mum: Akbar is my son, I called him and his wife. We already lost a child Abdul, now is the time to forgive. Let it be, just for a while, let us at least have some peace. Now Akbar you bring your wife in and introduce her to the family.

At first I though I may have to call an ambulance as dad was having another heart attack yet he was silent and so too, the house was silent. No one ever heard my mum speak out like that. I had not for years.

It was awkward, but would you expect anything less from the Sha household now.

Everyone else was close family and just did what most people do in awkward family in fights, act like nothing happened. I was glad they did.

Akbar and Christine came in. Christine fit in pretty well. She helped with the ladies and even smiled and made conversation with everyone. Akbar seemed happy too. Yet dad was just reserved. We ate. We maintained etiquette. We cleaned up. A little bit of conversation here and there.

Everyone slowly filtered out like a slowly squeezed fart. They were all waiting for more drama that never came.

Then there were five.

Akbar got up and said it was time to go.

Christine thanked mum and hugged her, she ruffled my hair and said bye to dad and waited at the door

He gave mum an envelope saying it was from Christine.

And he went to hug mum and she cried.

She whispered something in his ear.

Akbar went to hug dad.

Dad hugged him too, he actually held him, but he did not cry.

Akbar looked me in the eye and smiled.

Christine was smiling too. For dad that was big.

Akbar was misty eyed. I walked with them to the car.

He said you make sure that they are OK, alright? But remember I am a phone call away.

And I knew he would be back.

So my family was never normal, and never will be, not that there is a normal family any where in the world. Like most families we had issues that are unlikely to be resolved any time soon.

Whats next, I don't know. I can't predict.

Only time will tell.

In the experience department, I am one up. The question though is, if you had the choice would you want to go though the downs?

I know the answer for me is yes, as it is only then, you truly are grateful for the ups.

So I had a year left here to fulfill my government obligations.

This should be a brutal year that will be full of painful experiences that will scar my career for life thus making me a better doctor.

Has this internship done that? Made me better, and for that matter will this internship of life keep molding me into something better?

And will I be able to make a difference in this world so that I may reap benefits in the next?

I don't know.

I can safely say I am a better doctor now, I have changed. I have grown both as a person and as a doctor. I am not the same. And that changes everyday.

I know my dream has changed; now I go through the resus and the patient lives.

WHO AM I?

I am Ali Sha, a Muslim, a medical doctor, a son and a brother.

WHAT AM I DOING HERE?

Hopefully, trying to make a small difference. Taking care of my family, friends and patients, without forgetting God.

DID I HAVE A NICE DAY?

Today, watching dad hug Akbar I did. Watching Christine and mum clear up the table and wash dishes together I did. These are the days worth waiting for.

And so I wait for more.

I wait for more.